For my sons, Cooper and Casper
You're not just my sons: you're my sunshine

one:

– now –

I can't see anything. I want to open my eyes, but it feels too much effort and I'm worried it'll hurt. Everything hurts.

I feel worried, I realise – not just about the pain, but about something else. I can hear . . . ticking. A bomb? Is that what's making me nervous? No . . . that's not quite right. I think it's dangerous, but not a bomb. Grey is all around me, but is receding, ebbing away, so I wait.

I'm still in nothingness but now there's a change. Now I don't feel nervous . . . it is more than that . . . I feel *afraid*. What of? I'm not sure. My thoughts are heavy, slow and I know there's something wrong with me.

Then, like a torch beam coming closer in the dark, I realise my head hurts. At the back. This pain grows greater until it shines above all others. This is why I can't think properly. Perhaps I've been attacked? Is that why I'm afraid? I try to touch my head but I can't.

I can't move. This discovery is shocking and I lie still in the grey soup that is my thinking. I know there's something else I *need to remember.* My thoughts are leaden and slow. It's very, very hard.

Think, Lisa! I realise I know my name. I latch on to that. I am Lisa. I am Lisa and I realise my right cheekbone is cold and numb. I can smell the pine disinfectant I used yesterday and with it I understand that I'm lying on the slate tiles of my kitchen floor.

Abruptly, I open my eyes. With that, comes clarity in my thinking. Until now I've been half-unconscious, but I'm now present. The pain now shines like a lighthouse. I turn my head away from it and see the underside of my kitchen cabinet.

I am Lisa and I am in pain and I am lying on my kitchen floor and I can't move my body *at all* and I am scared because something has gone badly, badly wrong but I can't remember what it is and if I don't remember, then I will run out of time – is this true? Do I only have a certain amount of time?

Yes.

I have to be quick but maybe it's too late already.

I hear something: I wait ... it's a light, metallic sound. Mournful. I know that sound. It's a wind chime – *my* wind chime. I'm home. At the cottage in Hereford.

Now I hear something new. I hear screaming. I think: *Yes, this is what I was waiting for. I knew the screaming would start and now it has.*

I'm too late to save him.

Jack!

And I remember everything.

two:

– before –

I was careful to arrive before the estate agent. I'd left Jack asleep in the car with all the windows and doors open to give him a breeze. I was so glad to get the chance to explore and make up my own mind before any sales spiel.

I had gradually moved further and further away from the cottage at the top of the hill and had dared to walk down the long drive until I stood beneath the broad oak tree. From here, I could see right up to the cottage, and downwards until the drive swept out of sight behind rhododendrons to where I knew it met the quiet country lane below.

I wanted to be there first so I could get a sense of the place; it was a big decision for me to move somewhere so isolated.

I stood and realised just how *absent* people were, here. There wasn't a sound from anyone – not even a child playing or a distant car. Only nature seemed alive here. The end-of-summer leaves muttered above me, caught in the too-light-for-the-heat breeze. Somewhere a cricket lazily clicked its slow dry rasps, oppressed by the swelter. A war mongering wasp interrogated me. But there were no human sounds. The absence of people, to a town girl like me, felt stifling.

I must've been standing very still, because a woodpigeon landed heavily in the low branch above me. Listening to the pigeon's cooing call I told myself firmly that we could live here. That we could be happy here. Here the isolation would give us the peace we so badly needed.

I had never been to Hereford until that morning, when seven-year-old Jack and I gazed in awe as we drove over the Severn Bridge at dawn; the huge expanse of water beneath felt like a tangible delineation (*no, no, not the River Styx*) between the danger of the past and the safety of the future. As the sun broke the horizon, pink shepherd-warning skies reflected onto the great stretch of water below.

'Hereford,' I told Jack, 'is the least populated county in England.' I didn't add: *And therefore the perfect choice for us to start again.* He was silent, but I felt the crossing was like a rebirth; like we were leaving the death of our life before and crossing into something new. I felt it and I hope that he did too.

If this didn't work for us, I didn't know what we would do because I knew that we couldn't keep moving – I could see so clearly how much it was killing Jack. After we had run, I wasn't sure where to go, so we simply moved around, staying in three hotels in three months. But his anxiety had changed from his previous mild stutter into stomach aches and bitten nails. This cottage in Herefordshire had a lot to deliver: it had to be perfect. Jack couldn't suffer any more.

I wasn't sure I could suffer any more change, either. I was like a vase, broken all the way to the base, superglued up, but no longer confident of holding water.

This move had to work.

I looked around, wanting to see the view from my prospective new home. I could see across the hills for miles; my gaze drawn to the gentle swell of the hills and dipping valleys. But this summer there was very little green; instead it was a palate of pale brown; dust beige and muted gold. Although still only July, several weather records had already been broken and the fields were scorched and thirsty; the crops dying. Radio programmes dwelled on environmental anxieties; I wanted to, but I was afraid of something more immediate.

I could only think of Him.

But he wouldn't find us here; it was too remote.

Beyond the cottage gardens it turned back to farming fields. In the distance, perhaps a couple of miles away, I could see a single farmhouse. Beyond, that, an empty nothing.

I realised that, living here, Jack and I could go for weeks without seeing anyone. We could become shadows, unseen and safe.

A little settled, I turned my attention to what I hoped would be our new home. The stretch of the driveway suggested that there might be a grand house at the top, but there wasn't; instead there was a small brick cottage of simple design. Its roof was low, like a hat that's been pulled down too low on a head, with two eaves popping out at each end. Although I'd never been in it, I knew it had two bedrooms. I had assumed they were both upstairs, but now, seeing the smallness of it, I wasn't so sure. I didn't know because there was no floor lay-out on Rightmove and I was glad: it meant that no one could Google it and find out.

Another plus, I realised, was that I could hear the sound of the estate agent's car before I could see it. A silver Micra pulled into view, passed the scrub of small trees and stopped in front of me. A young man, with the engine still running, lowered the window: 'Miss Law?'

'Lisa, please.'

'Do you want a lift up to the cottage?'

'Thanks, but I'll walk up. I was just having a poke around.'

He drove on to the cottage and I strode up to meet him.

'Great for views!' he said, opening his door. 'You'll be king of the hill up here!'

And it was. The two acres of garden fell gently on all sides, with a flattish lawn to the west of the cottage and on the east, a sloped, shrubby area with a steeper gradient down to the road. The gardens could give Jack something idyllic in his childhood, I thought – perhaps the access to nature would make up for losing his school friends.

The man grabbed his iPad from the passenger seat, just as his phone rang. 'I'll ignore it.'

'I don't mind if you take it,' I said, wanting to let Jack sleep on just a few minutes more. 'I'll walk around the property.' To the right of the cottage, a bay window overlooked the best views of the valley. Neglected flower beds edged the walls. I wondered if

I would ever be the kind of person to rescue them – I wanted to, I wanted so much to be better than I had been.

I knew as I listened to the gentle, mournful sound of the wind-chime tied outside the kitchen window, I knew we could be happy here.

Here, we could finally be safe.

three:

– before –

Although I really wanted to see inside the cottage, I realised with a dragging anxiety that I would now have to wake a sweaty Jack who was stretched out over the back seat of our old Volvo. The journey had been long and the air con wasn't working, and he'd nodded off. I'd left all the doors open and had been careful to park in the shade. But he'd still be hot on waking; we were all hot, too hot and the suffocating heat felt like it'd already lasted forever.

I debated leaving Jack asleep in the car: it would be so much easier to look around this cottage on my own. Getting the cottage was such a big decision and I wished again that I had someone to bounce big decisions off. For a moment I missed my mother; the longing for her – or maybe just another adult to talk to – was so overwhelming, I felt glad for the privacy of my sunglasses.

'Shall we get started?' The estate agent opened the front door and disappeared into the darkness of the cottage.

I had to follow. I trailed obediently after him into the cottage, leaving Jack alone. Guilt snagged like skin on a fish hook, my mind whispering: *Don't leave him! You have to guard him!*

Stop it, Lisa, I told myself. I wanted to get a grip on my anxiety. How could I hold the estate agent up? He'd have another appointment lined up after this one, and getting Jack up and settled, ready for a viewing, would take too long. I regretted not being more organised.

This move would be a fresh start for us both; not just to give Jack stability, but to give me a chance at being a better parent. Someone organised, thoughtful, prepared; someone who planned ahead. Someone who filled lunchboxes with flapjacks carefully covered with beeswax squares; someone who folded their children's clothes carefully into drawers rather than wedging them in to fit; someone who patiently walked their children round National Trust gardens.

I stepped into the low-ceilinged hall, leaving Jack behind. I stood in the square room, trying to breathe slowly, not feeling like the calm parent of National Trust gardens or neat drawers. Instead, I felt compulsive and wild. The urge to dart back and get Jack was overwhelming. But it was too late – the viewing had already started. *Lisa*, I told myself: *focus*. Be better. If it isn't safe here, my rational self countered, then why are we moving here?

I inhaled; exhaled, centred myself.

I made myself look around. The room was small, with a diamond-leaded window on one wall and another small window by the oak front door. It smelt of lavender, old stone and dust. The estate agent talked about the versatility of the room, but I wasn't really listening. Instead I looked out of the small window. The car doors were open just as I had left them and I could see Jack's hand thrown back, his leg spilling over the side of the seat.

I relaxed a little.

I had spent many nights contemplating the facts. Although school would be a risk too far, I knew that I'd have to combat Jack's growing anxiety by allowing him more freedom. Here, I thought, checking again through the window, he could play in the beautiful garden without me constantly watching him.

'Would you like to see another room now?'

I hesitated – I had barely taken this one in. But as I stood there, I made a quick judgement that I could make it a welcoming place, right for me and Jack.

'Could I see the kitchen, please?

He led me into the room I always thought of as the most important. It had a family-sized table in the middle and a half-glazed door to the garden, windows on two walls and a plank door. I was charmed to see a baby-blue Aga. 'Does it work?' I asked as I placed my palm on its cool top.

'All gas safety checks are in order – you'll just need to turn it on.' He pointed to the far side of the kitchen: 'Gas hob and oven too, if you prefer. Very good to have the option when it's as warm as this.'

Above the hearth was a large clock. The ticking was loud – too loud in the small space, but I liked it, and I liked everything about the kitchen, including the slate tiles on the floor. I slipped my foot out of my flip-flop and pressed my sole against the stone. It felt icy cold. I shivered. After such hot days and nights for the last month, it felt good.

I also loved the low ceilings and thick walls; I realised that rather than feeling exposed and vulnerable here in the middle of nowhere, I could actually feel safe. The fact that I had left Jack out of my sight in broad daylight for the first time in forever – even if I hadn't wanted to – felt like a major triumph.

I started to realise that the plan to come to Herefordshire, which had started as a panicked Google search for the most isolated place in England, and then a search for a furnished and remote cottage, might prove not to be just a panic-made decision, but actually a good move. 'I could live here,' I murmured to myself.

'I'm sorry?'

I smiled at him: 'It's a lovely room.' I touched the Aga again and imagined it warm and drying wet coats after brisk walks; perhaps we could even get a dog – Winston – *no*. We could never, *ever* get a dog – I shivered, thinking, remembering his brown loving eyes, the feel of his leather lead in my hand.

We might never be able to achieve family perfection, but perhaps here, perhaps surrounded by these rolling gentle hills, Jack and I could find what we so desperately needed.

A loud tapping sound brought me back. Someone at the window. Both the estate agent and I jumped at the unexpected noise.

But it wasn't a person, it was a hornet. It was inside, trapped, whirring around, suddenly inches from us. A tiger-striped bullet, it raged against the diamond-leaded glass, its buzzing rude and loutish. What had it been doing so silently before now?

The boy-man stepped back, alarmed. 'Whoa! It's massive!'

He was afraid, I could see that. I'd never liked insects – particularly the stinging kind – but his fear made me feel maternalistic and I wanted to save him. I stepped closer to the window and laid my hand on the cool marble worktop. The kitchen might be dated with oak cabinets, but someone, a long time ago, invested in this little room. Holding my breath, I tried to open the window, but the catch was stuck.

I pulled on it harder, feeling panic rising in my chest. Inches from me, and so angry – like Him! – and I remembered the terror of Him. It's like he's here in this kitchen with me, wanting to hurt me again, always so angry about things I don't understand – have never understood.

The catch suddenly freed, the window opened outwards too easily under the pressure of my adrenaline, yanking my arm and shoulder with it.

The hornet bounced along the diamond-leaded window towards me, quick to move towards the rush of air. The buzzing was alarming . . . but then it was gone.

'Wow! Wasn't it loud?' The estate agent swiped at the layer of sweat on his top lip.

Feeling sorry for his embarrassment, I quipped: 'I bet you get tenants like that.' I felt pleased when he laughed and looked a little less embarrassed.

Another door off the hall revealed a small sitting room; Jack and I could be happy here.

I pictured myself tucked up by a fire, watching the telly whilst Jack was asleep upstairs. Then I realised that's all I would be doing. I felt a shudder of anxiety: I'd be living as a single parent where there was no park; no flat whites at the local coffee shop and no swimming pool. But even though that was true, I put my anxieties away. Nothing was more important than keeping Jack hidden.

The estate agent opened a door: 'A stairs in a cupboard! Isn't that a stunning character feature?' and I was charmed enough to agree. The stairs were behind the door; U-shaped and creaky. I followed him up, each riser groaning, to the top of the house where there were two low-ceilinged bedrooms built into the eaves at each end, with a tiny bathroom in the middle. We went to the first bedroom. It had leaded windows and was only just big enough for a double bed.

'This could be the master,' he said, 'Or you might prefer the views from the other bedroom – excellent as well, of course.' I followed him to the other. 'Both the same size,' he said, 'so you have the choice between them and then you'll have the added benefit of a guest bed or upstairs office.'

'I have a son. This will be his room.'

'Oh! Forgive me, your details said it was for a household of one.'

His manner, his young certainty, annoyed me for some reason. 'Jack's in the car.'

I was glad to see a shadow of confusion cross his face. 'Oh, I didn't see . . .' but he recovered quickly and smiled. 'This will be a great bedroom for him, I'm sure.'

I examined the wardrobes; the bathroom. Every step upstairs creaked and gave a little. 'Do you think this floor is safe?'

'A surveyor visited just last month – no woodworm and the joists are sound. It's a character property; adds to the charm.'

I followed him out onto the drive. 'I'm going to take it,' I said, agreeing that I'd come into the office to get the tenancy set up.

He held his hand out. 'Great, I'm sure you will be so happy here – you and your son,' he looked over to see Jack, but Jack's hand was no longer hanging out of the car and he'd pulled his leg in; I was glad he'd hidden from sight. Since saying it, I'd been regretting mentioning him. I told the estate agent's office it was just me for a reason and should've kept it that way.

I shook the man's hand.

'You'll be checking out local schools this afternoon, I'll bet. I understand the nearest one is in the village of Cleasong; it's outstanding and is only four miles that way.'

I looked in the direction he was pointing, but could see only farmland, and what might possibly be a farmhouse. 'Thanks, but Jack's going to be home-educated.'

I lingered, watching him drive away, my arms, despite the heat, wrapped round me.

four:

Listening to the screaming, I realise I'm too late to save Jack. I hear the wind-chime again and I realise that I'm wrong – the screaming is only the scream of mating foxes in the dusk.

Is that true?

Yes. Their crying sounds like tortured children and it's always scared me, misplaced city girl that I am. I'm from Brighton. And Bracknell. Now I live here in the countryside with Jack. I've been fighting for something but I can't remember what. It's hard to think when I feel so tired . . . I shut my eyes or perhaps the world is just greying . . .

. . . I'm drifting. My thoughts are the flashes of silver-sided eels in a strong, muddy river: brief, elusive, slippery. I can't be sure of anything . . .

Then, I'm in a playground I've forgotten about. I'm feeling happy: sunshine yellow happy. I haven't been here for a long time. Jack is on a swing and I'm pushing him. This is real: this has *happened.*

Jack is young and is wearing the cutest little short dungarees that show his pudgy legs, the type of baby podge that demands kisses and makes me want to squeeze them harder than I should. I read once that the word to describe this urge is called *gigil* – an overwhelming reaction to cuteness that the brain tries to shut down with aggression. I don't know if this is true but I know that the sight of Jack's squidgy legs makes me want to greedily bite them.

This is real – *this has happened.*

The sun is shining and there's only the wispiest of clouds in the blue sky. The June weather is lovely – warm but with no press of heat. Everything is green and lovely and fresh. Jack and I have the park nearly to ourselves; I even turn from Winston's *save-me* gaze through the railings of the children's area. I love that dog, but for now just want to concentrate on Jack; I don't want to have to think about anything else other than my beautiful son.

In this simple moment I love my baby and my love for Jack is simple and yet molten. Nothing is confused; nothing is complicated; nothing causes concern. He grew in my tummy and he is mine and I love him. The only thing that matters is that today it's just us and it's the start of summer and things might be different and things might improve and—

My lungs inhale suddenly as I lift my head off the kitchen floor and open my eyes again.

I'm back.

I see that the old lead-light windows are open and think: *The bugs will get in!* But the back door is very slightly ajar, swinging in the breeze, and I know that something much nastier than bugs has already got inside.

Everything instantly both hurts and is clear: Jack's dad has come for us.

five:

– before –

I remember when I met Jack's dad. I hadn't long trained as a nurse when I attended a blue-light evening for nurses, firemen and police. Nick had come in with a woman who he introduced as his boss, a rather thin blonde who I thought was interested in him, but he said he didn't mix work with pleasure – 'too messy'. Besides, she had a tinny, high-pitched laugh that didn't sound authentic.

He, on the other hand, was so very bloody authentic. He wore his dark blonde hair swept back, but when a wavy lock broke loose I thought he looked like James Dean.

He wore trousers that showed his muscly legs and shirts with short sleeves that showed off his blue Celtic tattoos. He wasn't particularly tall but he was good-looking in that square-jawed way that I'm just a sucker for. And when he spoke, boy, he could just talk anyone's knickers off. It might've been the words he used; it might've been the intonation, I don't know because I could never put my finger on it, but he was very sexy. And when he looked at me, I was glad he wasn't interested in Too Messy.

As we danced, he told me he was a police constable who had visions of becoming a detective. The music was too loud to talk properly, so we left to go to a nearby pub, where we sat in a dark corner, our hope big, eyes bright and conversation small.

Eventually, we left and walked to the bus stop. We behaved ourselves, released from the pub into the night, but we felt aware, so aware, of the possibilities. It was as if the electric ions that buzz before a storm were alive for us, pensive but poised. But if he felt it too, we didn't speak about it. Instead we talked in quiet voices, walked orderly as if to deny the huge amount of wine we'd drunk and the dark eyes we'd been making at each other all night.

We almost made it.

With only ten metres to the bus stop, I thought that it was over. I'd already started to think about how to say goodbye. I started to rehearse lines that suggested I didn't mind too much we hadn't made it to the next base. My cheeks started to flame and I felt both desperate and embarrassed that I'd read it all wrong. The pub had seemed a womb of possibility; the cold night the steriliser.

Then in a snap, it changed.

In one moment he'd moved me back into the shadows and kissed me lightly against someone's garden wall. It was that moment that changed the direction of my life.

At some point I must've drawn breath, but it wasn't for the longest of moments. The intensity of that kiss, mirrored the intensity of our relationship.

We'd only been together for two months when Nick asked me to marry him. We were in bed on a Sunday morning; it was still early and we were sleepy but happy. It was one of those perfect days when the sun fell through the sash windows of his flat, and we had nothing planned except rumbles of a possible Sunday lunch at a country pub and a bank holiday on the other side of another night filled with curiously dark, but incredibly erotic, sex.

I lay on top of him, my arms and legs star-stretched out, my hands finger-laced with his, my feet lying flat against his own.

It must've been summer because we'd lost the duvet somewhere along the way and neither of us looked for it. Instead we just stared and stared into each other's eyes. I stared at those blue eyes and felt amazed that I could have such an intense connection with another person. I'd never experienced anything like it – I just stared, fascinated, enraptured.

'Lisa,' he said, his breath moving my hair against my face. I giggled, but his face had changed, become serious.

'Honey?' he said trying again. 'I want to ask you something. I know . . . it's been no time, I know that . . . but even so, what I'm trying to say is . . .' In his pause, he looked so vulnerable, so afraid. 'I want to marry you.' His tone was serious but his words floated like bubbles. 'What I'm trying to say is – will you marry me? Lisa, will you be my wife?'

I knew it was crazy to get married so soon, when I didn't really know him. But I didn't care. Right then was the happiest moment of my life.

We loved being together and as soon as we were engaged we started looking at flats. But nothing was the perfect family home I'd dreamed of. By the time we walked into the Victorian flat we were to buy, I was seven months pregnant with Jack. We loved it straightaway. 'Look at the high ceilings!' I said in a hushed squeal, as we trailed round after the estate agent. We were a couple with vision. We could see past the peeling wallpaper, the dirty carpet, the dated kitchen and tired bathroom. Together, we opened cupboards, looked up the chimneys and angled our heads out of the bay windows, not caring that the estate agent stood in the hall pointedly looking at his watch and saying: 'If there's nothing else, I've really got to get going.'

We knew we could make it beautiful. It would take dedication, sweat and whatever money we had spare, but we could do it.

'Put the offer in,' I whispered in the kitchen, away from the estate agent's hearing.

'Now?' he asked. 'Before we leave?'

'We don't want to miss out. What if it goes?'

'We should think it over. It's all our money. And more – much more.'

'But we can't risk losing it. It's the best we've seen.' I patted my stomach. 'We'll not find a better one.' Money was tight; we knew I'd be stopping work soon and we would miss my nurse's wage. In those days, we still believed that I'd be going back after a few months.

'But . . .' He rubbed his cheek in the way he always did when unsure and thinking things over. 'But you said we were only looking at it to get an understanding of the market . . .'

I loved him in that moment more than I had ever loved him because I knew he was thinking about it only because I wanted him to. Even more than when I told him I was pregnant and he beamed with joy. Even more than when he introduced me to his widowed mother as if I were a princess. We loved each other a lot back then.

'Please, Nick!' My fingers squeezed his arm, perhaps a little too hard. 'I really want *this* flat.'

He squeezed my hand and nodded.

Nick was – and is – the love of my life. It was to my joy that we came together and it was to my shame how we parted. Much of what went on in our world was as dark as the shadows that we came together in, but I never could regret it because we had Jack.

Jack.

six:

– now –

I remember everything now.

Jack is very nearly eight years old and he is beautiful and he's *in danger.*

Now, every molecule I have is refocused and tuned to save him. I hope he's upstairs where I finally left him, carefully unpeeling my hand from his, as we do every night when he finally falls asleep. But I'm scared he's gone.

I'm scared he's been taken.

I know I'm in the cottage I rented a year ago; I think his father has found us.

The screaming of the foxes is now replaced by silent screaming in my head.

I know I've been hit. I know this is why I am grey and foggy and there's bright white pain at the back of my head.

I sit up. The suddenness of my movement makes my shoulders scream. I'm numb. I don't get more than a few inches without feeling the grey rolling back again, this time with the need to vomit.

I try again to touch the hurt, but I realise he has tied my hands behind my back.

Of course he has.

He. I can't, won't, use his name. When he cut me off by not using mine, then I did the same and burnt his name from my lips. Now he's just Jack's father. *Him.* That man. Bastard. Beloved. Breaker of hearts. Darling one. Destructor. Murderer. Mine. It's all the same.

What will he do now he has found his son?

This question beats in my brain like the *thrum thrum* of my pulse, each beat pulling on my meninges, feeling like the worst hangover ever. This is a question I've considered possibly every night since I bundled Jack up and ran. This is the question that has kept us moving, finally seeking refuge here.

I pull at my wrists, then try to sit up again, feeling sea-lion clumsy. It's harder than I thought, my balance thrown off with my deadened, so painful, hands and shoulders, but this time I manage it. The world lurches . . .

. . . Grey . . .

. . . Nausea . . .

. . . Fairground roller coaster . . .

I bring my knees up and rest my face against them, breathing slowly until the nausea passes.

Panic flares, but I force myself to stay still for a moment, to keep breathing deeply. I want to leap up and save Jack, but I'm worried I'll pass out again. I turn my head and look at the wall clock. Eight thirty: I've been out for half an hour.

I need a plan. There's a great possibility, I realise, that they are already miles away, perhaps even out of Herefordshire itself. I imagine him leading Jack through the back door, into the garden, and taking him by the hand across the green fields, all the time pulling him, his large fingers handcuffed tight around Jack's little wrist.

No – he would've put him in a car. I imagine one hand clamped across a silently screaming Jack's mouth as he holds his son across one shoulder, dropping him into the car boot. Then I start to imagine something worse – much worse.

I see it; I see them; I see the dark.

A vast, jagged iceberg drops into my stomach. I swallow against the cold, cold fear. I know I am close to losing it again. I have to fight this.

I need to search the cottage. If they are here, I will appeal to him, or fight him or whatever it takes. I know the police won't help me, I know they will side with him, but I will not lie here on my floor doing nothing.

I pull against my wrists and then move my fingers in an attempt to understand what's holding them. It's tight. It burns my skin. I twist round trying to see but I can't see much over my shoulder. I fight my bonds: whatever it is bites my flesh again and I understand it's not going to be easy to get free.

Twisting my legs underneath me, I clamber to my knees. Then I check behind me, fearing a blood puddle: but the tiles are clean. Shuffling nearer the oak cabinets, I decide to use the counter for support. I struggle to stand, but manage it, before flopping against it and then laying my cheek against the cold marble. It makes me feel better.

I want to understand what happened to me. I came down the narrow cottage stairs just before eight. I remember coming into the kitchen and going to pick up our dinner plates from the table . . . and . . .

Nothing.

He must have attacked me then, because I don't remember getting to the sink. Where *are* the plates? Not in the sink, not on the floor.

Then I notice the dishwasher door is ajar. It's not been left like that by me. I never use the dishwasher, I always wash up by hand. He never used to, even when it was the two of us, before Jack. It was one of the petty arguments we used to have at a time when we still had petty arguments. Inside are two dinner plates: mine and Jack's.

He stepped over me and opened the unused dishwasher and slotted in the plates as I lay on the floor by his feet.

My anger is hot steel, forged by years of his abuse. Sickened that he has brought his violence here, sickened in case Jack witnessed it, furious he would just step over me to purposefully make a mockery of me, I decide I'm going to have it out with him. Yes, he's bigger, stronger, more vicious, but suddenly I don't care. I am beyond seething. I don't even care if my recklessness is because of my head injury. It doesn't have to make sense: I just *feel* it.

I stand up straight and, reaching the kitchen door, I look into the hall and at the door to the stairs. It takes less than a second to decide to get free first. He'll be expecting me and with my hands tied behind my back, I couldn't do more than insult him.

I look around the kitchen for a knife.

seven:

– before –

I joined the queue for a coffee, then checked the café for my friends. This was my favourite time of the week – Friday morning, the beginning of the weekend, Jack enjoying his time with his nan and me being able to decompress by seeing my friends.

I spotted Issy, and mouthed: *Do you want a drink?* When she shook her head, I felt a stab of relief. I wanted to be generous but I couldn't help but be glad I was buying only for me – money was tight, and Nick kept talking about me going back to work now Jack was three. I had said I'd go back when he was one, and since then the subject seemed to come up every couple of months. But today, I decided I wouldn't think about it – today was Nessa's birthday and I couldn't wait to give her the dozen tulips I'd bought her, and – smugness beyond smugness – I'd made her my famous banana bread. I'd wrapped it carefully in brown paper and string and it smelt pretty darned special.

Coffee in hand, I wove through the tables to our favourite spot in the window. 'Hey!' It was only Issy, not little Lottie, and

I realised I'd never before seen Issy without her daughter during the day. Lottie was the sweetest thing, with matching red hair to Issy's, and she'd sit and draw for hours.

I looked around, expecting to see one of the others come in: 'No Nadia or Nessa yet?' I sat down without waiting for an answer and relaxed.

Issy smiled at me without meeting my gaze. 'Your hair is pretty like that.'

I touched it a little self-consciously: 'Thanks.' Normally I wore my hair scraped back into a ponytail. I changed the subject: 'I thought I'd be last because I've run late all morning. You haven't heard from the others?'

When Issy didn't answer, I looked at her properly and saw her avoidant gaze, the bottom bite of her lip – and just *knew*. Issy was so bright and confident and nothing ever fazed her but I realised from her nerves and the lack of her daughter and our friends that something was going on. This was no normal Friday coffee. Then I thought: *She knows. They all know.*

And even though I didn't truly believe that – even though I dismissed it as my paranoia talking, already it felt like the banana cake and the tulips and the stress of running late might all be for nothing.

'It's just us today.'

'Not even Lottie?'

'I asked my mum to have her.'

'You asked your mum to have her,' I repeated, shock dulling my voice. Issy hated her mum looking after her daughter – she thought her much too strict. Today had to be a special day if she'd actually *asked* her mum for childcare. Obviously whatever was going to be said, couldn't be said in front of small ears.

'Is there ... something going on?' I tried a smile, but my face felt stiff and false. I smelt the waft of banana bread from my string bag and felt ambushed. 'I wish I'd known that Nessa wasn't going to join us – I'll have to get these tulips to her somehow.'

'Sorry,' Issy said, 'maybe I should've said, but we . . .'

Now, I'd have to wait until Nick was back from work and then drive the tulips across town. It'd be late and I'd be tired. My irritation made me bold; if she was going to rip a plaster off, I suddenly wanted her to get on with it. 'Issy – what's going on?'

'We all thought it'd be better that it wasn't everyone today, just one of us. Otherwise . . . you might not feel comfortable.'

My face burnt; within that one statement, I'd changed my mind. I didn't want to know. This would be embarrassing and awkward and I just wanted to be anywhere but here.

Issy was lovely, but she always had that air of self-possessed confidence of those who've had wealthy parents and good schooling. She was a high-powered solicitor and I was only a stay-at-home mum. I didn't begrudge her – she was funny, sweet and hard-working. I really liked her. But I never felt like I quite measured up. Her bobbed hair was, as always, immaculate; my mousey mop rarely saw a brush. I lived in jeans and flip-flops; she loved tailored pieces. Her daughter wore neat dresses and ate biscuits slowly, whereas Jack was greedy and rubbed his dirty hands on his T-shirts. It was as if she was in control of everything, whereas I was just holding on to the edges of life.

'I've just remembered . . .' I said, fumbling for a reason to save me.

'Please don't go.' She lightly rested her hand over mine. 'We really care about you. So much. You're a dear friend and we all just love Jack.' Her eyes flicked away and I knew she was going to deliver a bomb; she squeezed my hand and said: 'This – what I'm about to say – is *so* important.' She took a deep breath: 'I want to get this right. Please give me a chance.'

I nodded and tried to smile a little. 'Of course, Issy. Whatever you want to say.'

Issy inhaled deeply, squeezed her eyes shut and said: 'We've seen the bruises.' There was a long beat and then she added: 'And we are concerned for you. For your safety.'

I let go of her hand to add sugar to my coffee and stirred very slowly, keeping my gaze on the moving spoon.

'We saw your cheek last week.' She barely paused before adding: 'And your eye just before that. And bruises, your finger . . . lots of things have made us think.'

For a moment, I felt like the noise of the people around us had turned mute. In the chaos of my life was this little island that I visited once a week, and I was watching it being smashed by a cyclone.

She looked so sad and I felt so sick, I just didn't know what to do. I had read once that if one wasn't sure how to answer a question, one should simply ask a question back. 'What do you think I should do?'

She inhaled audibly. 'We think you should leave Nick.'

I put down my cup and stared at it. I couldn't look up at her. The café felt hot – too hot. This was my nightmare.

'We will support you . . .' She gripped my arm. 'We've talked it through but, honey, I really hope that you see this is for the best, because of Jack.'

'Jack?'

'You must worry about the effect on him. We haven't seen him for a little while, I know, but we really care about him like we care about you.'

They hadn't seen Jack for over a year. When the women in our NCT gang all went back to work after a year, Friday was the only day everyone was free; Irene, Nick's mum, had agreed to look after Jack on a Friday and I was reluctant to change it not least because I had a little routine where I'd have a coffee with them first thing, then go straight on and do the family shop for the week. I'd tried Jack in nursery and he didn't like it, so the one day felt like a chance to get chores done.

But boy, did I miss him now. I wanted to cling to him and breathe him in and shut out Issy and the reality of what was happening. I couldn't think properly. I felt so hot and so utterly humiliated; all I could smell was the sweet fug of banana cake, reminding me of how it should've been. I realised Issy was looking at me like she expected me to say something. I clutched for my first thought: 'The effect on Jack?' I said, still stumbling to understand what they meant.

'Nick's violence. Obviously we don't understand –' she gave me a heartfelt shoulder squeeze – 'the extent of what you're suffering, but it can't be good for Jack.'

I swallowed against the dry of my throat.

'Nick might get worse.' She leaned forward and lowered her voice: 'What if he doesn't just hurt you but starts to hurt Jack?'

'No!' I said, loud enough to make other people turn around. I couldn't help it, but I worked to control myself. 'He would never hurt Jack. *Never*. He loves him, like I do.' I felt a flash of anger. 'What do you take me for? Do you think I'm the kind of woman who stands by whilst her man hurts her child?'

'I'm sorry, Lisa, we were just worried about if it gets worse and you felt trapped.'

Now it wasn't just the café that was hot – I felt volcanic. 'I'm so hurt you could think that about me! As if I wouldn't kill any man who'd threaten the safety of my child!' As I said it, an image from another time, another place, became so vivid: *the bloodied knife as it fell, used and dirtied, to the floor.*

The memory felt so clear, so powerful, so unexpected, tears sprang to my eyes. I couldn't hide them: I was too overwhelmed.

'Oh gosh, Lisa!' Issy stumbled for tissues, and like the well-prepared mother she was, found them and I mopped up my tears. Then there was a tense silence, where we'd both been bruised, her by my sudden hugely emotional reaction and me by her words. It was like a chess game where neither of us had the skills or knowledge to know how to move forward.

Eventually, I spoke. 'You want me to leave him?'

'No.'

I felt a wave of relief. Perhaps we could talk this through and find some way back to where we should be.

She gave my hand a quick squeeze: 'Honey, we want you to leave him *now*.'

I blinked. 'Now?'

'Don't think you're on your own. We've talked about it – we, the whole gang, are so desperate to help you both, believe me. Nadia says you and Jack can stay with her for as long as you need. Let's be honest, she's got masses of room. And you'll have all our support.' She reached forward and moved the stuck hair away from my sweaty forehead in an intimate gesture. 'Anything you need darling, *anything*.'

I jerked back, not wanting her to touch me.

She took my silence for possible interest and ploughed on. 'Think of it: Nadia's got four floors and there's only her, Ben and Matt. She's already spoken to Matt and—'

Spoken to Matt! Matt the high-powered banking exec who hankers after being a stand-up comedian and who Nick likes the most. Sometimes the eight of us got together in the evening – Nessa and George, Nadia and Matt, and Issy and Chris, me and Nick – but it's all ruined. How could Matt and Nick crack jokes over a beer, now? I realised, with sickening certainty, this big talk has killed that part of my life. Not only are our weekly coffee meetings trashed but also it seems that the part where I get to put on a nice top and nice shoes and have drinks with people who think I'm just like them, is also over.

Now at-the-moment-I'm-stay-at-home-mum-but-I'm-really-a-trained-nurse Lisa and policeman Nick Law will never be welcome around housewife Nadia Marshall and her husband Matt Head-of-some-big-banking-division; now we will never again sip gin and tonic, and eat nibbles from little bowls on their lovely patio. Now it's extremely unlikely that Matt would even let Nick into his house but even if he did, I know that every single one of them would be staring at Nick thinking: *Wife beater.*

And worse, they'll be looking at me thinking: *Target.*

I feel sick that they'll look at little Jack and think: *Victim.*

These people, my friends, are lovely people, and I wish it wasn't true, but I can't see how we can ever not be set apart from them now.

'. . . and Matt's agreed that you and Jack can have the top floor. It's got lovely views – you can see the sea from the Velux. Nessa says you can have her camping kitchen if you want to set it up and Matt and Nadia are happy for you to do that if you want your own privacy. Even if you don't, you'll have your own bathroom and be perfectly safe.'

Issy sat back and breathed out, evidently relieved that she'd delivered what was, undeniably, a difficult message to deliver.

But if it was hard to say, it was harder to hear. The thought of being stuck in someone else's top floor on my own every day with Jack and none of my things around me and no future, and no family unit, made me feel sick.

'Thank you,' I said, now it was my turn to squeeze her hand. 'I mean that, but . . . you're wrong. We *are* a happy family. We all love each other and want to be together. It's sweet of Nadia to offer us her house, but we don't need it. I'm tired a lot of the time – as you know Jack doesn't sleep well – and I'm clumsy. I know it just sounds like a cliché, but aren't clichés often true? When he sleeps through the night properly – when he's eighteen maybe! – I'll go back to work and I'll just be . . . more on it.' This time my smile felt more natural.

She sat back surprised. 'Are you saying we've got it wrong?'

I nodded slowly. I made myself drink my coffee as if it evidenced just how OK everything was. 'I know it sounds like the worst excuse ever – oh, I walked into the door! – but . . .' I shrugged. 'What can I do if that's what's happened? I can't tell it any other way, can I?'

A shadow of doubt crossed Issy's lovely face. 'No, I guess . . . not.'

'Look, I really appreciate the offer. But it's – I'm glad to say – just not like that. But it gives me a good excuse to go back to the GP for help with his sleep. I'll tell this to the GP to show just how bad it is for me, and who knows, maybe this time they'll set up a referral or something. Sorry.'

'You don't need to apologise.'

'I just feel, you've been so thoughtful, so kind, but it's all for . . .' I shrugged, warming to my role.

'For nothing.'

'Exactly. But, Issy, seriously, so, so nice of you. I'm lucky to have such great, thoughtful, *kind* friends.'

Somehow, our hands found one another, and for a moment we smiled hard at each other, as we gripped hands across the table. And then – and I still don't know why – Issy, with a deft and sudden movement, reached across with her other hand and pulled up the baggy sleeve of my loose-knit jumper.

I didn't let her – I just didn't move quick enough.

And there further up, on the soft flesh on the underside of my arm, near my elbow, was a burn, where, when frying Nick a couple of eggs and after a silly dispute about ketchup, a sudden shove caught the flame, and I saw it and then I looked up to see her staring at it – and I did nothing, because I could *do* nothing.

Because it was over. Even if she'd pulled up my sleeve and found no injury, I would've still understood that she didn't believe me. And I understood, as well as anyone, that once trust has gone in a relationship, it's gone. But she did find something, so the mistrust now went both ways.

Thinking that, I got up and kissed her goodbye.

eight:

– before –

Although the café had felt stifling, outside, despite it being well into autumn, it felt little better; the unseasonable warmth combined with a fine mist made it feel sultry, like a possible storm could suddenly erupt. Feeling breathless, I decided to pick up Jack early from Irene's – I felt unsettled and anxious without him. It was as if because one unforeseen event had occurred – *and that jagged, forgotten memory of the falling knife!* – then anything could now happen.

I knew Nick wouldn't like it; Irene loved her time with her only grandchild and Nick would grumble that I was spoiling the child again. I knew he was jealous of Jack's and my special bond, but after last night, I no longer cared.

What Issy didn't know was that last night, another terrible row had erupted which ended with Nick getting a bleeding hand and me receiving a bruised ear which I had covered by keeping my hair loose. But now I could no longer just wear full-length sleeves, dab heavily with the concealer, or let my hair fall about my face. Now I knew that they would be looking for signs of injury, I wouldn't be able to hide it. Now, they would be watching for any difference in my gait, any awkwardness in my sitting down – just anything that might show that I had an injury. Then, if I went to the loo they would watch the door and whisper to each other, worried, until they saw me coming back, and then they would resume some fabricated conversation. I knew I'd sit down, pink-cheeked, and try to hide my misery, but instead my heart would be breaking from their concern.

As I walked up the hill to the terraced houses where Irene lived, I'd realised I'd lost them. But as I pushed away the upset that I'd allow myself to process later (if only because I didn't want to arrive at Irene's in tears because it'd be too awkward to explain), I instead held on to the new determination I suddenly felt – their concern would not be in vain.

I wouldn't continue the way I had been. I resolved to make a change – a permanent, yet unknown change – before I turned out like my mother.

Feeling fierce yet fragile, I arrived at Irene's to collect Jack. Although I hadn't told her I was coming early, she was friendly and ushered me into her neatly kept terraced house. Irene was the most organised person I knew, her home prim with the same precision she applied to her tidy appearance. Irene – although a little too bossy at times – was worthy of respect: she'd had three boys, all one year apart, and I was lucky to have her help.

Jack was playing trains on the floor, but he ran to me. 'Mummy, home, home, home.' he said into my waist. Sometimes I worried about Jack's limited speech, but whenever I broached the subject with Nick, all he would say was that Jack should go to nursery so he could widen his social pool. It was amazing how nursery had become the panacea for every ill.

Normally, I'd be happy to sit and have a natter with Irene, but today I wanted to get Jack and go. My head was full of tumbling thoughts: it was if Issy had jump-started me out of inertia. Her solution wasn't right for me, but humiliated, I now felt determined to find one that was. A walk home via the park with my son was just what I needed to focus my thoughts.

I'd readied an excuse to decline a cup of tea without seeming rude, but she didn't offer, instead just dismissing me with: 'No, dear, you must get going if you're busy,' and let me go. Because she was so lonely, I'd never normally get away so easily, so I became gripped by paranoia: did she know Nick and I were arguing? Had he told her about last night? Did she see a future where I was no longer her daughter-in-law and she was already making the mental break from me?

As we left, Jack hugged me tightly and was so reluctant to walk, I hoicked him onto my hip. Despite the weight, I took the longer route home to give me time to think.

We walked the long road that bordered the park and I enjoyed being out of the suffocating café and away from Irene's. We walked amongst a line of sycamores, the russet, red and golden leaves lifting my spirits. I held Jack koala-close, pleased to have him to cling to. I breathed in his scrummy smell and kissed his face, allowing my tears to fall.

'Why are you crying, Mummy?'

'I'm just so happy to see you, darling,' I said, wiping my eyes. 'I really missed you this morning.'

Jack kissed my hand: 'I *always* miss you, Mummy, when I'm not with you.' I set him free to run around under the trees; I pressed the space under my belly button where Jack had grown. He'd been an impossible carry; but still I'd been sorry to give him up. I knew that each day that passed after his birth would see him move further and further away from me, until one day he'd be gone, leaving me all alone.

I always saw my parents' flaws so clearly that I thought I'd be able to just be the opposite of them and it'd all be fine. It was as if they had given me a rule book on how not to be: I only had to apply it in reverse and I'd succeed where they had failed. But it seems that life is more complex than that: it seems that there's more than one way to fail.

As Jack collected fallen leaves, I resolved to see my mother and ask for advice – she was the one person I could trust with the truth and still not feel judged by. Besides, she'd be able to tell if I was unhappy anyway – she always could. I could never hide anything from her, even though she'd been serving a life sentence since I was eight. I winced as I thought of the long journey from Brighton to Woking I'd have to make to see her, first by train, then by bus, to Send women's prison. But I knew it would be worth it – she would help me make a plan.

Jack brought me his bundle of leaves and together we threw them into the wind. He laughed and jumped for them and I delighted in his joy. His game lifted my spirits and I found I could manage a smile at the thought of what Issy would say if she knew that my mother was imprisoned for murder. I wondered if it would make her view my marriage differently.

I rather thought it would – and that she'd possibly view me differently too.

nine:

- before -

Two weeks later, my visit to my mother was booked in.

Nothing would stop me from my monthly visit to see her: I loved my mum dearly. But this time it felt even more vital – this time I counted down the days because I needed her help.

I always took Jack with me, but now I needed to go alone. There was no question, I'd been galvanised by Issy and was determined to take action, but if Jack was with me, I wouldn't be able to talk freely. If my mother was to help me make a plan, then she would need my innermost thoughts and feelings, and the details were not Jack-friendly.

First, I'd asked Irene if she could have Jack for the day, but it wasn't her day to have him and she had a busy diary. Normally, I would've turned to one of my NCT friends to have him, but that was now out of the question. Then, unexpected joy of joys, I realised that Nick was rota'd a day off on visiting day, and I'd asked him: 'Would you be able to have Jack?'

His response was to actually laugh. 'Not on my day off, love. I've got golf with the boys from work.'

But he offered me the car so at least I'd be spared the hideous train journey followed by the seven mile prison visitor shuttle bus.

If I were to take Jack, then I accepted that I had to do our 'usual', as I so quaintly called it. When Nadia had flown with their baby on a plane, she'd confessed to us that she'd slipped her daughter a little antihistamine, knowing it would make her drowsy. I'd never taken Jack abroad, but she'd given me the idea and I'd tried it. It worked and became part of our 'usual' routine for travelling to prison, alongside buying him a new book and a packet of something chewy that would take an age to eat. I always felt lousy doing it, but children's doses of antihistamine are pretty harmless and my training as a nurse gave me a little confidence that I knew what I was doing. I told myself that since he seemed to hate loud noises and the clanging and banging of metal doors could scare him, this would be better for him. That was true, but so was the fact that nothing was straightforward about visiting my mother in prison, so I found it easier to have him calm and a little drowsy. It worked so well, we even called it the Sleepy. 'Time for Sleepy!' I said, before telling him to 'open wide!' and feeding him the medicine.

He took the spoon from me and sucked it like a lolly. I'd tasted it: it was loaded with sugar. 'Any more Sleepy?' he asked hopefully.

'No darling, that's just the usual to help with the journey.'

'We are going to see Nana today,' he said knowledgably.

Yes, I answered silently. *And she's going to give us the solutions to our problems.* I had a quick thought about what was ahead of me and then said: 'Actually, give me the spoon back – now you're a bigger boy you could probably have a fraction more.'

A couple of hours later, as I pulled my Maclaren pushchair and the shame of still using it out of the boot, I wondered if I'd been too generous with it. Jack had slept the whole journey. He must've been the only small child never to nod off in the car, but with the antihistamine, he had and as I pulled him out, hot and sweaty from his car seat, he didn't even wake with the October air on him.

I put him gently into the pushchair. 'Mummy loves you,' I said, whispering into his hair. I felt terrible I was still relying on it for these journeys. He was three and should walk, but he was slow and would dawdle. I'd never got over the shame of walking into a prison to see my mum and I couldn't bear anything that made it slower and more agonising. I wish I had got used to it, but I hadn't. I was a bad daughter and a bad mother. Wanting to feel better by trying for a kiss, I didn't dare, in case it woke him. I think if that had happened, and he'd woken with a cry, I would've put him back into his seat and driven all the way home. I was close to breaking. My confidence at talking to my mum was waning – the drive had given me time to think and I'd become edgy with too much caffeine and speculation of what she'd say when I smashed the image of her daughter's perfect world.

But I couldn't let go of the look in Issy's eyes as she pulled up my sleeve and saw my bruise. My world had to change, whether I liked it or not.

And, as I approached the prison, the tension of disappointing my mum and yet needing a new authentic life, put me on the edge of breaking.

ten:

– *before* –

HM Send women's prison was my mother's favourite prison by far. She had been newly transferred here to this modern, brick building, which held the highest concentration of women lifers anywhere in the country. My mum said it was more relaxed, more respectful than the others she'd been in before, and she enjoyed the gardening detail she'd been assigned.

But even if she preferred it, the visitors were the same as the others: everyone drawn and pensive as we filed to go in. I always felt the oppressiveness of it, as I fell compliantly into line with the thin stream of visitors – mostly women, but some men and some children, too, as we stepped into the building. We'd file; we'd wait in line; bonelessly, we offered our bags and bodies, submissive to the searching. There, we were no longer in charge of ourselves.

I don't think I ever visited a prison without half-expecting a hand to drop onto my shoulder and a guard to say that a mistake had been made and I was no longer at liberty to leave.

I could do the routine with my eyes shut. I knew the drill better than most.

I passed the prison officer my ID and he checked me off against the list. I waited as another officer asked me to sign a declaration that I wasn't bringing in anything I shouldn't and then I was checked again, patted down once more and my pockets checked. When she'd finished with me, she scrutinised Jack's pushchair, and then I had to lift him out so she could examine where he sat, and also the back of him.

The first time I visited my mother in prison with Jack, I was outraged. She was still in Holloway then, and the austere Victorian walls had frowned dourly upon prisoners and visitors alike. Before I'd been pregnant, I'd seen other prams searched, but never thought much about it. But when my son, tiny then at only a few weeks old, was searched, my maternal instincts had kicked in and I'd shouted at them, creating a scene. I couldn't bear them searching his pram, running their hands over his Babygro back. It'd all felt so awfully Dickensian, so persecutory, as if the system was torturing the tiny and innocent.

But time has a habit of getting you used to things – things that once you'd never have believed you could possibly endure.

After submitting to the search, I pushed Jack's pushchair into the corridor to the waiting room.

The room was overlit and filled with plastic stackable seats. Around it sat about thirty people, some I recognised, some I didn't. When I first started visiting as a teenager, I hated the visiting rooms, because I never felt that my mother was the same as the other prisoners. But as the years went by, I changed my mind. As I got older, I got a clearer perspective and I realised that she was *just* like the other women. I think that prisons are stuffed full of women like my mother – women with similar tales of suffering, subjugation and careless violence – and always have been and always will be.

Sitting there waiting to be called in, with Jack still dozing in the pushchair, I rubbed a bruise I had hidden under my sleeve and realised I was probably more kith and kin with these female inmates than with Issy and the others. I just didn't *want* that to be true.

I thought this as I gently pushed the sleeping Jack. I loved him when he was asleep. His eyelashes were longer than most children's – longer than mine even – and they lay like a delicate kiss against his apricot cheeks. His mouth was a soft blush and if I leaned closer I could hear his gentle breaths.

My name was called by an officer with a clipboard. I got up with a small group and left the waiting room by a different door. Like obedient school children we filed down the corridor and stepped into the visiting hall.

Mesh covered the windows, restraining the bruised sky behind them. Harsh lighting glared. The room was dotted with low tables and grouped chairs, one orange chair amongst three grey chairs at each table.

I saw my mum lift her hand in greeting and I pushed Jack towards her.

She stood to meet me; she was taller than most women and broad-shouldered, perhaps a little overweight. She had chestnut brown hair that reached her shoulders when she wore it loose, but time seemed to stroke grey into it more and more each time I saw her. She gave me only the briefest of kisses: but it was warm and made me feel like I was wanted. It was all we were allowed in case I passed any contraband to her.

She held me briefly by the shoulders: 'My darling girl.' Then she stared at me closely, as if I wore my new loneliness as punch marks on my face. 'How are you, Lisa?'

'How are you, Mum?'

She stared at me with her conker-coloured eyes, seeing me better than anyone ever did. 'You've ignored my question,' she gently grumbled as she settled her large body back into her chair. She was wearing denim dungarees and they suited her. Her fringe had been cut shorter and I could see her eyebrows; they too seemed a little grey and I felt nerves crawl in my stomach that time was not standing still.

'I'm just tired,' I told her – this was safe ground. I was always tired.

She touched the skin on my cheekbones. 'You need more iron. And more fun.' It felt lovely to be touched by my mum – I've never had to doubt how much she loved me.

Her shrewd stare shifted to a sleeping Jack. 'You shouldn't let him nap during the day, then he'd sleep through the night. He's turned three and far, far too old for it – and for the pram.'

'Buggy, Mum – prams are for babies. All kids develop at different rates – boys can be a bit later with things. Besides, the travel here wears him out and trust me, *nothing* makes him sleep through the night – me and Nick have tried everything. Besides, if I woke him up now, he'd be a grumpy loud three-year-old.'

'Nobody would mind.'

'*I* would mind.' Irritation itched: I wanted to talk about more important things than whether Jack napped.

'You never slept either. Golly, you were a trial.'

'Trust me, the trial is travelling here,' I said, more stung now than irritated. 'One more disrupted night is worth the peace for me driving on the motorway or queueing to get into this *prison*, or when I'm being searched. Schlepping us two hours here and two hours back takes it out of me, Mum, and if he's asleep for some of it, then he's one less thing to worry about.'

She held the pushchair, her thumb skating up and down as if she was thinking hard about something.

Instantly, I felt annoyed with myself. I didn't want to admit I found the journey hard work, because I wanted to protect her from my anxieties. And this was not the mood I wanted to create. 'I'm sorry, Mum, I love seeing you, so does Jack – you know that.'

'I'm sorry that he has to see me here. I'm sorry that you did too. Hard for a little kid, I realise that.'

Hard for a daughter any age, I wanted to say, but instead I said: 'It's fine, I'm just grumpy, that's all. Tired – like I said.'

'I know you aren't yourself, Lisa. Are you and Nick OK?'

I made the mistake of taking a minute to steady myself. A cup of tea would help. 'Hold that thought,' I told her, begged two minutes and grabbed my purse so I could buy us both a cup of tea from the WRVS ladies.

When I came back, I nearly dropped the two plastic cups of stewed tea I was carrying. My mother had Jack out of his pushchair and he was sitting on her lap, laughing. Clearly, the antihistamine had worn off. Jack was holding his chin up really high, and she was looking under it, pretending to look for something. 'There! I found it – I knew the tickle was hiding there!'

'More, more,' he squealed and she gave him a last tickle before clasping him tightly to her large bosom.

Usually, I felt glad to see their bond as it made the journey worthwhile to reunite them both and I loved seeing how he responded to her, but right then, I felt cheated. I might be grown up, but *I* needed her.

I pouted, hating myself for it and for not speaking up: *You said I could talk to you!* I watched mutely as my mother started a new tickle game with him: 'Naughty Jack! Hiding my tickle from me . . . let me see if I can find it!' Jack laughed and begged for more.

I look round to catch the eye of one of the prison officers, but no one was paying attention to us.

'Can I . . .?' I said, reaching for him after a few minutes. I felt envious – of her or him, I wasn't sure. It wasn't just that I wanted her attention and guidance, it was that Jack had been so tense recently, and seeing him happy with my mother just reinforced the idea that perhaps it was because of me, because we were so close (*too* close, Nick said). 'I've got your tea here.'

'I'm just saying hello.' She continued her game without even looking up. 'And if you can't already tell, I'm ignoring you, Lisa, because you fuss too much. The tea will need to cool and Jack will not break –' she paused to blow a raspberry on his neck and his scream of happiness was so loud it drew glances (except from the officers) – 'nor will he smash or fall apart –' another raspberry – 'from a big, happy cuddle from his nana who loves him.'

I dropped my hands to my lap and waited, powerless.

The seconds and minutes ticked on.

Eventually, she handed Jack back. By the time she did, I was near tears with frustration. I had travelled for hours for one reason and it was being thwarted.

Apparently she noticed this: 'You need to relax more.' She set him up with his reading book and then reached for her tea. For a minute she simply sipped from her plastic cup and smiled at me. 'You're too tense,' she finally announced. 'I can tell you now, you don't get that from me.' She leaned forward, observing me like a new type of animal, as if trying to classify it for the first time. 'You get that from your father – he was always too uptight and it was *not* good for him. Now, come on, I want to hear from you. You've clearly got something on your mind and now Jack's had his cuddle, I want to hear what's what.'

I wanted to confide – felt desperate to – but how could I now Jack was awake? He sat settled, reading his book, but I never trusted that he wouldn't soon pick up on what we were saying. It was crushing, because I desperately wanted to seek her counsel, but it was now out of the question – the chance was gone.

'I'm fine,' I said brightly, feeling anything but.

'You know what fine means in therapy terms?' She didn't wait for me to answer: 'Fucked up. Insecure. Neurotic and over-Emotional. Get it?' She laughed and I burst into tears.

She dried my eyes, and I tried to laugh it off, but it was too accurate. Eventually, she said: 'I'm sorry, darling. You're so fragile.' She dabbed at me with a tissue, kissed me on the cheek and then sent me a poison dart: 'Perhaps you should go back to work, Lisa. At your age, you should be building your career.'

'I hear that from Nick all the time.'

'How're your finances?'

I inhaled, trying to keep calm. I had not come here for this. 'Well, two wages are better than one.' I'd been hoping to sound sarcastic or ironic or something but it was lost on her because she nodded as if I was simply stating an obvious fact. 'But if I went back to work, Jack would do what?'

'What do other people do? Send their children to nursery?' She smiled. 'It'll do you good to have a bit of time apart. You spend too much time together.'

I glanced at Jack – his eyes were dutifully following from left to right and after a pause, he turned a page. But I didn't trust it. Jack was always so smart.

'How could I spend "too much" time together with my own child?'

'Because love needs time to breathe. It doesn't hurt to miss someone a bit.'

Like I had to learn to miss you? I nearly asked. But I didn't because I'm not that mean.

She wrinkled her nose and leaned in. 'You were a good nurse. You shouldn't give it up.'

'I could've been a terrible nurse and you wouldn't know.'

'I know *you*.' Her eyes narrowed. 'I know you try hard at everything you do. And you're kind too. And smart. How could you not be a great nurse if you try hard and you're kind and smart?'

'Maybe I pinched the patients.'

'Well, go and pinch them again, Lisa, before you forget how to or before your training gets so old they don't let you. You should be busy; it suits you.'

'Things are great the way they are, Mum.' I was lying but I couldn't do anything else, because I could just *tell* that Jack was really listening to every word we say. I wanted an honest conversation, but with an audience, that wasn't possible.

'You'd have your own money again,' she persevered. 'It'd give you more . . . *control*.'

The way she emphasised her last word made me think she'd selected the word with care. Did she know something? Had I given something away?

'If you have your own career, Lisa, you can be more independent. That can only give you more . . . *options*.'

I struggled for what to say, because it felt like we were talking about my problems. I wondered if she knew, but I was unsure. 'I tried nursery and it wasn't a good fit for Jack.' *There* – I caught Jack give just the quickest glance up at me. He *was* listening. We cannot, I decide, have this conversation now. 'How's the gardening, Mum? You said you've been growing some veg?'

'Nursery does children good,' she said, ignoring me. 'They see other kids their own age; it helps them socialise.'

'Well, obviously, but it doesn't suit them all. Did you pick your Brussel sprouts yet?'

'You loved nursery.'

'I was different, I—'

'Different, smifferent. You've just got to persevere. That's parenting – and you know it. You've only tried one – I can't believe that they're all the same.'

My breath felt like it was burning in my chest. There was so much I hadn't imagined about becoming a parent. I would've never been able to guess at how hard it was – how relentless, how demanding, how boring it often was. Getting a kid to poo on a loo – who knew it would require such effort? But of all the things – like making interesting 'recipes' out of mashed veg or coordinating outfits – what I could *never* have been prepared for, was how political it was. How judgey everyone thought that they had a right to be. And that judgement was what I struggled with the most. 'No one perseveres more than me – and he's where he should be, safe with me.'

'What's this nonsense about being safe? Why on earth would you worry about his safety?' She wrinkled her nose again. She does this a lot when she doesn't get her own way. 'You're not thinking about when you were a child and—'

'I don't want to get into this now.'

'Well, honey,' she said with a little laugh, 'we could wait until I come over to yours on Sunday, for that roast you promised me.'

Her sarcasm dug deep. I've never had my mother visit any home I've lived in. I've never cooked for her; she's never seen a single thing I've ever chosen for my teenage walls or my adult home. One day she was there, then she was gone. And she never came back.

'It was bad,' I said. 'You can't understand: you weren't there.' I was still talking about Jack's short stint at nursery, but I think we both knew that I was talking about other things as well.

She must have, because she leaned back and looked around the room. Normally I could read her expression, but then I couldn't. Instantly I felt bad – she didn't want to leave me, she just wanted to protect me. It wasn't until I had Jack that I realised just how awful it must've been for her. It must've been torture. Perhaps it still was.

The silence stretched on between us. On the other side of the hall, a prisoner had started to raise her voice to her male visitor. My mother watched them, the whole time rubbing her pinkie fingernail against the pad of her thumb – back and forth, back and forth. It was a sign that she was agitated. I know this is because she views the other women as her responsibility. She's been here five minutes yet she's already queen of this prison too, top dog again, unofficially in charge. She's earned her place as a lifer, but how she's made it to the top after only five minutes at Send, I don't know.

Maybe I wouldn't want to.

'Do you know her?' I asked, indicating subtly with my head in the direction of the angry prisoner. Of course she did, but I wanted to hear that she did, that that was the reason for her annoyance. Not me.

'Shhh,' she said, and continued to watch.

I thought: that's it now, she's annoyed and now she's not going to say anything else to me until the end of the visit. We'll have to wait out the rest of the time in silence.

I was free to get up and leave any time I wanted to, but only once had I done that to her, walked out in front of everyone, before the bell rang signalling our time was up. Everyone would see; everyone would know we'd had an argument. I knew that Mum was so proud of me, her only child, and I loved her very much and would never want to suggest anything other than that.

But we didn't sit in silence because the other prisoner's argument stopped as soon as it started, and then Mum relaxed and started talking about her gardening. I played along, asking questions in the right places, but all I could think about was that I'd come here for a plan and I'd now leave without one.

When visiting time was up, my mother reached for me and hugged me, clearly not caring that it wasn't allowed. I inhaled her smell and felt ridiculously comforted by her embrace. The relief brought tears stinging to my eyes.

'I'm sorry, Lisa, if today hasn't gone well. I'm sorry if there was something you wanted to say but couldn't. Honey, I know you don't like writing detail in your letters, but they don't read them as closely as you think and anyway –' she rubbed her thumb down my cheek – 'the screws do understand that people have problems. You mustn't feel judged. We are all just people on God's earth, trying to make it out of the scrum alive.'

I nodded benignly, determined not to torture her with emotion, but as I turned to leave, she gripped my arm and looked me in the eye. 'Lisa. Listen to me, darling. I think you're a great mother. But I want you to think about what returning to work could give you – the opportunity to earn your own money and be your own woman. I want you to have your independence.'

She tightened her grip and when she spoke the next line, her voice was meant to be a whisper, I think, but sounded instead like a hiss: 'I don't want you to suffer like I did.'

My heart stopped beating, I swear, as I thought: she has seen my bruises. *She knows.*

Finally, she released me. But when she bent to kiss Jack, he turned his head into my skirt and stayed there.

We both pretended he was tired, but perhaps my mother understood that Jack had heard her conversation. I picked my son up and settled him on my hip, and pushed the pushchair away from my mum.

It always hurt so bad to leave her there. Worse now that I'd seen her grey hair. Her recent request for parole had been denied – there was no clear end date to this.

I never looked back at her – never – but that day I did, and saw that she was standing there, watching me go. I wondered what she was thinking. But if she had any regrets, it didn't show because she smiled and she lifted her hand a little, giving just the most subtle movement of a wave. Queen-like, really. She *is* my queen; my hero.

My mum.

And for some reason, then, I re-remembered the forgotten, long-buried memory of my mother dropping that knife onto her bedroom carpet. I remembered the crimson tide of the duvet, white cotton then red. It was *so* sudden: so quick. Red before it fell from her hand.

This time, the memory was less abrupt for the remembering. And strangely, it didn't knock me to the floor again. For some inexplicable reason, it seemed to do the opposite. I knew that I was always afraid of my father and the memory of my mother letting go of that knife didn't fill with me fear, but instead filled me with confidence and peace. Finally, *finally*, she was in charge. I didn't understand it, but I didn't question it either because I was so filled with radiating love for her, I simply lifted my hand in response to her goodbye.

Even from my distance, I could see the golden delight in her eyes and I wondered how many times she had watched me go, my face turned away from her, waiting for me to turn back as I just did. All these years of my not turning back to give a final goodbye feels like I have stolen from her. This patient, stoic woman as strong as Greek marble. She gifted me treasure and I love her.

On impulse, I pressed my fingers against my dry lips and blew her a faithful kiss. And then I realised we must've seen the same corny film, because she pretended to catch it in her fist and grinned a conspiratorial smile that creased all the way into her deep laughter lines.

Then, I decided, my mother was wrong about my being like my father.

Even better, I realised I didn't need her advice because I already had so much more than that. I know I will work out my own action plan, because I am her daughter and as such, I carry her with me. Really, I am so much more than me alone. Her bravery is mine – and that could take me anywhere.

eleven:

– now –

There's an empty slot in the knife block. The gap yawns ominously, as obvious to me as a lost tooth. It's the mid-sized one that's gone – wide blade, smooth edge. The one I use for chopping vegetables. But we had omelette, chips and peas earlier, so I know I didn't use it. Now I can only think of that missing knife. I know what it means – he means business.

Well, so do I, I think, white hot with the heady fire of indignation, injustice and anger.

I can't think about Jack dying but I do anyway. I promised myself I'd stay focused but I can't. I'm trying to stay strong but it's like there's a little pop-up window that's opened in my mind and it's running a film of the unthinkable.

I'm doing what any decent mother would. If you see something – a situation which is toxic and dangerous for your child – then you do what you can to stop it from happening. I know I've not always been a very good parent, but I'm trying, I'm still trying. Even now, I'm still just trying to be better.

And that's why we are in this cottage, in this nightmare now. This pop-up video in my mind has been what I've feared for a long time. This is what I've been running from.

Is it happening tonight?

Is it happening now?

Galvanised, I lean over the countertop and clamp my mouth down on a knife. The steel handle is cold and heavy between my molars. A nerve registers the metal with a lightning bolt, but it feels good, like it's wired straight to my brain. Like a jolt to a dead battery, I instantly feel more alert. I know I can do this.

I get a strong grip on the handle and slowly, steadily, pull it away from the wood. I feel like a contestant in a sick TV game show: *'Will Lisa Law be able to complete this challenge?'* It feels so real I realise I've taken a major blow to the head. The knife starts to rise out of the block, and I hear the *'Oooohhhh!'* of the imaginary over-hyped audience, but it gets to a point where I can't pull back any further. I haven't got the reach to change the angle.

It starts to slip.

I let go and it slithers back into place. *'Aaahhhh!'* commiserates the audience. They were certain I was going to do it. I swallow against the saliva that's pooling in my mouth, not even minding that I'm half mad. At least they're on my side.

I feel like screaming. I lean right over the countertop and slam my head against the knife block. The block goes down with a bang. I hold my breath. Instead of the spike of victory I should've felt as the knives splay across the countertop, I feel scared because the bang of the block was loud – *really* loud.

This cottage is so old and creaky; I know after a year of living here that no one can move around it without someone else hearing. If he comes downstairs, I will hear each step across the landing, and each step on the stairs.

I wait, still not breathing. Like a hare caught on a road at night-time, I listen for danger.

I don't breathe, I don't move: I wait.

There's nothing. But my mind whispers: *No one heard you because they're no longer there.* They've left, gone into the night, running –

No.

The worst has already happened.

No.

The knife block is on its side and the knives are freed.

I clamp the knife handle between my teeth, before I realise I've been so fixated on getting it, I hadn't realised the futility of it – how am I going to use it to cut my hands free?

Stupid, muddy brain.

I twist my head round as far as I can, moving my wrists to meet my mouth. I arch my back, yoga like, and crane my neck. But it's not even close. Not even a little bit.

If I really push myself, I can just about see my hands. They are so darkened with blood, they no longer look like mine. But I don't care – only Jack matters. I focus. I try for another arch, another push to do the impossible, but I already know it's point-less – I already know it's not even *near* working. I'm only doing it because I don't know what else to do. *Think, Lisa.*

Perhaps I can wedge the knife to saw back and forth against my ties. I drop the knife back onto the counter's edge.

I turn my back to it and grab it first try. Hope surges. I hold the handle, cold in my hot sausage fingers.

Inching round, I trap the knife between me and the wall so that the blade can press against my bindings. It takes a few fumbles but when I angle it just right, I know I am pressing against them. It's painful, because whatever it is that is tying my hands together puts even more pressure on my wrists, but I keep going.

'Lisa is going to have another go, ladies and gentlemen! Isn't she just the grreeaaatttesst contestant we've ever had?'

I can't achieve the sawing motion that I'd hoped for – I can't get the range of movement. The ticking of the clock is taunting the pressure of time.

Eventually, finally, I put the knife back on the counter and stare at it like a lover that's betrayed me – it gave me a hope of something that wasn't real.

I need to try something else. I cast around the small kitchen, desperate for a solution. The food mixer; the washing machine; the sink; all these are useless to me.

Then I see the gas stove.

twelve:

I see the gas stove and think: *Fire cuts through everything*.

Including me. Do I really want to do this? I look at the gas ring and think how the fire will cut my flesh. I'll do anything to save Jack – but there must be a different way. Anger and fear and being knocked out have made me hasty. I just need to take a second to be logical.

It comes to me in an instant, a bright and beautiful *ta-daaaahhhh!!! My handbag is in the hall!* Everything I need is in there – my phone, wallet and car keys. Yes, I decide, of course! Logic saves the day. Relief washes through me – and I almost smile at my fervour: no burning needed today.

I look out into the hall first, frightened as I peer round the door. The stairs door is shut. By the front door is a shoe rack and I can see my bag on top where I normally leave it.

I look around the room; it's gloomy, lit by a single lamp. It's a small room, set up as a dining room when we moved in, but because we eat at the kitchen table, I squeezed in some small sofas and now we have a second sitting room. It doesn't function as a hall: halls are for people who have visitors.

But he's not there – there's nowhere to hide.

I take a deep breath and then with light feet, run to the door. Bending down I pick up my bag handles with my teeth and then, feeling triumphant, turn and run back to the safety of the kitchen. But before I get there, I realise what is wrong with what I have just seen.

Only Jack's little shoes are in the rack. All mine are gone.

On tiptoes I enter the kitchen and drop the bag down on the kitchen table. But I feel deflated – he's a step ahead of me. With careful, short moves, I bite the bottom of my leather bag and coax the insides onto the pine table. But really I'm thinking about him taking my shoes. There were several pairs there – trainers, sandals, welly boots. In my mind's eye, I see the gaps on the rack, and one by one the contents of my bag is emptied. Lipstick, a hairbrush, a used tissue, some wrapped individual mints that I must've got from a curry house about a hundred years ago and other detritus from my life. But really I'm seeing the gap left by the welly boots. It tells me what I won't find in my bag.

When everything is on the table I look at the contents. Just as I thought: no phone, no keys, no wallet. Even if I wanted to call the police – which I don't because there's no point because they'll only side with him – I can't. My mobile is the only phone in the cottage.

I also won't be driving out of here. I realise I was sort of thinking I'd be able to drive the car for help. Somewhere in my brain lurked visions of me holding the steering wheel with my mouth, which I realise now was just ridiculous. Already, I can feel my cognitive function improving. As if I'd be able to negotiate the curvy country lanes steering with my mouth!

Ridiculous, desperate me. But as ludicrous as the idea was, I still feel crushed it can't happen.

No money either – so I can't even flag a bus down. Not that there's a bus stop within a mile of here.

I breathe deeply, trying not to cry. Instead I run through the facts. He's here – he's taken my shoes and phone to stop me from leaving. He tied me up and knocked me out. Perhaps he doesn't want to kill me, but he certainly has something in mind.

I want to tiptoe up the first few stairs. Even if I don't reach the top, I want to try and hear if they are in the cottage still. It's risky – the stairs door will squeak and so will every bit of wood I step on. It makes sense that if I am going to try and bust my hands free, I do that first.

Just in case.

I look back at the gas ring. Whether I like it or not, if I don't want to face him with my hands tied behind my back, then it's suddenly become idea number one again.

thirteen:

– now –

I look at the gas hob. The reality of burning whatever is tying my wrists from me without properly being able to see, makes me feel ill. But he's a killer, a killer of many, and I don't have a choice. I purposefully remember the stretchers carrying the dead and the blue lights flashing in the dark and remind myself that there's nothing he won't do, no risk he won't take, to get his way.

Just as he's bold, I need to be bolder.

I turn back to the gas ring, I will not fail now. I will only face him with my hands freed. Perhaps I can keep it as an element of surprise. I need anything that will work in my favour.

Backwards, with fumbling, fattened fingers I turn on the ring closest to me and then click the ignition. *Tisht, tisht, tisht.* It flames sapphire. I am not afraid of anything except for Jack's safety.

I hear the *shusshh* of the gas.

Over my shoulder, I can see it perfectly, but when I raise my hands up to the flame, my shoulder blades rise up and block my view. I won't be able to get an accurate aim.

I count: 'One, two –' and even though I can't see what I am doing, before I can say *three*, I push my wrists back into the flames.

fourteen:

– before –

I left Send prison with Jack. As we walked through the gates, I stopped to put Jack into his buggy but as I turned to my beautiful son, I paused. He kicked a stone and I thought: *how long can I keep doing the* same *thing?*

Then: *am I really being the best parent I can be for Jack?*

My childhood memory of my mother dropping her knife and then, just now, seeing her watching me go, made me realise that despite what she'd done, she had never stopped watching out for me. The fact she'd been better than my perception made me want to be better for Jack. Things had to change – and it was going to start now. 'Darling, I think you're a big enough boy not to need your pushchair anymore. What do you think?'

He looked up at me with big, pretty eyes, considering my question.

'Could you walk like me? I wouldn't want to push you into school next year. Maybe some of the other kids might think it's a bit babyish.'

His forehead wrinkled with the consideration, then he nodded: 'I can walk.'

Dropping a kiss on his head, I took his hand, pushed the redundant buggy with my other. My boy was growing up. It was a stark thought: things changed without me doing anything. Nothing would stay the same.

The walk made him grumpy, but we stuck with it. By the time I got back to the car, I felt on the verge of something significant. Tired, Jack had started grumbling before I'd even started the car, but I put on an audio children's story and he settled down to listen, letting me settle down to make decisions. Even as we crossed Ockham Common, the narrator's voice spoke of *The Faraway Tree*, and my heart spoke of freedom. Sometimes driving had the same effect on me as walking – it helped me think *properly* – and I was determined to use the headspace to make a plan before I arrived home.

On the M25, the lorries thundered past; the driving towards the coast loosened my mind and it felt almost hypnotic. As cars overtook, as I overtook others, I went through possible option after possible option and what became clear was, all choices led to needing money.

And I had none.

Nick controlled our money; I've always been uninterested in anything practical and mundane like paying bills, but that lack of control and lack of any personal income meant that I couldn't siphon any money from our account without him knowing. With that inability to access cold hard cash, I accepted that, as I turned off for the M23, I would have to return to work.

Once I'd made the decision to find a nursery for Jack and to sign on with a nursing agency, I actually felt exhilarated. The idea of having my own income felt empowering. It would give me control.

I still had my own bank account. I'd opened it years before I met Nick; it was currently empty. I would fill it with my own wages. I would give the nursing agency the details of that account, and then I would transfer the bulk of the cash into the joint account. Nick wouldn't know how much I left in my account and nor would he be able to complain, as it was exactly the arrangement he himself used.

By the time I'd arrived in Brighton, I felt amazing. I realised that my mother had given me a plan – she'd told me what I needed to do, and after circling around different options, I'd realised she was right. But like all good decisions, I needed to decide it for myself. I felt intoxicated and saw so clearly how I'd allowed myself to be trapped.

Keen to act, as soon as I was back home I parked Jack in front of the TV and made phone calls to both nurseries and the biggest nursing agency in the area.

When Nick came in from the golf course, he smacked me on the backside, produced a doggy treat for Winston and gave Jack a packet of sweets. It was clear then that he'd been drinking heavily at the clubhouse, because he'd banned Jack from having any sweets, saying that they were bad for kids.

I ushered him to sit at the kitchen table.

'I've got to get changed,' he complained.

'In a minute, I just want to say something first.' I didn't like him drinking too much, so I put a cup of tea in front of him. 'I've got news!' I announced.

His mood darkened as he eyed me over the top of his mug. 'Please don't tell me you're pregnant,' he said, his tone plunging from joyous to dangerous in a single second.

I blinked, stung. It'd been a long time since we'd talked about trying for another baby, but Nick had always been the keen one, trying to persuade reluctant me. I wasn't aware that he no longer wanted another child and it told me then how much our relationship had slipped over the last year. I'd thought it, but to hear it back from him felt disorientating.

'No, actually. I've got a job interview at a nursing agency. I'm going to see them on Friday at ten o'clock, when your mum has Jack, and then I'm viewing three nurseries that afternoon.'

He was so surprised, he slopped his tea. 'You're going back to work?'

'I've decided it's time.'

He looked so surprised, it was almost comic. 'When? How? Why?'

I shrugged, feigning nonchalance. 'Jack's three now and I thought I should use my training before it gets so old they don't let me,' I said, parroting my mother. I smiled at the thought – she really had done her job without even trying to. 'In fact, before I start back, I'm going to do a short refresher course to bring me up to date.'

'Well . . . that's just fantastic!' Then his eyes narrowed a little with suspicion. 'And that's it? Don't think I'm not overjoyed, it's just I've pointed that out to you in the past and you've always said you didn't care.'

'It's for Jack too,' I said. I watched him drunkenly lift his mug. No wonder he hadn't wanted the car – he'd got tanked at the golf club. 'Obviously, Jack will be starting school soon. I still think it was great for him to spend his early years with me, but I can see it's just as important to prepare him for the next stage.' I smiled, as if the answer was obvious: 'So I am!'

'Well . . . good.' The booze was addling his thinking, but he was catching up. 'I agree. It'll be good for him. Mum will be pleased too – she told me she wants a break.'

'Oh! Do you think she could carry on for a bit longer? I don't want to sound mercenary but we'll have to start paying out for four days' childcare and although I won't be working full-time, we need the childcare so I can say yes if I get offered work. Paying for five days might tip the balance of making it financially viable.' I took his hand. 'Honey, if she could keep going, just while we get him over this transition period, that'd be perfect.'

'I'll talk to her.' He looked down and rubbed Winston's velvet muzzle. 'But what about Winston?'

I looked at our lovely dog and realised I've been so focused on Jack and the logistics of getting back into work, I'd overlooked him. 'Maybe Irene?' I put the kettle on and offered more tea to buy thinking time; Nick could never drink enough of the stuff. 'Really, it wouldn't be that often. The course is full-time, but when I'm working, there'll be days during the week I won't be and you're often off during the week, so I suppose we're only talking a couple of days a week.'

'She loves Winston!' He got up from the kitchen table and actually hugged me – for a moment I stood in his arms, and then I reached up and hugged him back. I shut my eyes and exhaled. It felt so long since he'd done that, it felt strange, mechanical, almost like we were acting.

'I'm so pleased, Lisa! This is amazing.' The kettle rose to a boil and switched itself off. The relief of a way forward was immense.

'What's amazing, Mummy?'

I opened my eyes to see my beautiful Jack standing in the doorway. His large eyes looked pensive – perhaps seeing me and Nick in a hug was so unusual, it actually made him nervous.

I let go of Nick but I didn't tell Jack about my plans for nursery – not yet.

Distracting Jack with a biscuit, it felt sensible to wait until Friday and all the dotted lines were metaphorically signed. Just in case.

fifteen:

– before –

Within a month, I'd put the early stages of my plan into action and had started work.

Initially, my plan worked ridiculously well. I'd completed my nursing knowledge course and had started with the agency, working anywhere between one and five days during the week. I couldn't work weekends because Nick often worked then and the nursery was closed. Even if Nick was off at the weekend, he didn't like me working – ironically, he complained about missing out on 'family time' which I read as: *I don't want to look after Jack on my own.*

Irene still had Jack on a Friday and filled in when needed with Winston. Nursery was booked Monday to Thursday, which meant that if I didn't have any work, I had lots of time on my hands. I didn't earn much but I took solace in my savings rising steadily each month. Looking at my bank statement gave me a feeling of security that I'd lost since I'd given up work to have Jack. Looking at my increasing funds kept me on track when things were difficult.

In a way, work itself kept me on anchored, too. Surprisingly, I actually found it enjoyable being back on the wards. In small moments, I puzzled why I'd pushed against it so long. I put on my uniform and it was like putting on a better version of myself. I liked Nurse Lisa more than I liked Wife Lisa or Mummy Lisa. The variety that agency work brought also gave me lots of benefits, with the added advantage that at my regular gigs, I got to know the staff well, sometimes even going on nights out with them, which helped plug the gap of losing Issy, Nadia and Nessa. I still hadn't ruled out getting back in touch with them; after all, they had just been trying to be kind. But the idea of it appealed more than actually putting it into practice, so it just never seemed to happen.

It also helped us out with family life – us all being out of the house more, and away from each other, simply made us more peaceful.

Even better, I also started therapy.

I went on my own every Wednesday night, telling Nick I'd joined a book group. If he noticed that I never seemed to be reading any books, he didn't say. If Nick worked late, I organised a babysitter. The fact that I had money to pay for that and the therapy meant everything to me. Although Jack struggled to settle into nursery – perhaps not surprising given he'd had me to himself full-time and then was in daycare full-time – I determinedly dug in. He needed me to be stronger and money gave us a future with options.

When I went to the therapist the first time, I'd simply introduced myself, told her about my family and then pulled up my shirt to show her my stomach. When she'd seen, I stood up, unbuttoned my jeans and let them fall, so she could see my thighs, too. To reveal my injuries myself felt amazingly powerful – it was as if I was holding my head up and saying: *Look at what's happening to me.* For the first time, I was calling the abuse out. Going to work had empowered me – now the process had started, it felt as if I could only grow stronger.

'Your husband hits you,' the therapist said.

I'd wanted to answer her in a strong voice but, sitting in the darkened plant-filled room, with its womb-like quality, I cried the release I needed instead.

The therapist didn't say anything, instead she passed me a box of tissues. It felt like I cried for an hour straight. At the end, I stood up, thanked her and left. Because of the crying, I thought I'd be too embarrassed to go back again, but by the following week, I found I was looking forward to it.

The next week, I only cried for forty minutes, which felt like an improvement. After I had been going for two months, I stopped crying and instead spent the time processing what was happening to me.

The therapy kept me on track and, although it slowed my savings, I continued to put money steadily away, and before I knew it, Jack had started school.

Of course, therapy was good for more than talking about my family; it was also needed to talk about my most secret secret – the one that no one knew.

That my addiction problems had started again.

sixteen:

– before –

Codeine. Codeine. Codeine. How I loved thee from the start.

Addiction is a powerful curse. Like all addicts, there comes a time in your life when you realise firstly that you are addicted and secondly, that you have to make a choice. You either keep going on the merry-go-round with all the bright lights and fun that it offers (and if you think it doesn't offer fun, then you've never been addicted), whizzing round and round and round, or you choose to step off.

One of my darkest secrets was that by the time Jack had started school, I was already on the merry-go-round of drug dependency, hanging on (look-no-hands!) and enjoying the whizzing lights. It was inevitable that those who lived with me knew I was an addict. I accept that they did not get to see the bright lights, only the dulled, vomitus side of me. But still I held on, with white-knuckled determination.

Addicts *are* determined – you have to be to deal with the criticism, the shame and the hassle of getting hold of the good shit. And as an agency nurse, who was clever and determined, it was all too possible to get hold of what I needed.

But as much as I totally accept that being an addict was my fault, the start of my addiction was not.

After a terrible pregnancy, where I'd nearly been hospitalised twice for dehydration because even a sip of water would make me throw up, the midwife assured me: 'You'll have a lovely birth. Very straightforward – it's always the way if you've had a tough pregnancy.' But it wasn't the case.

I woke in the night and Nick drove me to hospital. Within minutes my ankles were up in stirrups. I was given pethidine which made me feel very sick, very spaced out. Everything slowed down, until Jack's heart rate showed he was in distress, then his birth became very fast. I remember feeling so cheated it wasn't the promise of the "lovely" birth that had kept me going through the tough times.

I remember the fluorescent lights, the blinding agony and the panic as a more experienced doctor was paged. A midwife later hinted darkly that I'd mistakenly been given too much pethidine, and I certainly felt like I was tripping, with the strangest and strongest certainty that I was in a horror film, and when the senior doctor all but pushed the younger medic aside and came at me with something held high and glinting in the light, I think I started screaming and screaming.

When Jack was finally out, he was whisked away from me to check for skull damage before I could even hold him. I was whizzed down to surgery. Afterwards, a nurse felt she could confide to me as a fellow nurse, that mine was the worst birthing injury she'd ever seen. 'Honey,' she said, her hand on my shoulder, 'you were split so badly front to back, that if it had been any worse, you'd been peeing through your ear.'

I smiled back at her, not caring because by then I had a syringe driver full of morphine. All my fear for my tiny son and my own pain was dulled from a shrill scream to the smallest of whispers, as the morphine washed contentment through my veins.

With my postpartum complications, my own GP, who'd had a similar birth story herself, felt very at ease prescribing me large doses of codeine. Some check-and-balance failed to happen, and by the time it did and they turned the tap off, I was already long addicted.

But I did the right thing – I stepped off the roundabout, stuck with the withdrawal and came out the other side. I was glad to be shot of the embarrassment of it all. I've always been someone who likes to do the right thing. I have a huge sense of justice and it felt wrong to raise a child and not be clean.

So that might have been the end of it except for a nasty row about me giving Jack a half-packet of Skittles, which resulted in my finger being dislocated.

It hurt very badly, but rather than go to the hospital, I popped it back in myself and dosed myself up on paracetamol and ibuprofen. I had been due to work and nearly used the injury as a reason to turn it down, but needed to get away from Nick. He was very much on edge at this point. He was very fragile, and not only had he started drinking too much, but he had also taken up smoking again which had always been a massive bone of contention between us. Even his hair had started to fall out. He had never been a vain man, but I think it reminded him that his life was out of control and he didn't know how to help himself.

Looking back, I don't think either of us was doing very well. We were struggling with the collapse of our marriage and the vision we'd had of family life. Nothing was like we'd thought it would be and the violence was making me scared and him sour. Therapy gave me an outlet to talk, but Nick was a very macho man and he probably didn't even confide in his friends. I'd made an appointment for us at Relate, but he refused to go, and I didn't have the energy to push it.

Our sex life had long since dwindled away. There had been a nasty incident, when late at night, drunk, he'd tried to have sex with me. He'd held me down by my wrists, each of his legs pinning my own, and I had struggled, hissing into his ear that I hated him. In the end, he'd collapsed into my shoulder, sobbing, crushed by his own violence and impotence.

As he lay there, his tears mixed with my own, I think we both knew how much our dream was broken, and perhaps we hated ourselves just a little more.

We were stuck, unable to go back, unwilling to go forward.

So the day of the Skittles argument, desperate to get away from him, I selected the correct bandage from my extensive, pilfered-from-work first-aid stores. Then I had *the* idea.

Like most nurses, my own home first-aid kit was second to none. Like most nurses, I didn't think twice about taking home a half-used roll of Micropore, some 'spare' dressings, some Steri-Strips. I winced at the bandage. And then I had what might have been one of the most defining thoughts of my life: *I bet I could get some decent painkillers at work today.*

As I fetched my car keys, I realised that I was looking forward to going to work and I was already mentally shopping for something better.

And so started my second, secret addiction.

Nick knew about my first addiction and had actually been incredibly supportive. But the second time, I kept it fiercely hidden. There are advantages to anything if you look hard enough, but I didn't have to look very hard for the advantages to codeine and Valium. They improved how I reacted to the world, and with it, things improved at home. For example, Jack didn't sleep through the night until he started school and before then, there was still lots of crying and restlessness, but the codeine stopped me from getting too maudlin about being permanently exhausted.

But when Jack turned five, I realised that Nick had known about my drug abuse. And it only happened because I'd been careless.

Every birthday, my mother arranged lovely gifts from prison. Because she couldn't send anything herself, her sister, my aunt who raised me after my own grandmother died, took on the role of gift organiser. My mother told my aunt what to buy and my aunt packaged it and sent it.

Jack loved getting his Nana parcels. On his fifth birthday she sent him a plaster-of-Paris Peter Rabbit money-box kit. It was bigger than the average money-box, a sizeable thing. We'd never made anything like it before and when he'd first ripped open the delivery package and we saw what was inside, my heart sank because I thought he'd hate it.

I was surprised when he seemed to be intrigued by the kit. He turned the box over and over, looking at the pictures, and he silently mouthed the words as he read the box-front instructions. I hated mucky art things and thought he'd start it and then lose interest, so I distracted him, tucked it away and forgot about it.

But a couple of days later I had come home from a difficult shift at work and had found Jack and his dad very proud of themselves. There had been a sudden death on the ward and dealing with the traumatised relatives had been upsetting. I was in no mood to find the clean kitchen I'd left now covered with mess: powered plaster-dusted surfaces; wet plaster-smudged faces and my unread *Marie Claire* laid out as a half-arsed attempt to protect the table. They'd mixed the plaster-of-Paris in my favourite kitchen jug and hadn't bothered rinsing it, so the now dry plaster coated its insides. But reddened with achievement, Jack sat on his dad's lap and they both held up the rubbery, liquid plaster-filled mould like it was something amazing.

And instead of forgetting about it, they seemed obsessed with it. They prodded the foul-smelling thing with interest every minute, Jack asking his father over and over: 'Is it ready yet?' and then it became every hour, and all I could think of was the trauma of the time of death being called and then the new widow screaming. Then, when nobody helped me trying to tidy the table for tea, I lost my temper and that was that.

Two days later, I went shopping. When I came back, I was annoyed to find them painting, the table a mess again, and Jack's school uniform too, but the result was beautiful. It'd come with little plastic paint pots and now Peter Rabbit was the right shade of brown, with white-and-black eyes and little blue coat.

'Jack did it all himself!' his dad said, and paint-smudged Jack grinned.

'It's lovely. Very well done.'

'No, Lisa, I mean Jack really *did* paint it all by himself!' He beamed at his son and stroked Jack's heavy fringe out of his eyes. 'I mean he did every little bit of it and I just watched!'

And it did look good but the next day it looked even better. Jack, who'd never really made anything, saw the whole project through and finished it by opening the final pot and giving it a coat of varnish. It gleamed and sat in the prize spot in the middle of the kitchen table for a month, until I finally wanted my fruit bowl back and put the Peter Rabbit in Jack's room.

And when it was there I could finally stop thinking of my mother. Because I don't know if she remembered or not but she'd bought me one of those kits when I was a kid. I'd opened the paint pots before making the cast and used them to paint a picture. I thought she would be impressed, but she only scolded me for not using the kit properly. She told me I was too impatient. I had so few memories of living with my mum before she was sent to prison, I was sorry to be reminded of a negative one.

But my sad childhood and extra cleaning aside, I was pleased that Jack was finally showing some passion. Then one day I'd had too much codeine and made a very stupid, very regrettable mistake.

seventeen:

– before –

My love for codeine meant that I sometimes took risks.

I'd been able to take more than I'd hoped because I'd done an agency shift at a private nursing home and the senior nurse on duty was a very lovely, very unobservant woman.

It felt great to have a proper stash and I was feeling a bit off because it was my mother's birthday and, when push came to shove, I just missed her and wanted to be with her, and although it'd been years, I wished I could turn back time and use the poster paints differently. I knew it seemed like a strange thing to get hung up about, but losing her at just eight-years-old was just painful. Every time I went into Jack's room, seeing the Peter Rabbit opened up old wounds of missing her and missing her and missing her, and I just wanted to escape feeling crap.

It was a lovely day in June and the sun was shining; it had been a hard spring because Nick was working extra shifts to pay for the new bedroom carpets and a few other bits and bobs we'd splashed out on, and I was feeling low.

So I popped an extra tablet and maybe a small amount – maybe even only a couple of milligrams of diazepam – but it made all the difference and I finally felt candyfloss happy.

I'd put my new headphones on so I could listen to my music without Jack covering his ears. With Nick out of the house I could clean as much as I liked without any snide comments.

I had cleaned the kitchen and the bathroom and had moved on to the floors. The carpets simply dazzled me in their loveliness – we'd bought them only a month ago and settled on a soft grey in a wool mix and I loved to keep them clean. We'd also – because it seemed silly not to when we had new carpets – bought a super-flash hoover. I just loved it! I loved running it over and over the cut pile, feeling it pull up all the dirt so there was no muck left behind.

At the time I felt as if I could hoover up the filth out of my life: but I was wrong.

I was hoovering, headphones in, Queen loud in my ears and singing loudly, when Nick came in.

I jumped just to see him. I hadn't expected him to be home for hours, so to see him in his police uniform there in the doorway alarmed me. I glanced at the bedroom clock and was stunned to see it was after seven. The music still blared in my ears. He was saying something but I couldn't hear him and I was having trouble adjusting: where had the time gone? I thought it was four – definitely no later than five. But now . . . all that time had passed me by.

What had I been doing?

And where was Jack?

I think I just stood there blinking. I knew it took me longer to order my thoughts when I was on diazepam and codeine together. I didn't always like it but I accepted it because it was worth the feeling they gave me.

Then Nick took a step towards me and I knew I was in trouble.

He looked furious: eyebrows drawn into a line; blue eyes stormy; large hands up and gripping the air as if already wringing my neck. He was mouthing something but I couldn't hear. I could tell he was shouting, because his Adam's apple was jumping up and down as if it believed if it bounced high enough it could escape out of his mouth. When the idea amused me almost to a giggle, I realised that I was stoned – too stoned.

He strode closer and with one hand yanked on the wire and my headphones popped from my ears.

'You.' *Bam*: he pushed against my chest. 'Silly.' *Bam*: again. 'Bitch.' *Bam*. The last time was hard enough to make me swing my arms wildly to stay upright.

With the other hand, he thrust broken pieces of something (a plate? no, a mug? no, not sure) under my nose. 'What have you done, Lisa?' he shouted.

I blinked, unsure. What had I done? I'd been in another world, a place where the carpet became clean in smooth easy strokes, the music had been all-consuming, and everything had been lovely. Fun; mellow; lovely.

'You don't know, do you, *Lisa*? Because, as fucking usual, you're out of it!'

It was confusing. It was horrible. Without my earphones, without the music, I could hear Jack screaming somewhere out of sight. The change was abrupt. The information overload was too much: Jack was upset; his dad was white with fury; I was in big, big trouble; something was broken. He thought it was me – was it?

I thought I had been doing a good thing by cleaning the flat, but it didn't seem to matter. The soft grey carpets had never looked better but it didn't matter.

Nothing mattered because I realised that he knew about me: he knew about my tablets.

Could he? Is that what he meant?

My mind went slow: replaying his words. *As fucking usual, you're out of it!* I held on to the hoover, my hands clenching the handle.

I blinked, uncertain.

He stared at me, his thin face twisted with fury. 'How long do you expect me to put up with this shit?' he said, his question now full of rattlesnake warning.

I scrabbled along the wall to get away from him. I could get no further because our sofa blocked my path. I could hear the warning in his voice. What 'shit' was he talking about? What did I have to defend? The chair pressed into my back legs. I wanted to get away; I glanced past him thinking I might be able to dodge and weave and be free. But now I could see, standing in the doorway watching it all, was the crying Jack. He was cuddling his new soft plushie Peter Rabbit (because everything now was Peter Rabbit this, Peter Rabbit that).

His father grabbed me by the shoulders, his fingers talons in my flesh. I didn't see him but he leaned in so close I could smell cigarettes on his breath. 'You. Are. A,' he hissed, '*Disgrace.*'

Jack finally seemed to have stopped crying. He'd plugged his mouth with his thumb and rubbed and rubbed the rabbit's ear against his face.

'You're an embarrassment, *Lisa.*' I could feel his father's spittle spray against my face. He pushed me much harder this time: *bam!* Maybe because I wasn't looking at him but instead at the rub, rub of Peter, I fell back easily, bouncing off the wall from my hip, onto the sofa.

The impact forced my jaw up, banging against my top row of teeth. The impact jolted my brain and forced me back to my husband. He dropped the pieces at my feet, his voice cold: 'You were just so jealous.'

I squeezed my eyes shut against the pain: I did not want to see. Yet after a breath, I opened them anyway.

I saw what he held. The brown; the carefully painted blue. I had broken Peter Rabbit. Then I had a flash: I remembered banging Jack's bedside unit with the vacuum; I saw it wobble . . . but then it had gone. I don't know what happened afterwards. But I do remember I wasn't thinking too hard. I was just singing and hoovering, singing and hoovering, singing and hoovering. It'd been such a nice day.

He stepped forward again, his jaw tight, his eyes hard.

I put my arms over my head to protect myself.

I wanted to have my headphones back in and listen to Queen and watch the carpet stripe as the vacuum lifted the pile. It felt good and orderly and neat and controlled.

But this was a mess of shouting and thin, reedy screaming as a top note trying to be heard. The screaming rose even higher and I wasn't sure if it was me or Jack. It was all such a blur.

I couldn't see him but I kept my eyes squeezed shut and tucked my head behind my knees making myself into a ball. But as frightened as I was, the codeine and diazepam made it a manageable haze. It was as if I had a thick duvet over me and even though his words landed like blows, and my mind fluttered like a nervous bird with questions, none of it was too bad. I couldn't *quite* feel the impact of any of it through the duvet of the drugs.

As the codeine coated me in eiderdowns, and I felt the kicks to my kidneys, I felt that nothing was going to change. It was then that I decided my therapist was right: it did have to change. It was time to pack a go-bag.

eighteen:

– before –

Just when it felt like nothing was ever going to change, everything changed very quickly. A week after the attack I'd received because I broke Peter Rabbit, following the ideas I'd explored with my therapist, my go-bag – clothes, money, etc. – was packed and hidden in my wardrobe. Of course, I dreaded my husband finding it, but I piled things over the top of it and hoped for the best. Now I was poised for flight – just one more raised voice and that bag would've been in my hand and nothing would've changed my mind.

It'd been nearly two years since I had started my plan. It'd taken that long to save a decent fund, but I was there now, both financially and – after my therapy – emotionally too.

I remember Jack had just broken up for the Easter holidays. Irene still helped out during the school holidays, but on that day she'd been ill and unable to have him. We'd been at home together and, woken from a Valium-induced nap, I'd become aware of Nick's shouting. Getting up, I followed the shouts into the front room.

Nick lay collapsed on our brown leather chesterfield, crying and rocking back and forth like a toddler. In his hand he held the bloodied broom. In front of him, Jack was standing just out of reach.

Winston lay on the floor, clearly dead, and Nick was crying with regret; like Jack he was usually hard, as if the release of emotion was a struggle. I stood in the doorway, gripping the door handle. I could smell his beer. The only strong emotion I saw normally was anger flashing in his blue eyes.

I had gone years without seeing him cry and now this made two days in a row . . . things were becoming unravelled, fast. As I stood there, doing pathetically nothing, Nick's howl reached a new higher level of anguish. Then he looked up and reached for his son. Jack stood in front of him, face expressionless. 'Jack . . . come here'.

Jack reacted, snapped out of his stasis. He clutched his hands to his cheek, his eyes pure rounds of fear. And I finally noticed a dribble of blood slowly running from his nostril.

I think I yelled: 'What have you done?' They didn't even notice me.

'Please,' Nick begged him. 'I'm sorry, Jack. So sorry. Please forgive me.'

Sorry.

A dead dog and a bloodied son. The word hangs in the air. This was new – Nick hitting Jack – but the apology was so pointless, so redundant and powerless, it felt like an affront to be there at all. *Sorry?* A dead dog and we have *sorry?*

I think about Issy warning me of this – and I dismissed it. I said it could never happen.

Jack shuffled away from his dad. Instead, he stood in the corner, next to the painted original Victorian shutters that I had personally sanded and painted with three coats of perfect Silk Sigh White. I loved those shutters, but I knew I would never look at them again without thinking of this moment. My son turned his head away from us both and stood so close as if he was examining my work. There were two imperfections about where his head was, two hairs that came away from the brush unnoticed, now caught forever in the paint. It bugged me more than I knew it should, those hairs. When I cleaned I always trailed my nail over them, hoping to knock them free. It would leave a chip in the paint, but then I knew I'd have the excuse to make a repair.

Nick stared at his son who stood in the corner by the imperfect paint. I could see Jack put his hand to his nose and then look at the blood on his fingertips. It made me frightened of what was going on in his mind.

He was only five years old. What had we done to him? Now his pet dog was dead. Things could never go back to what they had been. Never.

I wished I could chip this whole day out of my life. I wished I could just sand down the damage until it was gone and start again with another coat of Silk Sigh.

Nick reached out, his hand outstretched. There was a smear of blood on his finger. 'Please,' he called out in a voice so thick with emotion, I barely recognised it. 'Jack! I'm sorry I lost my temper!'

The word *sorry* seemed to hang in the air, as thin as smoke and as vulnerable, before it instantly evaporated into nothing.

Nick realised that Jack wouldn't turn around for him, so he collapsed to his knees, and bent to pick up the broken body of Winston. The bulldog had always really been Nick's idea – he brought him home as a puppy when Jack was just a baby. I was annoyed at first but then I fell completely in love with Winston.

Nick dropped the broom and picked him up, the back part of his body flopping: his spine was broken. *Snap.*

Snapped with the power of what? My thoughts sped, each blurred and smudgy with panic: the dog was dead and I grasped through the haze that, as a family, we'd finally reached *the* impasse. There had been a sequence leading to this and now that wouldn't stop; now nothing was going to stay the same. I felt it clearly in that moment, through the muddle: *now it's all going to get worse.* I didn't know how, but I was right, because within two days Nick and I were finished, for better or for worse.

Really, the way we'd been functioning, it was about time.

But I couldn't be relieved about it – there was no relief in the dog being dead or what came next.

I looked at Nick, on his knees with our dead dog, a silent bellow of anger and sadness ripping through me, making me step back. My marriage was over and it *hurt.*

Sorry.

I know about temper: I grew up around it. How that sudden silent seizing in the amygdala and the release of catecholamines means rational becomes irrational within a heartbeat. Fire like that can just live in blood.

I pick up the broom, just to look at it really. Just to see the smudge of blood on the handle more closely, and seeing it, I thought of Issy pulling up my jumper sleeve and exposing the bruises. Not for the first time, I wonder what could happen to me.

He must've known that we couldn't come back from this. I thought: *How is this horror my life?*

I felt the snap again. Blood hot; beating heart. I looked at my son, eyes wide with fright, blood-smeared. Then I turned, reaching for something, desperate to spear the anger with something possible. Then: *Nobody lays a finger on my child*. I held the broom tight. White knuckles. Then brought it down again and again on my husband as he cowered under my rage.

I was never a victim. This is because I always knew what others, like beautiful Issy, did not. I have a hard edge: there's a point beyond which I will yield no more. It's that knowledge that kept my chin up, kept me in my home, because really, what is a broken rib? What is that single, slim, white rib or finger or bruise, when any time you want, you can change your world?

nineteen:

– before –

Three days later, Jack and I were alone. We queued for train tickets at Brighton train station. Then we sat on the cold, metal benches and ate the sandwiches I'd bought from a café.

By our feet were several large suitcases and my go-bag. Apart from our clothes and a few of Jack's toys, we'd left everything in the flat. The furniture, the car, the sofas – I'd laid claim to none of it. It was too dangerous. All the effort of the refurbishment: sanding the woodwork, the careful cutting in, the bookshelves I'd helped build . . . it was all just nothing to me now.

It was cold and I tightened Jack's coat, buttoning against the chill. But my own I left open. Some things you can't be shielded from.

Our train drew into the station. I stood up and pulled my bag over my shoulder and then, with careful arrangement, laid claim to the rest of our baggage except Jack's own, small ruck-sack. I indicated to Jack that he should take my free hand. He did. I wrapped my fingers tight round his and smiled down at him. Sometimes you don't have the answer, I knew, but some-times any answer is better than none. Whatever had happened in the past, I was determined we'd leave it all there. We had a new start ahead of us and we had to look forward.

As we stepped up onto the train, receiving a little help from strangers paid for with 'Oh, thank you!' and 'If you don't mind, that'd be great,' we settled our extensive baggage and then ourselves.

Seated, I rubbed the condensation from the window so I could see clearly. Looking out, I saw nothing of Brighton's vibrancy, only the grey station platform pocked with discarded chewing gum, dropped litter, and in the shadows, a homeless person as wanted as a dropped Subway cup.

Because I needed to see it again, I took out the letter and read it all through for the zillionth time. When I got to the end, I took a deep breath, folded it up and returned it to the zipped-up compartment in my handbag. I was done with my home town and this letter confirmed it – anywhere was better.

When the train finally pulled away, I leaned forward and seized both of Jack's small hands in my own. His sweet face looked up at me; he was so young and it all seemed so impossible. I wanted to say something important, something memorable, but in the end all I could say was: 'We're leaving.'

And that seemed enough for him.

It was enough for me.

twenty:

- now -

One.
Two.
Th—

Then into the flame. Nothing. Then: instant! So instant! Think of Jack, I think, already panicking. It's worse than I thought it would be. Searing doesn't cut it. It's like the ring of fire in childbirth without any pain control. At least then you have no choice, but I have to hold my wrists, my hands, over this flame because I can't see where to hold it. My fingers too – they're over the other side of the ring of fire, I thought.

A bright point – this agony is a bright point, larger, and then larger still, a rising and exploding firework. Now it's a star; a sun; vast and all-consuming.

I can't do it, I think, panic rising high, so high, that I can't think of anything else. *Can't do it, I can't do it, I can't do it.*

I smell something like food – cooking meat. It's me! It's me! I'm cooking myself!

I start to shiver. Then it's gone. My subconscious is now screaming what my conscious already knows: *Too hot, too hot, too hot.*

I'm worried I'm screaming. My jaw is clamped shut and my ears hear nothing, but I'm not sure there's not a thin, high wail emanating from me.

When I know I can't stand any more my mind clears. I can only describe it as a nirvana. Maybe it's just adrenaline, maybe it's a higher power come to help me. But it works.

Through it all I think: *Jack.* I see his eyelashes – so long, longer than mine! His blue eyes with the dark ring round them that makes them so unique. I see his face, so serious until something makes him laugh and then he erupts in the funniest laugh I ever heard.

Jack. This second thought is the important one. Through the fire I feel my love for him. Just like his terrible, terrible birth, after which I swore, never again. I have handled pain before – that is what I tell myself when the smell makes me so sick and the fire is so bad that the world greys again.

I think of Nick.

twenty-one:

– now –

I wake on my kitchen floor. This time the grey recedes quickly and I immediately know where I am. I am sharper; I feel the difference to before. The burning in my wrists and hands is ragged and rabid, an uncontrollable animal that stalks my mind, not waiting for me to open my eyes, before sinking its jagged jaws into my wrists, but I want to know.

I move my arms to test . . .

Yes. I am free.

Now I can get to Jack.

I shut my eyes when I bring my hands up in front of me. I feel the thrum of my heart in my hands as I lift them up.

I don't want to open my eyes and see the damage. But there's no time to waste, so I do.

twenty-two:

- before -

Just five days after Winston's death, everything was different. Sometimes, one thing triggers another thing and before you know it, your world has irrevocably changed. I suppose it was several things coming together that finally ended our family life forever, but mostly that awful, terrible last straw that I don't think about even now, that happened two days after Winston's death – but also the letter, which I carried with me as Jack and I arrived at our new home.

A new town; a new home; a new us. This available-now-and-also-furnished flat was just behind the Bracknell high-street shops. Finally, my diligent savings had been put to good use.

My son stood nervously behind me, unsure. I rattled the key in the lock, muttering under my breath. When it gave and opened, I stood on the threshold and hid my sigh.

I'd only been here once, just two days ago. Although Jack had been with me, he'd sat, uninterested, playing a game on my phone. I was still so frightened after the terrible event that I'd had to hide my shaking hands from the lettings agent.

Then, it'd been a bright sunny day, a counterpoint to my misery – and the sun streamed through the windows. Inside, the flat had smelt of fresh coffee. Today, it was rainy and we'd had to dodge a huge puddle by the front door where the drainage must've been blocked and now I was standing in a flat that smelt of gravy and old socks. Of course, I realised, inexperienced me had been hoodwinked by the homely fresh coffee smell.

Now, I stepped into the thin corridor of a hall and looked at the grubby carpet tiles and couldn't help but compare it to the carpet of our last oh-so-lovely flat. We'd never been well off, but this . . . this felt like I'd been plunged into a world of poverty. Perhaps I'd rushed things a bit.

No. No choice, I reminded myself.

'Well, this is it!' I said to Jack in a too-bright voice. 'Don't forget we will put plants around the place –' I glanced through to the small sitting room and the tired sofa – 'and brighten the place up with throws and pictures! And I can paint it too, so you can pick any colour for your bedroom walls.' My thin laugh bounced in the low-ceilinged, characterless space.

Five-year-old Jack peered round me and stared, his bottom lip now protruding, looking like he was going to cry. Boys his age don't care much for throws and pictures. They want their dads. They also want their old school. They also want their grandma, Irene.

What did I want? I wondered, looking inside the grubby faux-wood kitchen cupboards. I wanted safety. I wanted change. I opened a drawer and saw a dead woodlouse. I wasn't sure this was it.

After Winston and then . . . what happened next, I'd picked up my phone and pretty much picked Bracknell off a map. It was a panicked decision to leave Brighton.

When I'd seen it, Bracknell had seemed like enough distance to start again. It had several hospitals and lots of care homes, so there was plenty of opportunity for work. A phone call to the local authority had told me I could secure a space for Jack at the nearby school; it was small and only a short walk away, which felt perfect. By living on the high street, we had useful shops on our doorstep and great connections Even better, Bracknell was only thirty minutes' drive from my mother's prison. At the time, it'd felt like the perfect decision.

But today, I could see the reality. When I got a car, I wouldn't be able to park it nearby. The recent rain had overflowed the drains. The overcast April sky made the flat feel shabby and cheap, because it *was* shabby and cheap. Although I'd saved enough for a deposit and the first few months' rent, I couldn't afford to be extravagant. Moving away from Nick also meant moving away from Irene. I felt terrible for her, effectively walking out of her life, but it also meant that I'd be limited to how much I could work and therefore earn.

I planned on taking nothing from Nick – it felt safer that way.

But despite it all, I still missed my husband. I missed his large hands rubbing my back when I was upset; I missed his pragmatic way of looking at things; I missed his logos to my pathos. But I wasn't going to stand in this empty '70s box with Jack looking at me with large blue eyes, waiting for me to react to what we had lost.

'Well, this is good, isn't it!' I had to be bright about this because we were only here because I wanted us to be – because I thought it was right.

I took hold of his hand and led him round the flat, but I didn't linger in the bathroom because it had no window, and its brown dirge colour scheme made me feel like my life was so far off its rails it couldn't even see where it'd left the tracks.

But this was somewhere safe, where no one knew us, and I had to be strong. It didn't matter that my nerves were still gossamer thin from yet more tears from Jack. I didn't blame him – he was five and understood that he'd left his home forever.

It was all so terrible.

Poor Jack, my heart bled for him. I looked at my little boy standing by the back door. I knew there was an alleyway that ran down the side of the flat, and it led to the high street one way, and the flat's small yard the other way. He looked pale and I thought: *I'll show him the yard.* I wished it was a garden, but there was no pretending that it was anything more than a barren, six-metre-square paved concrete area.

'Jack, there's a yard out back – do you want to see it? I thought we could grow tomato—'

'No!' His hands had balled to fists. He took a step forward. With his eyes narrowed, he looked just like his dad.

'Jack . . .' My tone was at best placatory, but I didn't have any words. He was owed a tantrum. What could I tell him?

'I want Daddy.'

I forced myself to breathe in. And then out. 'We've talked about—'

Jack started crying. 'I want Daddy, please, Mummy, *please.*'

People talk about their hearts breaking, and right there, I felt physical pain. 'Daddy is fine and safe and well but we just can't see him at the moment because . . .'

Jack looked around the kitchen area and I saw it through his eyes. The Formica worktop was scratched and chipped. The window above the single full run of cabinets overlooked the dark alley, and only the bobbly privacy glass was softened by a fat-splatted blind.

'It looks a bit unfriendly here, but we'll cheer it up. We'll make it home.'

'But what about *Daddy*? Is this because of what Daddy did?'

'All you have to understand is that Daddy isn't living with us anymore,' I said again, using the most calming, patient tone I could manage given that we'd had this conversation five hundred zillion times. 'We've decided it's for the best.'

'Best for who?'

That was a good question and one he hadn't asked before, and for a moment I was stumped. Unable to answer it in a way that he could understand, I said: 'You come first, Jack.' And it was true. I had always put him first. I was standing in a shithole and he was looking at me like I was the emerging turd and yet we were both standing here for him.

But sometimes, when I lay in the dark thinking about the different ways my life had gone wrong, I wasn't so sure. It seemed that everyone else was the turd and I was the paper they used to clean up their shitty mess. The thought angered me. *Actually, it's best for you, Jack.*

'Best for me how?'

I took a step back and hit the radiator behind me. My hands reached down and touched the coldness. The paint was rough and chipped. How could I have said it aloud? I shook my head a little – I didn't say it, I didn't.

'Why is it best for me? I want to go home.' He bit his lip and I knew he was about to cry.

I wanted to grip him tight in a hug, squeeze him and say yes, all right, we will go home. Tomorrow we will wake up and go to the DIY store and chip the hairs out of the paint and sand the living room and paint it fresh all over and everything will be perfect.

But it wasn't as simple as that. If it was, I would've done it already. I felt sick. This new flat was so disappointing. It was so tiring being a parent. And I so hated – *hated* – being on my own.

'I want to go home!'

He said it but I felt it. Jack shouted: '*Home, home, home,*' in a chant as he backed up against the kitchen counter; it was like we were opposing fighters backed up against the ropes of a boxing ring. He then threw his head back and began to scream.

twenty-three:

- before -

Two weeks after I'd moved Jack and me into the dreadful flat off the high street, I took a train, another train and then *another* train, before getting on the visitor bus, to visit my mother.

The journey was a huge disappointment. I was now carless; because our car had been a present from Irene, I'd decided to leave it with Nick. Without it though, the trip was as long as it had been driving to Send from Brighton.

The travel got to both Jack and me. By the time I got off the bus, I was on the verge of a full mental breakdown. I'd once did a rotation on a psychiatric ward during my nursing training, so I had an idea what I was talking about. Now we'd given up the buggy, I was determined not to go back, but I missed it when Jack dithered. With the gate in sight, I took his hand and tried to tow him faster, but he complained: 'Ow, Mummy, don't pull so hard!' An old man, walking in with us, turned to glance at me. Feeling judged, I felt the tension in my jaw tighten and I loosened my grip on him.

I realised I was brewing for an argument and felt a twinge of shame. I told him: 'Sorry, Jack, it's just that we *have* to get there on time,' as if he didn't already know.

As we walked through the outer gate that seemed to define my life, I glanced down at my young son, and finally felt my heart properly soften. His large eyes looked up at me and I realised again that he was so beautiful, sometimes I just forgot what a precious, precious gift he was.

I knew I was angry at him; angry at Nick; angry at myself and what our family had become. It was so far from where we'd wanted to be, it was such a scrunched up mess, it made me hate each one of us. But at the centre of it, I saved the most hate for myself.

Each of us were victims. However, Jack was the biggest victim of us all. I thought of me and then of my mother. And then of my father. Jack was my father's victim too. Like throwing a stone in a lake, the ripples of his actions many years ago were hitting against Jack now.

As I took my hard, plastic chair, I realised that I wasn't stressed from our horrendous journey, I was frightened. I was frightened of what my mother would say about my news.

I sat opposite her and it started straightaway.

'No smile today?' She didn't look at me as she said that, instead looking at Jack who was reading a *Horrible Histories* book. He loved them, but I didn't trust him not to be listening anyway. 'Jack,' I asked to test him out, 'want a sweet?' He didn't raise his head. Mollified a little, I paused, listening to the sounds of the visiting room. Lots of voices; someone weeping; someone else hacking a stubborn cough; maniacal laugher cackling from some other place. Jack turned a page.

'Nick and I . . . we are . . .' I made myself look at my mother.

She leaned, her broad hands laced together on her lap, her body motionless, waiting.

'He's gone.' I glanced at Jack, but his eyes continued to track the words on his page.

She raised an eyebrow, her blue eyes staring. 'Gone? Where?'

'I don't know.'

'You don't know where your husband is? Or are you telling me that Nick's left you?'

'No.' My mouth was dry. 'It's me – *us*. What I'm trying to say is, it's not really him that's gone, I suppose.'

'You've left him?'

I glanced at my son and mouthed: *we've separated*.

She blinked and for the first time, perhaps ever, I saw her looking unsure. But she soon rallied. 'Are you and Jack are still in your flat?'

'No. It's under offer.'

'*What*?' She took an audible breath. 'You've left and the flat has already been put up for sale? What on earth's going on?'

'It's what I wanted.' But even as I said it, I couldn't believe it. It went under offer before the details were even produced, going to the first couple who viewed it. Now the hairs in the paint are their problem, but I'm not stupid enough to think they care.

'But it's not too late to change your mind?'

I can't go back, I mouthed. My throat ached. I reached for my son but he moved away from me. It was a subtle move, a little leaning away, but enough for me to know he was listening. But what could I do? I had to tell my mum and it wasn't like he didn't already know.

'But is Nick still in the flat?' I could tell by her voice that she was angry.

'He's wrapping things up.'

'And where's he going? And if he goes, can't you just stay?'

I could only shrug. I wanted to try to touch Jack again, but didn't dare. I couldn't take his anger – not when everything I did was for him. When he was older, I told myself, then he would understand. Love is so controlling: nobody tells you the leash it becomes.

'Lisa! Stop playing silly buggers. I want proper details, the full facts. Are you two talking at all?'

'We email.'

'And where are you living?'

'Bracknell.'

'Bracknell! You've left Brighton?'

'I had to.'

'Is he still seeing . . .' *Jack?* She mouthed the last bit, careful eyes watching him.

I shook my head.

She looked at me with shrewd, impatient eyes. 'So all this happened, when?'

'Two weeks ago.'

'What, just out of the blue? I've been seeing you every month and you say everything is fine, but now I find out your marriage is over, you've left your home, and, what, I presume you must've moved Jack out of his lovely school, too.'

How do you know his school was lovely? I felt like yelling. But I didn't say this because I didn't want her to feel bad about what she did and didn't know. 'Mum.' I tried for calm but my voice still carried a tone of warning. I paused and watched Jack. He carried on reading and eventually turned a page. I didn't believe he wasn't listening, but I had to have this conversation. 'No, not out of the blue,' I said eventually. 'And I think you know that.'

'I don't know anything. You don't tell me anything.'

'What can I ever tell you?' I cut a glance at my son. 'I have him with me, what can I say?'

'You could write.'

'I'm no writer. Besides . . .' I glanced down at my hands. My pale pink nail varnish was chipped. 'You know how I feel about them being read.'

She sighed and sat back. She seemed to think for a while. 'Jack?' she said, but he carried on reading. She tried again. When he continued to read, she said it again, but louder and sharper this time.

He looked up over his book. 'Nana?'

'How grown up are you feeling?'

'I'm five – but nearly six! I'm big now.' He stood up. 'See?'

My mother nodded as if she was impressed. 'I can see you're old enough for this. I'd like you to go up to the ladies over there –' she said, signalling at the WRVS stall – 'and all on your own, bring us two teas and something for yourself. Maybe a bit of cake?'

He hesitated.

'Go on, Jack,' she said. 'Ask for a tray to carry the drinks.'

'Mum, he's only—'

'He's old enough for a little responsibility. Give him some cash, love. Please.' She turned back to him. 'Crisps if you want, instead of cake.'

I relented and opened my purse. He skipped as he headed towards the tea stall. We both watched him weave across the room, through the groups of women meeting their families.

'How is this affecting Jack? It must be such a lot for a young lad to take on, away from dad, new town, new home. He must miss his friends and his school dreadfully.'

'I had to do something, it wasn't – we couldn't stay. Besides, it wasn't right for him. It was too . . . too . . .'

'Too much like school?' she shook her head. 'Just like you – you were just the same.'

Thoughts explode like fireworks. How does she know what I was like at school? I realise my nana or Auntie Janice must've told her. I remember bunking classes, and moving around from school to school, but the memories aren't as sharp as they might be and it was a period in my life I don't like to think about. I want to yell: with you in prison, I couldn't concentrate! Dad died, you got locked up, then even nana died – but I don't. Pressing half-moons into the pads of my thumbs, I mantra: *she did her best, she did her best.*

Instead I said: 'His new school seems great; besides, kids move schools all the time.'

Her mouth tightened. We both look at Jack standing in line for the drinks. He looks so little. 'So before Jack comes back, first I've got to know why and second I want to know where you're living and what's it like.'

I was prepared for this. 'The why is simply that we were arguing too much. I don't want Jack growing up around that. The second is that I'm temporarily renting somewhere. The truth is it's a bit grotty, but I'm hoping that the sale will give me some money for a deposit on something else. I'm going to get a job and I know Nick won't see me short, so we'll do what other people do and just get by.'

She raised a sceptical eyebrow. 'You've made this huge move just because of a few rows? Couldn't you just go to Relate?'

'It wasn't just a few rows, and besides, we tried Relate,' I lied. 'It had got so toxic, it was safer to just go.' I meet her gaze, confident now that with the last bit, I was back on truthful ground.

'Safer?'

'It's better for us.'

'And how is Jack with all this?'

My fragile confidence deflated in an instant. 'I admit, he hates it,' I confessed. 'He hates the flat, he hates not being with his dad, he hates . . . *me.*'

I wanted her to touch my arm and tell me that it wasn't true.

'I'm sure he does,' she said instead. My mother was never one for subtlety. If she had been, my life, I know, would be very, very different.

'And Nick, how has that been left, apart from the emails?'

'He's out of our life for good. It's better that way.'

'He doesn't want to see his son anymore? Not even a little bit?'

Her incredulity was starting to annoy me. 'It's for the best.'

'Because of a few toxic rows? I just can't believe this is the way forwards. Try Relate again. You've got to consider what's best for Jack.'

She continues, but I let it wash over me. It's done and it can't be changed.

When she'd finished, we sat in silence, watching Jack still talking to the WRVS ladies. They seemed to love his company.

'It was a big disappointment to me that you married a flatfoot,' she said finally. It felt like a conciliatory gesture. To emphasise her point, her nose wrinkled as if she smelt something bad. A habit from her time in prison or perhaps her protesting years, holding a banner, yelling: *I smell bacon*. I thought of my mother, dungaree-wearing even then – I've seen the pictures of before I was born – campaigning for CND and Greenpeace. She's always fought against the machine. She never let any bastard grind her down.

'Well, I suppose I have to trust your decision that it was the right thing to do,' she said finally.

I felt a flush of annoyance: it was my marriage to make a decision on, not hers. 'Trust me, it was the right decision. If we'd stayed together, someone – and not just the dog – was going to die.'

She started as if I'd electric-shocked her. I thought she was going to ask about Winston. She'd never met him as dogs weren't allowed in prison, but she liked animals and always took an interest. Instead her eyes narrowed and her face flushed and she said: 'You think this is my fault? All the troubles in your life are my fault?'

I sat back, challenged. I felt like saying: *No, no, no, how did we come to this?*

But I knew.

I shouldn't have mentioned death. Or maybe I wanted to. Maybe I wanted to say it so she knew how I felt. Really I was thinking: *Yes, your fault, your fault, your fault.*

You should've left him.

I think it but instead I say carefully: 'Not yours . . . maybe. Definitely Dad's.' The maybe felt like an act of defiance I'd never have felt capable of before. To even include my mother's actions as being even possibly attributable to the mess and violence of my life, felt dangerous.

We never talked about my father. Never. This was the closest we'd come to talking about the spider's web of our life. But all this time, he'd sat at the heart of it, dark, poisonous, waiting.

She opened her mouth to say something, but Jack was suddenly there, with a lady from the WRVS who carried the two mugs of tea. He held his packet of Hula Hoops, one hand snaking in and pulling them out. He'd pushed his finger into the pale hoops before biting them off, just as I had as a child, and I wondered if anything ever changed over time. Or if everything would just keep repeating itself through the years, ad nauseam.

If that was the case, where did that leave me and Jack?

twenty-four:

– now –

I look at my hands and I am shocked.

They are already swollen. Burns cover both wrists like wide cuffs. The backs of my fingers are also red, with a peppering of white blisters, but my palms are clear because I clenched my fists.

My right wrist is white fire, compared to a more manageable burning on my left, but they're not completely useless – far from it.

I glance around to see what it is that bound me, but it's pinged off somewhere. I don't care, it's time to save Jack.

I grab a knife from the knife block – noticing the empty slot again – and head to the bottom of the stairs. Gripping it, I pause – listening. I don't want to open the door, but I can't hear anything. Holding my breath, hearing the *wham-wham* of my heart, I gently grip the door and ease it ever so slowly back. *Please don't squeak, please don't squeak.* It will, though, I know, and I suddenly get an idea. I nip back to the kitchen and get a bottle of vegetable oil from the cupboard and then try to squirt as much as I can onto the hinges. I feel both brilliant and ridiculous. Then, I try to open the door again. I'm rewarded – the door eases back without a sound.

I take a few deep breaths, my head swimming with the adrenaline and lack of oxygen. I pause at the bottom of the stairs, looking up. Because it's a U-shape, I can't see the landing. I'm going to have to go up. I'd rather climb Everest.

I swallow and try my foot on the first stair, placing it right to one side, hoping that the boards are less worn there and therefore less squeaky. Then slowly, so slowly, I increase my weight.

The riser starts to creak and I stop, hesitate, then continue. The creak starts again, but it's more a weak sigh than a loud complaint. And I'm up!

I repeat again, feeling so nervous now I'm fully on the stair. Pause; breathe; slow leg movements until my foot is on the next step and I gradually increase pressure. The same again – creaking, but not too much. I hope and pray and keep my grip on my knife.

I pause again. Wait – I hear something . . .

I can't breathe – I'm not sure what it was that I heard. My heart is so loud in my ears it's all I can hear.

I decide to try again. The next foot goes up and the difference is immediate. A heavy creak of betrayal. I freeze, feeling that I've wet myself a little, and curse myself for trying. I don't move, I don't do anything . . . but I hear . . .

. . . definitely voices.

Someone *is* upstairs. I feel both relief and terror that I have to go further up – I have to find out for sure that Jack is all right and that it's his father with him. A guess is not enough, even if it's an educated guess.

I slowly start to transfer my weight again but stiffen: I hear heavy footsteps. The floorboards run across the squeaky joists so I hear him before I hear a bedroom door opening. I think, from the direction, it's Jack's bedroom. I crouch a little lower, shut my eyes and grip my knife: I desperately hope that I'm still too low in the stairwell to be seen. And then:

'I'm just going to the loo, Jack, choose a story and I'll be right back to read it to you.'

It's him; it's him; it's him!

Then: *Jack's alive; Jack's alive; Jack's alive!*

I hear him cross into the bathroom and I'm almost crying with fear and relief.

There's peeing, then the loo flush and he's back out on the landing. There's a pause: has he seen me?

I don't dare to open my eyes but I must, I know, because I can't defend myself with my eyes shut but I'm just too scared do it. Lisa, do it now – there's no one there. No one. Relief.

Then he pulls the light cord and I hear it ping up and hit the mirror and it's a little darker, then there are heavy steps back into Jack's bedroom. I smell woodsmoke and I realise he's lit a fire in Jack's bedroom. Something Jack's always wanted but I've never allowed. So typical of him to swoop in and be the hero. The door clicks shut and for a moment I allow myself to lean my forehead against the wall and shut my eyes again.

I'm dizzy with new information and the adrenaline dumped in my system. I realise that I have to decide now if I am going to go up and challenge him (then what? How far will you take this? He has a knife too! What about Jack?) or if I can do something else.

I feel much less brave than even a few minutes ago and so desperately want to do the something else. Feeling pathetic with my kitchen knife and not liking the idea of charging into Jack's bedroom wielding it as he's having a story read to him, I decide to retreat back to the kitchen to regroup. I push my knife into my waistband at the back where it digs a little against my T-shirt, a reassuring pressure. I can hardly attack his dad in front of him. To confront him, with Jack there, is out of the question.

But what else is there when it seems I'm out of options?

twenty-five:

– now –

I retreat to the kitchen and think of what I've never truly forgotten. I have pain relief – good pain relief.

The.

Really.

Good.

Shit.

And I really need it now. Both addiction and genuine pain mean that the constant underhum of wanting pain relief is distracting and I want it dealt with to clear my thinking, so I can concentrate on what's important.

Inside the larder, on the top row, I have a store of medication in a locked tin box. The key is hidden on the top shelf, in an old paint tin. Tentatively, I reach for the tin and the box with careful, throbbing hands; when I open the lid, for the first time since I have woken I feel an eddy of calm. I probably shouldn't have too much with a head injury, but my burns are screaming and I need to be able to forget about them.

Inside I see the neat contents, laid out in rows. I know exactly what I've got in here. Some people might think it's silly that I've got a sign-out sheet but as a nurse I know with these drugs – DF118s, morphine patches, OxyContin from America – you've got to be sure what you've taken and when.

I really want an Oxy, but I know it's too strong, and I cannot risk too much. So I select the right dose of Ativan, knowing it'll help enough but not too much. A little Valium too – just a bit.

I dry swallow them with a love and a gratitude that once I might have been embarrassed about.

Already feeling soothed, I turn towards the door. I gasp: my bladder threatens.

I see a face in front of me, pale in the gloom.

I shut my eyes, lifting my hands even higher to protect my face.

It's over, it's over.

twenty-six:

– now –

The figure is in front of me. In the gloom it takes me a second to adjust.

It's the worst and longest second of my life.

I see the hair first – the wild hair, pushed up into new angles. I see the eyes: crazed holes of despair.

I've seen this figure before. I'm haunted by this person.

I see the hands raised . . . ready for . . . these hands are going to hit me!

It's only when I flinch away that I realise it's me. *Just me.* The dusty mirror on the back of the door is showing me my own reflection in the gloom.

As I start to steady, I want to look in the mirror and see myself. I turn on the light. The sudden brightness shocks my eyes, but only for a moment. I twist my head from side to side, examining closely to find some sign of damage. Perhaps infuriatingly, there isn't much. My ear is reddened; I've obviously been slapped or perhaps that's where I took the blow, or perhaps just from lying on the cold floor.

I have to push forwards. Feeling better for just taking the pain relief, I think through my options: I can't call anyone. I have no shoes. No money. It's four miles to the nearest village. I can't use my car. I don't know anyone who lives nearby – there isn't anyone nearby. That's the bad news.

The good news is that Jack is upstairs and is apparently having a bedtime story. He didn't sound hurt or upset but seemed content choosing a book. He's with his dad, which although it is a disaster, Jack will be happy about because he does love him. I feel reassured.

What might be the worst news is that I've been assaulted, tied up and by taking my keys and phone and shoes, his dad is expecting me to stay here – forcing me to. Why? Suddenly, I see that it isn't Jack who is in danger, but me. By making the bedroom warm and reading him a story, his father has made sure Jack will soon fall asleep. Then when all is quiet, he will come down to see me. He has come here to punish me. Jack is safe – if anything was going to happen to him, his father has already had ample opportunity to harm him.

It's me he wants to harm.

Immediately, I see I was right not to challenge him. Instead I've got to do the opposite: I've got to get out.

I mustn't be here when he comes for me.

But that means leaving Jack.

It's not for long though, I tell myself. I have no choice but to get help – perhaps I even have to consider the police. What's clear is that we will never be safe here again – we will never be safe anywhere again. What he's done tonight means I have to think fresh on old ideas. And if that means calling the police and risk losing Jack, so be it. The truth is, now he's attacked me, tied me up, perhaps I have grounds to get them to listen to me, side with me. Although he'll say I made it up or I did it to myself, there's still a possibility they'll believe me.

The back door is still ajar and, stepping outside, the air is cold in my face. I take another step, contemplating the shadowy garden, the darker fields beyond. I look at my socked feet, grateful the ground hasn't seen rain in nearly two weeks and my socks are thermal. It's not much, but it's something.

I place my foot gingerly down outside onto the stone step. I briefly consider another weapon, but looking around the garden, I don't need light to know there isn't anything. There are no tools because I don't have any. I've never seen a log lying around and if there was, how would I find it with no torch? And if I did, how would that be any better than a knife? I feel the reassuring weight of my own, tucked in my waistband.

I draw my fleece around me and stare into the night. The wind lightly blows in my face and I think about how I've never got used to how dark the countryside gets in Herefordshire. It's not like town life when the street, house and shop lights lift the dark. Here, in the countryside, there's nothing to puncture the night.

Just me, in the darkness, shoeless and running ... where? Cleasong?

The moon is only a fingernail crescent, offering no light. Even as I stare, the black crosses it and I realise that with cloud cover, as soon as I step away from the spill of kitchen light, I will be running blind. I leave the patio, and for safety, run under the concealment of the shadows. Now I am truly in the dark. I take a deep breath: the air is heavy with moulding nature, warm, yeasty and rotting.

I hear a noise behind me, and then the sound of a badger barking nearby, and my fear is as a touch on my skin: I am not alone.

Here in the dark, something is with me.

Something, no – *someone* – is standing here in the garden shadows with me. The night is so dark, there is so little light, but I can sense them . . . like a single candle in a vast cave, my sight barely breaks the darkness. But I look, look, look. Who is it? Is it him? It can't be – he's upstairs reading to Jack. Even so, the feeling that I am not alone sets alight my nerves and, broken from my inertia, I shoot into the night.

twenty-seven:

– now –

I make it only a short distance before I trip in the dark and then I stumble over something and half fall into the border plants. I'm so adrenalised it takes me a minute to draw a decent breath, before I look back, owl eyes to where I was standing – I was so, so sure there was someone standing with me in the dark.

I feel my heart *wham-wham*, sure . . . and then less sure. I was so frightened, but as I centre myself, I see nothing there except shadows and my heart eases. I stay watching, crouched in the gloomy far edge of the garden, looking back across the inky sea of lawn, to the cottage. The feeling of being spooked has already passed: it was visceral but has now gone.

Perhaps . . . it's just a side effect. Perhaps.

This is what I tell myself.

But it had felt *so* real.

I'm hidden by the dense canopy of the huge rhododendron bush. I'm no gardener, but I remember learning that rhododendrons drop poison onto the ground underneath them to stop anything else from growing; perhaps this is how they manage to proliferate – killing everything else. Its thick, leathery leaves brush against my cheek, as if it doesn't want me here, as if my presence will draw another more efficient killer.

I cower amongst it as I listen to my breathing slow. Normally I'd use my hands to steady my uncomfortable crouching position, but instead I hold the burning, thudding things in front, so nothing touches them anywhere, not even themselves. The painkillers are working now, and although my hands are incredibly painful, it's dulling to a muted, manageable soreness.

Something scuttles near me and I almost flinch, but I don't because it's not him. Rats and badgers can't hurt me. I reach for my knife, tucked in my waistband. It's gone. I look back across the lawn, but I can't see it. I hate myself for losing it so quickly.

Without it I am truly helpless. I can't stay here, not doing anything, just waiting.

If I'm going to Cleasong, it'll take a long time. I'll have to head down to the road. I consider that I could flag down a passing car but we rarely pass other cars out here, particularly at night. Even if there was traffic, they come hurtling around the corners. The road weaves and bends with high hedges on either side. There's only a grass verge and that's non-existent in places. I would be very vulnerable stumbling on the road in my dark outfit – and it'd be incredibly dangerous to try and flag them down. If I die out there, roadkill, then no one is ever going to save Jack.

Looking out into the night, I remember the distant farm. West, in the direction that the sun falls, I don't know anything about it, but I've seen the house and outbuildings as I've stood looking at the sunset. Although I don't know who lives there – or even if it's occupied – I suspect it's my best option. It's certainly a lot nearer and there's likely to be a farmer and dogs and help. I'm pinning all my hope on an idea in the distance, but right now, it's the best I've got. Worst-case scenario, I'll push on to Cleasong if there's no one there.

I turn back to whisper to Jack that I'm not leaving him but instead going to get him help, but what I see then dumps fear into my blood.

Upstairs, the curtains in Jack's room have now been drawn.

Pulling Jack's curtains closed is the last thing I do at night. I check on him, shut his curtains, then clean my teeth and go to bed. Jack loves to lie in bed and see the sky as he goes to sleep. He loves to see the stars; we've even angled his bed so he has the perfect view. When we lived in town, the light pollution was so bad it meant he couldn't really see anything of any worth, but it's wonderful here in the dark of the countryside. It's been a surprise and a delight to discover how much Jack loves stargazing. Only yesterday, I was scouring the internet looking for a bargain telescope that I can surprise him with for Christmas.

But the curtains are shut already.

That means that Jack might already be asleep, and if that's the case, his dad will be coming to look for me.

I plunge on, hitting my hedge, and push, fighting, my way through it. I emerge on the other side, scratched, falling forwards onto a field, but the cottage is behind me now and I don't look back again.

twenty-eight:

Jack. I could only think of him. His name held on my breath and my heart. My feet tramp plunging, pistoning, ploughing on through the mud field. My wet, socked feet are already numb with cold but I punch forward, not looking back.

Fear keeps me running – pushing me forward.

In my mind it's like he's right there, running close behind me, his breath on my neck. Sometimes he's carrying a broom handle, sometimes a petrol can. But in my worst dreams he holds out Winston to me in his arms – an awful offering. Winston is still alive despite his broken back, his back legs flopping. And as he holds the dog, yelping and whining in great pain, he's always laughing, his face the same grimace of humour that I imagine he had when he killed Winston.

The air is cold as I pull it into my throat, but it burns in my lungs with the exhaustion of running, still running.

I want to concentrate on the ground, the things underfoot that cut my ankle. But somewhere a fox barks and I think of Winston again. Winston is significant – not only because I loved him – but because his death was the start of this. If he hadn't killed the dog, perhaps my life would be different; perhaps Jack's life would be different.

I run.

The ploughed furrows mean that each step jolts me, sometimes up, sometimes down. I click my hip, my knees jar with the unexpected rough cadence of the ground, but still – panting, I run on. I won't let myself think of the past; instead I keep my eyes on where I need to get to, and then I reach the other side of the huge field and I'm forced to stop because the other side is a hedge.

In a place where everything is just shadows against shadows, layers of black against black, I nearly slam into it.

My first thought is to turn to see if he's behind me, but I already know he isn't. The ploughed field I've just run across stretches behind me. Blind eyes search the dark: but I can't detect any movement. He could be there . . . but I can't see him and I just don't *feel* him.

If he was, I'm in no position to fight him. But still I wished he was here ready to grab me.

Because instead it means that he's back there, in the cottage, on the other side of the pulled curtains, with Jack.

I bend, drawing great lungfuls of air into my chest, then afterwards, it's my stomach that's heaving and I think I'm going to be sick. I want to drop to the damp earth and die. I feel worn, broken, used up. I wish I could just give up, let the cold take me in the night, but I have to keep going. I have to find a way to save Jack. I have to get help.

My eyes have adjusted to the lack of light. I can't see through the hedge, exactly, but I stand, freezing numb feet in the damp mud, and try to find the best way through. Looking up and down, I can't make out a gate. It's through the hedge or nothing. Only then, I notice the moon glint back from something in the hedge. I move closer: *urgh*. It's a wire fence.

It's banked up and thick with weeds. It's hard on my feet. They already feel ruined. When I was running, I was aware that I was stamping on the occasional stone and I feel it now.

It's too dark to see properly despite the thin moon, but through the hedge it seems to only be wires, pegged in by metal stakes. I part the wire and begin to climb through. Then my city-girl mistake: electricity *bites*.

The shock is not too much but I fall back, surprised.

A scream rips forth and I sink to the ground, beaten. I lie and scream all my hurt and fear at the moon. I have endured worse than tonight, but for some reason, it's this sting and surprise that means I cannot stand *any more,* and it defeats me.

I think of my dropped knife and I don't think I can get up again. I don't think I can face another electric shock. I don't think I can run across another field without shoes on.

I think I'm screaming a lot. I think he could hear it a field away. Like the beating wings of an insect, drawing a bat to it, he will find me in the dark and he will consume me.

I have run out of bravery.

I cannot go on.

twenty-nine:

– now –

I'm lying on my back in the cold field, my eyes shut, unable to
go on – *I just can't, I just can't* – when suddenly I instinctively
know – again – that I am not alone.

Someone's here.

Now.

Watching me.

The thought is as clear as lightning: at once both illuminat-
ing and chilling and infinitely dangerous. I don't want to look,
but my eyes are traitors and snap open. For a moment I just
lie there staring into the dark, not breathing, not moving, but
simply listening as if my life depends on it.

Perhaps it does.

The stars emerge from behind a cloud. I can't see the cloud,
black against black, so it's like a magic trick. All the time I stare,
I think: *Someone is here.*

Is it him?

At first, I thought, yes. But now . . .

. . . I think: *No.*

But who else would be standing in this dark field? It doesn't make sense. Why would they be here? How would they know that I would stop here? Or if he has followed me, then why am I still alive? My stare is fixed, waiting . . . for a noise . . . to be attacked . . . I don't know . . .

And then it's like the pressure drops. Someone has stepped up to me but I'm squeezing my eyes shut. I don't want to see. Then I feel a chill on my neck.

And I know they are there. I might be guilty of many things, but I am not guilty of imagining this.

Enough.

I'm up and I'm running and I plunge into yet another bloody hedge and the electricity bolts through me again as I reach the other side but this time it doesn't hurt too much and something jabs my cheek but I wrench my face away and I'm under one of the wires and climbing over the other. I understand two things: one, that the thought of the electric fence was worse than the reality, and two, I am more afraid of standing in the dark with an unknown presence than running in the night.

And so it is that I find myself running forward again, scratched, poked and hurting afresh, but moving closer to the farmhouse – relief layered upon relief – and it has its lights on.

I have finally found help.

thirty:

– now –

I struggle across the last field, but hope has helped strengthen me and I can move faster. Something flying hits me in the face – a moth perhaps, its dusty wing touching the corner of my open mouth, but it doesn't slow me.

The house lights puncture the night. As I get closer, I feel a burst of extra power. Perhaps he'll have a Land Rover and he'll drive me back as we both hatch a plan. He'll have dogs too – perhaps the best thing.

I pant and stumble in the dark, but the house looms bigger and bigger. I have nearly made it. I didn't think I could, but I have. There's one final hedge. When I reach it, I realise that the farmhouse garden is just behind it.

I tuck my burnt wrists back under my fleece, but now they bother me less than my feet. Now my feet are crying; tomorrow they will be screaming.

And then I think: *I might not be alive tomorrow to hear them.* I actually start a little in the dark as if the thought surprises me. It shouldn't, because it's always been there – a low thrum of concern, a low beat very, very nearly undetectable when there's the cacophony of all my other challenges. But here it is. I pause, almost amused. Is this the right response to the thought that I might die tonight?

Yes, the drugs help – a lot – but I've been here before. How many times have I thought I might die?

If I do, I just hope that Jack lives. With that, I push through the hedge, now not even caring if it gives me a jolt.

It scratches me. My feet kick through where the hedge is denser. My right foot stubs against a thick stem. But I keep going.

And I emerge on the other side.

I'm standing in a garden; the farmhouse is just in front of me. I pause, dragging air into my aching lungs. I stare at the building. It's great to see it, for my journey to be over, but it's not what I expected. It's not the architecturally lovely thing that my cottage is, but a large 1970s box with large windows and a flat-roofed extension to the side.

My breathing slows. A farmhouse that has a farmer is still a farmhouse, no matter what it looks like.

I hear loud music. It's spiky, shouty and sounds angry. This is just the type of person I need! The doorbell is the same – new looking. Whoever lives here takes care of things. I'm hoping for practical and strong. It all feels so positive.

I ring the bell and hold my breath.

thirty-one:

– now –

Somewhere in the dark, across the field behind me, a fox screams again and I'm reminded of waking up on my floor. I hate that sound.

When Jack and I first moved to the country, there were many things we struggled to adjust to. Planning ahead, even for milk, was something that took a few weeks to get right. For just about forever, I'd been making Jack a warm milk – just a small amount so he didn't wet the bed – before he went to sleep, but many times we ran out of milk and there could no longer be a quick dash to the shops.

It wasn't just the practical problems of being isolated that was the worst thing, more that it also didn't provide the feeling of safety I'd been hoping for. After fleeing, we moved a few times, staying in hotels, not really sure what we should do. But when Jack started to show severe anxiety, I realised we needed something more permanent. This had seemed like the answer. Homeschooling and not yet having to register with a GP meant that we were instantly harder to track. There were no links with me to Herefordshire – I'd never visited the place before and knew no one who lived here, so there was no reason to look for us here.

It should've been the ultimate place of safety. Rolling hills of nothingness – our idyllic cottage should've felt like a haven.

But it didn't.

The nights were just so dark. The evenings were horrendous, bringing huge moths or maybugs and crane flies that flew drunkenly into the house and left us breathless with the feeling of being hunted. Dark shapes moved across the lawn at night; I clutched myself as I whispered: 'Only badgers,' but undulating bodies in the dark made me skittish.

Now, standing here on this lawn, white security lights casting indigo shadows across a blued garden, the screaming feels like an echo of what might be happening to Jack right this minute. Even though I don't believe it, I still think it whilst I wait for this door to open.

I shift from one foot to the other – it feels too difficult waiting. I want to yell: *Hurry up! Help me! Now!* I have come all this way; it has been hard. My boy needs saving.

The door opens a fraction.

I swallow against the dry of my throat. The door seems to be opening too slowly. What's the problem?

It suddenly doesn't feel right. The door is still opening . . . but so slowly . . . and I still can't see who is opening it.

It's not just my impatience that makes this seem wrong, too slow. There's something else. The sense that this isn't a straightforward someone-answering-the-bell-and-coming-to-the-door is overpowering. Perhaps I've made a mistake – perhaps this is not where I should've come.

I take a step back.

The door opens and the figure begins to emerge. They are brightly lit from behind, so a silhouette, but as they become a little clearer, my voice catches and dies in my throat.

Along with any hope of help.

thirty-two:

– before –

I came home from dropping Jack off at school one morning, hung up my jacket, kicked off my shoes and walked through into my kitchen and saw *him*. Sitting there. At my table.

Emotion slammed into me. Jack's dad was back. I'd known the day would come but the knowing and then having him there, drinking my tea in my favourite mug, did not make me feel any better.

The time passing had meant he was both Nick-like and yet not: older, his hair was a little longer, but most notably – he had obviously been weightlifting. He'd never looked stronger. The way he eyed me when I walked into my own flat, he'd never looked more dangerous. His shoulders seemed broader than I remembered and his blue eyes looked sharper, more alert, as if being away from me and Jack suited him, had helped him find a focus that had eluded him before he left.

The shock was terrible. I hadn't seen him in so long and yet here he was, lounging at my kitchen table. I'd never achieved blanking him entirely from Jack's life, but this time the silence was so long, I'd *hoped*.

'What's the chance of you making me some breakfast, Lisa?' he asked, giving me the impossible grin and a hard stare at the same time. 'I'm starving.' He drank from his mug: 'And I'd love a refill.'

'What are you doing here? This is my flat. How did you get in?'

He got up and started rummaging through the cupboards. He found a sliced loaf and popped two slices down before answering. 'If you won't do it . . .' he said, whilst I watched him with a sense of disbelief, my heart banging in my chest.

He waited until it popped up, the sound of the toast making me jump. He saw my sudden movement and laughed. 'Jumpy! Surprised to see me?'

'You don't live here.'

He moved me away from the fridge and retrieved the margarine. He pulled off the lid and said: 'You shouldn't eat this rubbish. You know they put colourants in it, don't you? Margarine is actually grey.' He then took a knife, scraped out a wodge and spread it thickly on his toast. 'I hope you don't give this crap to Jack.'

'The corner shop was out of butter.' I put the lid back on the tub.

'Have I just missed the school run?'

I don't even breathe.

'Ah, yes.' He takes a hungry bite and chews it watching me. 'I expect Mrs Turnbill, at St Joseph's, is taking the register just as we speak.' He checked his watch. 'What am I talking about! His first lesson will be nearly over.'

My bladder froze. How long had he been watching Jack? How long had he been watching me? I shut the fridge door that he'd left open and saw a letter for a school trip and the colourful certificates won by Jack at school: '*Top Speller!*', '*Kindness Award of the Week!* and '*Perfect Pupil Politeness!*' all pinned under magnets to the door. Had he broken into my flat before? I tried to think if there had been any signs of it – moved things – but my brain felt like glue.

He took a huge bite of toast and chewed it, watching me with narrowed eyes. 'I've seen him in the playground. I don't think he likes it.'

There was so much danger in this, I wasn't just suddenly lost in the ocean, but there was a tidal wave coming straight for me too. Despite it, I wanted to ask: *Why do you think he doesn't like it?* And: *Does he look scared?* And: *Does he have any friends? Is he lonely . . . like me?*

Suddenly I was so lonely.

Not the loneliness that most of us get on a Saturday night when all our friends are out, the wine is gone and there's nothing on TV. But that suffocating, black, damp mould that sits in your chest and spreads like an infection; that disables the rational mind and makes you want to reach for the paracetamol. That damp cold that can lie across your lungs and heart like a heavy secret that stays there even when you're standing in a busy room at a drinks party. That lies behind a rictus grin reminding you that there's no one who loves you or understands you.

I never used to feel like that. It's only since I lost him.

But now he was back, leaning against the counter, pushing the last of the toast into his mouth and switching the kettle on again as easy as if he lived here, and I'd ignored the feeling since I saw him, but I couldn't lie any more: I was so pleased to see him. Because between us was only ever a love story. A bitter, broken tragic story, but there was always a love that no one ever understood. Not even me.

Suddenly the separateness between me and him was so enormous, so overwhelming, I just wanted to drop to my knees and beg him to come back. As scared as I was of him, I wanted to tell him that I loved him. That I missed him. That I was sorry for all the things I'd done, that I got wrong, that drove him away. I wanted us to be a family again: him, me and Jack.

I gripped the edge of the Formica but instead I wanted to jam my hand in my mouth so I didn't ask him to walk with me on the school pick-up. I wanted him back despite what he'd done to me, what he'd done to Jack.

But it was too late, I knew that. To think it, yes. To say it, no. So instead I managed to say: 'I don't like you being in my flat.' And I sounded cold when I said it, as if I meant it.

'Why not?'

'Because you didn't ask. Because you don't live here.' It was all I could manage. I could have said that to anyone and perhaps the reasonableness of this disarmed him because he only nodded as if he agreed with me.

He finished a slice of toast. 'To be fair, I only broke in because I didn't think you'd let me in.'

'Because?'

He shrugged. 'Because it's been such a long time? Because I didn't think you'd want me being around Jack?'

'I don't. It's better . . . now it's just me and him.'

'I want to see him.'

I felt my throat close up. This is what I dreaded. 'Why?'

'Because he's my son. Because I want to be a good dad.'

'*No.*' The abruptness of my answer was born of the certainty of my feelings. I would not allow it.

He watched me carefully. 'You don't have a choice, Lisa. He's my son and I want him with me.' When I didn't say anything, he threw a bomb into my life. 'I want full custody. Drug addicts shouldn't be allowed to raise children, should they?'

I looked at his raised eyebrow and knew that he'd started a war. 'Get out of my flat.'

He stared at me a brief moment. Then – surprising me – he calmly put down his toast, picked up his coat, and walked out of the door I now held open.

He did not look back.

thirty-three:

– before –

A week after his sudden toast-eating visit to my flat, I received a message saying he'd set himself up in a flat round the corner from mine and told me that he wanted regular access to Jack. *Fuck that*, I thought. Shortly followed by: *Fuck you*.

After a sleepless night, the following morning I went straight to a solicitor. I sat in the waiting room rehearsing over and over again what I would say.

From the start, everything about the solicitor's office was disappointing. I wasn't sure what I'd been imagining, but it wasn't what I got. The floor was a dull green lino and the chairs were constructed from metal and foam. The solicitor was a woman about my age and she wore an ugly blouse. She insisted on taking lots of details I didn't want to talk about before listening to what was important.

'He's not a fit father,' I said and I told her why.

She wrote everything down but she didn't seem surprised or concerned. All the writing and no action made my chest ache.

Then she said: 'We need to take action today.'

Hope flourished – I finally thought I was getting somewhere. 'Good!' I said, wanting to kiss her hand in gratitude.

'First you need to read this guidance.' She passed me a copy of something I didn't want to read. 'Then we need to fill out a specific court form. You need to be prepared that you're going to have to attend mediation with the father because . . .'

As she talked through the process, I nodded along, but inside my hope began to wither. It became clear that it would take ages, during which Jack would spend unsupervised time with his father where anything – *anything* – could happen. I thought of Winston. I thought about my bruises and injuries he'd given me. She showed me the forms I would need to fill out and explained about his rights, and I just felt sick. To challenge him, she wanted crime numbers, complaints to the police and witnesses – I had nothing. Within just ten minutes, all my hope had died.

I excused myself to the toilet and didn't go back.

Now I understood I couldn't fight for Jack through a long court battle; nor could I sit around and trust other people to do what was right for him. Jack needed something quicker than that, but I didn't know what.

After the solicitor, I'd trudged the streets, lost. I didn't see the spring flowers, only the dark, restless clouds slipping across the sky. Eventually my mind turned to the school pick-up. I changed direction and thought I'd allowed enough time, but I must've been lost in my thoughts, because when I got there I realised I was a little late. And not just a little late for the teacher, but a little late to do anything about the horror I witnessed.

I saw it all as I made my way across the busy school playground, filled with mums and dads waiting, some already leaving with their children, a melee of dogs tied to the fence, scooters and bikes.

With his back to me and hood up, I didn't see him at first.

Jack did.

I saw the teacher lead the class out onto the playground. I saw Jack in his yellow spring rain jacket. I saw his face – not looking at me – suddenly yell as he punched the air. I watched his happiness in slow motion and could only wonder how he could remember his father so instantly when he hadn't seen him for over a year. His huge smile was like the sun coming out, full beam, summer bright, and he shouted: 'Daddeeeeeee!' and without waiting for permission, he broke rank and ran towards his father. Like a scene from a movie, he flung aside his school bag. His father then picked Jack up and swung him high and around. Everyone turned to look. They hadn't seen each other in months and months and it looked like the joyful reunion it was.

Jack's teacher, Mrs Turnbill, looked at me, unsure. She'd never met Jack's father and was only permitted to discharge Jack to me and sought my permission now with a raised eyebrow. I found myself nodding *yes*. What could I say? They had every legal right to see each other. Besides, I could hardly make a fuss in front of everyone.

Instead, I was forced to pick up the abandoned bag from the ground and then lag behind them on the way home from school, instantly demoted to second-best. Jack held his dad's hand and bounced and hopped the whole way back to what was obviously the new flat. Not once did Jack turn to look at me. Instead I had to endure seeing his upturned, enraptured face, the whole way. Reaching the flats, I trailed up the stairs in the super-smart block of flats I'd watched being built only last year, but with a creeping dread that I would have to do this journey again and again. Jack's giggles and laughter bounced off the stairwell walls, almost mocking me to hear his joy amplified and multiplied.

At the top, they opened a door and Jack stepped into his hall and his dad turned and blocked my way.

His dad: my son, my Jack.

Two Jacks; father and son.

Me, already at 44 a grandmother to a six-year-old.

Jack turned back to see me. 'Granny?' he asked me, 'You don't mind if I stay with my daddy for the weekend?'

I could see the hope in his eyes, could see how much he wanted to be with his dad after all this time. How could I, as just his granny, not simply say yes? The solicitor had given me no hope of anything else.

So, I nodded, terror cold fingers around my heart. Side by side, I could see how different my two Jacks were – one sensitive and concerned, the other – just dangerous. Like the contrast is their ages, I felt the sharp contrast in raising them both. Never before had I wanted Nick's calm, kind reassurance more. Then, standing there, looking at our son now grown, I ached for my ex-husband's gentle touch.

My son smiled at me, alligator. 'Sorry, Granny, I think it's best that I spend some time on my own with my son, don't you?' Then his smile deepened, gouging deeper into flesh: 'But don't come back for him until Sunday morning. I've bought Jack new clothes and a toothbrush. Sunday. Thanks, Mum.'

Mum.

Cruel, cruel, cruel. Standing there, as he barred my way to Jack, he knew what he was doing when he called me *Mum*. He hadn't called me Mum in so long, not since he was fourteen when, after a row about him tracking mud onto my new, immaculate, cream carpet, he started calling me Lisa instead.

But then my Jack chose to call me that – just so I knew my place. We stood on his doorstep and it was such a rare moment that he looked at me – properly.

'And give me his school bag. Jack told me on the way home that he does his spelling homework on a Saturday morning.' He had his hand out for it and I looked down and saw that it was in my hand.

The bag handle was nylon material; rough. I gripped on to it, reluctant to give it up. It was as if it was all I had left. He was even taking our routine of spellings. I imagined them having a lovely breakfast on a Saturday morning, getting the spellings done before heading off to the park or town. That was our routine and now it felt like he wanted everything from me.

I always gave him everything.

It took everything to raise him.

He took it all.

'I do appreciate you stepping in for *my* boy. Granny.'

My.

Stepping in. So temporary.

And with that, he took Jack into the dark inside, like a calf swallowed up by dark water; as he shut the door, all I could think of was Winston, the dog he killed by hitting his spine with the broom, and the terror for my grandson, now alone in his care, took on a new, higher pitch, silent, yet shrill.

thirty-four:

– before –

I stood there, staring at the door shut against me. The memory of my son's voice mocked me. To come back and claim his son from me, I suspected, was all for this moment. To call me *Granny*, was just to hurt me. To remind me. Because although I loved Jack like he was my son, he was my grandson. Of course my son – *my Jack* – was all grown up now, and, even though he'd become a father to the sweetest little boy ever – *his Jack* – he himself was still as spiteful as he'd ever been.

My Jack of a thousand kicks and punches. His Jack with the stutter and pupil awards.

My son was back and now he had decided to reclaim his abandoned son and play Daddy – and there wasn't a thing I could do about it.

He didn't have to say it, but I heard it like he wanted me to: Jack is *mine*, not *yours*.

I remember the day he killed Winston. I shouldn't have taken to my bed that day; shouldn't have left my son unsupervised with Winston. I was just so upset. I had received a letter from his school; the contents were so painful that I'd necked 4 mg of diazepam and pulled the duvet over my head. I was so exhausted by being his mother, I just didn't even want to see him.

The letter was the formal notice of what I already knew. I had been told by his headmaster that they wouldn't have him back after Easter, that he was being expelled. But until I received the official notification, I'd still dared to hope. The letter killed that hope.

A week before the Easter term break, he (not *Jack*, it can't be since beautiful Jack now shares his name and my son refuses to call me Mum, I just won't muddle the two) – *he* had assaulted another boy with a pair of scissors, so badly that the child's earlobe had to be stitched back on. What was worse was that they'd had to persuade my son to give the earlobe back so they could put it on ice.

By then, the school had had enough. I didn't blame them – the violence, the tantrums, the spitting. Urgh, the humiliation of the spitting! That became quite the thing for him in his first term. He hated that I left him. He would cry and cling and then when I finally tried to escape, he became angry, punching and kicking me. The teacher and her assistant would restrain him and try and calm him down. But if he couldn't get to me, that was when the spitting started. He used to try so hard, a whole body effort to try to get the spit to hit me, it was like watching an '80s football hooligan.

The first year of Jack starting school was the hardest because of the judgement. The teaching staff were excellent and I couldn't fault them. But that first year, I know they blamed me and Nick. I know they must have wondered what went on in our home for our son to be like he was. I made sure that Nick and I spent lots of time working with the staff to try and find a solution for bettering our son's behaviour. Then, when they knew us well, I could sometimes catch them looking at us, the question in their eyes: *Well, if not you, then why . . .?*

I don't know, I wanted to scream. *You tell me!*

And it wasn't just the judgement of staff I feared, but the parents. When he first started in reception, there were lots of making-friends activities – meetings up in the park, picnics, play dates where the mums would drink coffee and their little ones would have fun. Except it was never fun with Jack. He seemed to take delight in refusing the simplest of requests. He would be obstinate, aggressive and downright rude. One particular play date, he'd requested fish fingers, only to then refuse to eat them, and the fish fingers had ended up being smeared on the poor woman's wall. It was all so humiliating. When they stopped inviting him, it was actually a relief.

It was that relief that made me give up Issy, Nadia and Nessa so easily. His difficulties were starting to become apparent, even at two. It was in their children's company that I started to realise something was wrong. Sure, their children had tantrums, but his lasted longer. He was also noticeably rougher than their children, and was more likely to cause disputes, break toys and be defiant. And bite! How he loved that from the start.

It was no coincidence that Irene started to have her grandson for me on the day the NCT always met up. I don't think they missed him. They probably thought he was difficult because Nick was abusing me, but Nick never raised a hand to me.

Looking back, my only regret is that I should've just told Issy the truth, that time in the café twenty years ago. It would've been a relief perhaps to share it with someone other than Nick.

Now, if my son had been little now, it would've been very different for me – for all of us. Now there's the internet – I could've Googled to my heart's content and perhaps used that to help me with the GP. But I doubt I would've had to – there's labels now, diagnoses that everyone is much more familiar with. There's proper processes for schools – it would've all been easier. I could've accessed help groups and chat rooms, like Mumsnet, to give me advice, support. There would've been prescriptions as a last resort. Twenty years ago, the world was a different place.

I did my best. I tried to create support. I once took him to the doctor and explained about his behaviour problems, but the doctor looked at me with a puzzled expression and offered to prescribe me antidepressants. I wanted to yell at the stupid, confused doctor: *It's not me!* This is not because of me! I am like this because – and only because – of *him*!

I remember how, after I'd taken our son to the doctor, Nick tried again the following year. He took him to a different GP, but came back silent yet clearly angry. He didn't tell me what that doctor had said, but neither of us ever tried taking him again.

After getting nowhere with the doctors, when I went back to work my plan A was always to earn money to access private counselling for my boy. Nick and I agreed on most things, including being both staunch supporters of the NHS. Obviously as a nurse and police officer, we believed in strong state provision; we were against private schools and private healthcare and Nick felt that by going down the private route, we were somehow traitors to our own kind. But I was desperate. With my own money, I secretly paid for therapy for Jack, but he only went a few times before refusing.

When it was clear there was going to be no change soon, then my plan A moved to my plan B – therapy for me, to help me cope with him. And after he hurt me so badly over the broken Peter Rabbit, before Nick finally calmed his own anger enough to intervene, I thought that one day he might kill me, so I packed my go-bag. It was for an emergency if I needed to get away from him. I never thought I would choose to leave the son I loved so much, but I could see a situation in which I might *need* to. But I also couldn't desert Nick – not when we'd been so united.

Then he'd killed the dog on the day I'd received the school letter. I knew then just how dangerous it was getting, but I didn't know how to keep my son with me and keep us safe as a family.

And as if that wasn't bad enough, there was what happened two days after that.

Then it was that I had no choice but to use my go-bag, just not in the way I had envisaged because I'd had to take Jack with me.

I think of that now, how my son was then, and what he might be like now. But I can't stare at this door, lost in the past, any longer. Instead, I have to accept – for now – that Jack will be with his dad this weekend.

thirty-five:

– before –

I took one last, reluctant look at the smart grey door to my son's flat and headed home.

As I walked, I passed sycamore trees; their autumn leaves reminded me of a different walk home, in a different time some twenty years before, in a different town. I thought then of Issy and the crew. I thought of my son then, when he was small and how we had walked through that park in Brighton and had thrown his collected leaves into the air with delight. Although bittersweet, it was a rare, easy, uncomplicated memory.

Because his birth was so bad, Nick and I had never had another child, so when Jack stopped calling me Mum, it was as if I stopped *being* one. He alone had the power to make me Mum and he alone denied me the power of being one. With a mother then still in prison, I felt almost motherless and childless, too.

I felt like I'd lost part of my identity.

Even after he'd had his own baby, he wouldn't acknowledge my rightful role and call me Granny. I remained just 'Lisa'. Even when he wanted my childcare, it would be: 'Here, Lisa –' he'd say, passing me his baby when Jack was small – 'look after Jack for me, will you?' And then he'd walk out of the door and some-times not come back for days.

But *now* he managed it. *Now* he wanted to cut me out from his son's life, now he managed to call me 'Mum' and 'Granny' – just to make a point. I already knew little Jack wasn't my son, but he felt like he was, because I was the one who had looked after him after his mum died and my son left.

But now Jack was back.

My Jack who was so, so different to his Jack. Mine was bold and adventurous, whereas his was nervous and scared of the shadows. Mine loved reading, but his didn't. Mine was action-focused whereas his loved studying the stars. Mine would never sleep but his would nap too readily. Mine was violent and killed his own dog, whereas his was gentle and loved animals. Mine was expelled whereas his was a perfect pupil. The list went on. If they hadn't shared the same physical features, I would've doubted they were even related.

But looking after my grandson had boosted me because it'd shown me that I could get it right.

Or, rather, that I had, because now it seemed, it was all over for me. Again.

I arrived home. In the kitchen were the ingredients I had laid out for our highly anticipated cooking session: a bushy basil plant, a pale gold bulb of garlic, pine nuts, and in the fridge, alongside our home-made tagliatelle, a chunk of parmesan. Jack had talked about nothing else this morning getting ready for school. Tonight was to be the culmination of our cooking project: home-made pasta with home-made pesto. We made the pasta yesterday, passing it through my KitchenAid. It was messy, our faces were smudged with flour, the dough under our nails, but at the end, we stood back and high-fived each other at the sight of our thin pasta over the pasta tree, the strands draping like willows.

Feeling bereft, I started to put the ingredients away. I touched a green, shiny basil leaf, its peppery smell pungent. I put the plant on the windowsill, ready for another time.

If there was going to be another time.

Then the fear that I might never get Jack back overwhelmed me, and I collapsed onto a dining chair.

Later, much later, I sat up. The back of my hand was reddened and wet where I'd rested my head as I cried. The room was now dark and I realised I was cold.

I sat thinking about getting a jumper, but felt too nervous to go into my bedroom. I always kept a small supply of codeine in there, tucked in a box on the top shelf of my wardrobe. To collect a jumper meant being too close: the thought of the codeine glowed like a beacon in the dark. Even though I'd been clean for years, I kept a stash to prove it. It was my: *Fuck you, codeine, I could take you if I wanted but I* don't *want to.*

But now I did.

That cold compulsion, that deep and dark desire, replaced the sunshine that Jack shone into my life.

And I found that I wanted to very much.

thirty-six:

– before –

That Friday night, I resisted the codeine by getting up from the kitchen table and pouring myself a glass of water which I carried into Jack's bedroom and set on his bedside table. I then took off my jeans and bra, and wearing just my T-shirt and pants and socks, got into his bed. When I found Bunny on his pillow, I started to weep again as it still smelt of Jack. I didn't trust my son: I didn't know if Jack would be well cared for or even if he would come home. But as overwhelmingly stressful as that was, I was determined not to give up my sobriety. Jack needed me to stay clean.

It was Jack being born that'd finally helped me get clean in the first place and after six years I held onto my sobriety tightly.

But before that were many years of codeine abuse. Really I would've liked to have given up after Nick and I broke up, but it was too traumatic.

Living alone with Jack and trying to be independent was also a trauma on its own. But after that miserable trip to see my mother in Send prison when I told her my marriage was over, I decided to take control. If not of the codeine, then of every other area of my life. Within the same week as visiting my mother, I bought a car and started applying for jobs. I'd loved agency work, but now I was a single parent, I needed more structure.

Nick emailed after a few days. First of all he begged me to return. It didn't take long for that to stop, however, and then I got news that he was moving to Gloucestershire following a big promotion. He visited every few months, staying with Irene, and sent housekeeping money and my share of the proceeds of our flat. I was satisfied with the arrangement, now he was at a distance.

Nick was helpful and supportive too in other ways, and sometimes, in the first year or so following our separation, we would talk on the phone like we had before our relationship had turned sour.

I found a great job as a nurse working nights in a nursing home called Sunningdale. It was a beautiful Victorian building, with twenty-four residents. Then I found the perfect childminder – a single parent with a child at Jack's new school. I would take Jack to her house two days a week at 7 p.m., in his PJs. He would sleep over and I would collect him in the morning, dress him for school and drop him off, before I returned home to sleep. I'd be up and ready to pick him up from school at home time.

Lillie was perfect for Jack: a bit of a hippy, she didn't mind his tantrums, even thought them a form of self-expression, and because his friend was there, he soon packed in any bad behaviour and settled into the routine.

Two shifts of night duty, with a bit of agency, meant I was earning a full-time wage. I'd never worked in private nursing before, and although I missed the NHS, I was earning enough money to buy a little house with a garden.

I stopped stealing codeine from the agency shifts when the internet developed – I simply bought what I need from there. Although it wasn't without difficulties, it was emancipating and I was finally able to let the agency work go.

I stayed at Sunningdale and, as Jack became older and more independent, I was able to take on more responsibility and was promoted, which meant moving away from night work.

Two other major events happened that helped. When Jack was ten, I inherited quite a lot of money from my aunt which gave me financial security. The second, only three months later, was my mum's release from Send prison. She had been inside since 1983 when I was eight until I was thirty, a total of twenty-two years. Her sentence was high in the first place: her lawyer told me that the fact that she was female and killed her husband meant she had a heavier sentence than if she'd been a man killing his wife. And then, as respected and liked as she was by the prison officers, she still had a tendency to get 'involved' with the other women's lives and parole had passed her by time after time.

With my mother moving only two miles away, it meant that Jack could visit her after school if I was working. He'd often cycle over to have tea with her and they'd play cards together; she remained his champion.

Jack and I sometimes went ten-pin bowling together; he'd complain that it wasn't often enough, that I was always working. It's true, I did work a lot. As a single parent, it was important to me to have financial security; it allowed me to take care of my mum a bit, as well as take care of Jack. I also loved the serenity of Sunningdale; the quiet atmosphere and the sweet nature of the residents made it a very peaceful place to be.

By the time my son was seventeen, I barely saw him anymore. I always kept his bed made up for him, and kept his favourite foods on my shopping list, but it wouldn't be unusual not to see him for two or three weeks at a time. He would never tell me where he'd been. It was stressful not knowing, although I was always delighted to see him when he drifted home – but admittedly that would wear off within a few hours. But sometimes we would jog along OK and sometimes he would stay for three or four days.

Then one day, when he was eighteen, he came home and told me his girlfriend was pregnant. I didn't even know he had a girlfriend. The baby was born, and sure enough as I visited the new family in hospital, he said, 'Look, Lisa, look at how lovely my baby Jack is.'

'You can't call him Jack! *You're* Jack.'

He laughed. 'In the old days, people always called their first-born son after themselves. I'm just being traditional. He's Jack Junior.'

Selena, his pale, monosyllabic girlfriend, held the baby out to me to hold and I took his beautiful weight in my arms. 'Junior,' I whispered to him.

'No,' my son corrected, 'never Junior. His name is *Jack*.'

Even as a tiny blanketed baby, he looked out at us all with lovely long lashes. As I whispered to my new grandchild, his name, the first time I said his name, the word felt like dust in my mouth – it felt like going back in time.

Jack.

But the feeling passed in a second and I became overwhelmed by the surprise at how joyful it felt to hold the baby to my chest and breathe in his smell. It was like all the stories I'd read about the instant rush of love mothers experienced. Because of my son's birth, I hadn't been able to hold him after he was born and the pain and the drugs meant I never had the suddenness of that feeling. But now I was feeling it for real. I whispered *Jack* for a second time into his tiny, delicate, soft pink ear and I realised how much I loved him. Baby Jack! It was so different from the start – and I was so different with him. The name Jack lost all its connotations and became reborn. Selena encouraged me to have Jack as much as I wanted. The slight, pale, near-silent teenager showed little interest in her baby, and so it felt like I was a mother again.

So it was me who pushed his pram through the streets. Even that pram was on steroids compared to the old one I'd had my son in – I bought Jack the best, a Bugaboo, amazed at how it could turn on a dime. It felt like motherhood but newer and fresher and easier. No sore boobs, no vaginal stiches or postpartum bleeding. Just this tiny person who was so easy to love.

And the best bit? He responded to me! There was a point to picking him up when he cried because he would stop. Stop! Maybe not immediately – he was a baby after all – but he could and would be soothed. This was a child I could make a difference to. Gone were the horrendous nights that I'd had with his father. His father, who screamed every night until around the time he started school, which meant broken sleep for years. It was like being reminded that I was normal, that I was OK, that I could be good where I once felt like a failure.

When Jack was six months old, his mother, Selena, was found dead with a heroin needle still in her arm. The shock was terrible and I vowed then that I wouldn't be an addict too.

Jack deserved better.

So – for him – I became clean. Decision made, I cut down carefully, on a reduction programme I'd designed myself. It was very difficult and I suffered with headaches, cramps, chills and diarrhoea, but for Jack, I did it. Clean for the second time.

Jack and my son moved in with me, but my son had started flitting in and out again, initially just disappearing for a day, then a night too, until eventually, he'd be gone sometimes for weeks at a time. I never minded – I liked being in charge. Then one day, when Jack was four and just a month shy of starting school, his father told me that he wouldn't do it anymore and just left for good.

Nick visited when our son walked out on me and little Jack. We discussed the idea of notifying social services, but decided against it. Nick was impressed with how much I had it under control and was content to leave me to it and return to his life up north; he'd been promoted many times and now lived with his wife and two daughters tucked up in a house near Cheltenham which I assumed was as beautiful as his wife. But as different as our lives were, we were united on protecting our son and keeping his options open with Jack.

But my ideas of keeping our son's options open soon changed.

Jack and I had a beautiful long and wonderful year together. Jack's stutter began to lessen and he seemed to grow in confidence without his father around. He moved up to Year 1 and thrived. I never could see any sign that my son had been abusing his child, but Jack certainly seemed to be happier without him around.

Now, as I lay in his bed clutching his bunny, I wondered if Jack was happy now.

For most of the night, I thought of both the past and the now. Questions puzzled relentlessly in my head: was Jack happy? Was he safe? Did my son have a job now? How was he paying for that smart new flat? Did he really mean to stay? Was this going to happen again? Was this going to be a new routine or was Jack going to be mucked about yet again with his father upping and leaving?

And the question that burnt more than any other: did my son hurt his son?

After all the injuries he'd given me over the years, I lay there, tortured that Jack was in danger and it felt like there was nothing I could do about it.

thirty-seven:

- before -

On Saturday morning, feeling fragile, I got up, still holding the bunny toy, and rang the only person who could help. Nick. To his credit he answered – he always did.

'Nick, Jack's got Jack.'

He swore and called out to his wife. I heard her answer and he came back on the line. 'Sorry, Lisa, we were about to go out, but it can wait.'

He always paused his life for me when it came to our son. I don't know what she thought, but it felt like he was still prepared to suffer with me. 'I don't want to interfere with your day.'

'It's just food shopping, Lese – I've got a minute. I've been meaning to ring you anyway.'

I still loved it when he called me Lese – it made me feel that I belonged to him. I told him what had happened.

'Well . . . this is good, isn't it?' he answered, not sounding surprised at all. How was it that I'd been blindsided, but he thought it was all perfectly to be expected? 'We always wanted him to come back for Jack and to face up to his adult responsibilities.'

That was true, I knew it was, but it just felt abrupt. 'Is he going to do a good job though? Jack's so young.'

'I checked again recently, he still hasn't got a criminal record – he's never done anything wrong. It's possible that he –' I could hear the shrug in his voice – 'just finally grew out of being a shit.'

It felt good to hear Nick's levity. It made me feel that I was in it with someone; that I wasn't alone. Then he said the perfect thing as usual. 'Lese, I know you'll get Jack back. Jack just wants another try at being a dad. He's older now and—'

I heard his wife calling him.

'You go, Nick. You've got stuff to do. I feel better; I can wait it out until tomorrow.'

'Anne-Marie can wait a sec. I just wanted you to know—'

I heard her calling him again, louder this time. 'Honestly, Nick, I get it. I'm not alone. I geddit.'

I geddit was something I used to say to him a lot when he would over-emphasise a point. He laughed at the memory – I did too. I promised to call again on Sunday and hung up.

Hearing that Nick thought it was a good idea made me feel a little better. I tried to be productive and tidy the flat, to get on with jobs that needed doing, like cleaning the grout in the bathroom.

As I scrubbed, I thought about Nick. I thought about how I missed him, how, despite being married to Anne-Marie for years, he still felt like my husband.

Nick tried so hard to be a good husband, a good father. To his credit, he always tried to do his best – not just with our son, but also with me. He would come home from work as promptly as he could. It was difficult to clock out on time as a copper, and I think his desire to look after me drove a wedge between him and his bosses at work, but – love him – he did it anyway. He would come home, make me a cup of tea and then when things were really bad, he would examine me, looking for scratches and bruises. There was a bad time involving an iron burn when he lost it – badly – with Jack, and another time when I needed stitches to my lip. Plus, the broken finger of course, and several broken ribs. And a broken nose. I had suffered, but I think it took courage for Nick to walk out of our front door every day and not know what he'd come back to. He was unable to muscle our son into good behaviour, so in some ways I think the abuse was emasculating. He knew he should be putting a stop to it, but like me, just didn't know how. It was so hard not getting help from the GPs, but then, bad behaviour in children just wasn't medicalised.

We tried to be self-sufficient and read up on what was available – not much then – and made plans which, to our credit, we stuck to. We tried it all. Nothing worked.

Now, things would've been different. Most likely, Nick would've been investigated, but this was before, when people looked the other way to domestic abuse and I was left to make excuses about clumsiness that were instantly believed. I know, as a nurse who'd done a few stints in A & E, that I'd seen injuries to wives and suspected, but it wouldn't have occurred to us to do anything.

It sounds so stupid, so improbable now, but times change.

I think if we had all been born later, it might've been OK. Now people are more *aware*. Behaviour problems have found medical recognition. Someone, somewhere, would've been able to offer us support. At the time there was no Google search, no help groups. At the time, we thought it was just us. And when you think you are the only ones, you don't talk. You keep shtum. It's hard – even as adults being abused by loved ones – but you fear the not being believed, the nothing changing, the shame of being found out and not being understood. Nick worried about people thinking he was an abuser, but not able to put them right. Both of us found it easier to bear the shame of people thinking he beat me rather than us trying to find a way to find a way to say: *No, you're wrong, it's our son.*

Nick and I have had our problems, but he was a good father and a good husband. In many ways, he will always be my hero.

I wish someone had asked. When he and I were still in a good place with each other, if someone had raised a question, we would've cried out in response, glad for help. But instead, we were on our own with it and we just didn't know what to do. We loved our son; we just kept hoping he would grow out of it. Besides, what else could we do? We could hardly just give him away as faulty goods. *Sorry, have you got another one? We think this one is broken.*

Don't think that there weren't dark moments, during dark nights, when I didn't think of it. But it was rare.

But on we went and on went the bad times that kept amassing like stones in a cairn; they built up, defiant against raw elements, until there were too many to take down. Sometimes, I would stand, metaphorically hands on hips, and *just look* at my life. And not believe.

There were just so many times, so many stones.

We all heaped our stones on that cairn. Not just our son. Nick and I brought our imperfections to our family life.

But a huge one, the stone that started the topple, was the death of Winston. Like the key all those decades later, the dog's death caused a huge earthquake through our world. What he did to the dog changed our family forever. Winston was so lovely. In some ways, he was like Nick's and my second baby. But as soon as our son was old enough, he made it clear he didn't like our family dog. Even as a twelve-month-old, he would throw his Lego bricks at him.

By the time he was three, I no longer allowed him to be alone with Winston. Except that one time, the day of the letter.

Despite what I might say, I didn't blame Nick for making the most of his freedom from us – I never have. Through it all, even when he found happiness somewhere else, with his new family, I never begrudged Nick for trying to squeeze some joy from his life. If I ever felt envy creep up on me, I remembered him on his knees, body bent over our dead dog, the terribleness of his heaving, silent sobs, and then that final moment when he raised his head and looked at me with huge, helpless eyes, and I could see the pain our union had brought him.

Finally, standing back, my home was clean and it'd become evening. I felt proud of myself: surfaces gleamed, I still hadn't touched the codeine, I'd survived my first day without Jack and I'd worked a little bit more of Nick out of my system. Suddenly starving, I ate two bowls of cereal. Then, with aching shoulders and knees from the day's chores, I gave up on the idea of TV and went back to Jack's bed. I thought I'd be awake all night, counting the hours and minutes until Sunday morning, but instead, feeling almost peaceful, fell asleep.

In my last waking moments, in the dreaminess and honesty of near-sleep, I wondered who I was looking forward to seeing more: Jack or Jack.

thirty-eight:

– before –

When I went to pick Jack up on Sunday morning, I got there for 9.30 a.m. I had been awake since 5.00, but thought that any earlier and I'd risk being labelled difficult. My son came to the door, already dressed. He was clean-shaven and had a cocky look in his eye. 'Bit early, isn't it, Lisa? Jack's just eating his pancakes.'

I was too surprised to argue when he shut the door to – albeit left ajar. I was surprised about everything: surprised he was letting Jack come back to me even though that was what we'd agreed; surprised my son was up and dressed at this hour, surprised he'd make his son breakfast, even more so, Jack's favourite.

When Jack came to the door, he looked happy and relaxed. He was dressed in clothes I hadn't seen before – they looked nice. More surprise. Even better, he was clearly pleased to see me, but not too eager – not enough to suggest there had been any concerns for him.

My son simply handed over Jack's school bag. 'We did his spellings homework. See you next Friday,' was all he said before he shut the door in my face.

Jack's flat was only fifteen minutes' walk from my own. As I walked home, feeling much better to have Jack's hand in mine, I asked about his weekend. He said his dad had taken him to London Zoo, and that they'd had fish and chips for dinner. 'Not both nights?' I asked.

Jack giggled. 'Both nights,' he said. He looked at me, his face lit with amusement.

'Hmmm,' I said, before Jack giggled again.

'What's so funny?'

'Daddy said you wouldn't like me having it twice in a row – but he let me choose.'

I smiled back at his laughter, and actually – to my utter amazement – realised I meant it. I liked the idea of them having a shared joke. I liked the idea that Jack had been a bit spoilt. I even liked them poking fun at me a little – perhaps I was being too optimistic, but it felt affectionate.

After the terrible worry I'd suffered, I was delighted for this peaceful anticlimax. Not only was Jack safe, but he was happy. I'd survived. My son had stuck to his word and I had Jack back, when he said I would. I relaxed – the tiniest, tiniest fraction.

Within three more weeks, I began to even feel magnanimous. Jack had always sung to himself, but now he was never without a tune. He'd started to ace his spelling tests and told me that: 'Daddy showed me a new way to learn.'

Daddy.

Part of me simply glowed to think of my own son finally finding his way with his own boy. It wasn't just that it was a good thing for Jack, it was also great for my son. It felt like he was waking up to his responsibilities as a parent. Of course, it made me feel good about myself – how I worried I had screwed my son up! – but Jack was so rewarding, so delightful, how could his father not find it wonderful to have him in his life?

The possibility that he'd just get bored and stumble off as he normally did remained, although the permanence of his new flat gave me something to hope for. And when he turned up the next week and the next, I relaxed a tiny bit more.

I was impressed with the flat. I was never invited in, but it was in a very nice block. He must've been making good money, although how, I was still unclear. When I asked Jack if he knew whether his dad had a job, he said that he worked in 'phones', but whatever that meant, I never found out. Although I was pleased, I still struggled to mentally align this successful, working man to the stoned teenager who was so resistant to work. Sometimes, in darker moments – usually on Friday nights which remained hard for me – I thought of leopards and spots, but I also recognised that he was older and time and regret could change anyone. Plus, Jack was older too, and to the fickleness of someone like my son, possibly more engaging than a baby.

The best thing I could do was watch and wait. But how could I not want the best for my son *and* for Jack? After all, I loved them both. I didn't ring Nick back either – I didn't want to push it with him or Anne-Marie. I'd save him for emergencies, I decided, and week after week, there was no emergency.

But it didn't take long for it to go wrong.

I still always attended the school pick-up on a Friday, and then one day, just eleven weeks after my son started turning up, he simply wasn't there. I saw Jack's wide-eyed search amongst the waiting parents for his dad. Clearly confused, in the end Jack allowed me to take him home. He tried to hide his tears from me, but he was only six. I hugged him close and promised to ring his dad. He didn't answer when I did.

That weekend, I did my best to lift Jack's spirits. But I felt let down too – again I had been too easily trusting. I thought we wouldn't see him again, but then the next Friday, he was there in the school playground as if nothing had happened. Jack ran to him and my hope withered.

After three months, the arrangement continued to deteriorate. But we never discussed it – if I tried, my son simply shut me down. Our only contact had always been, and continued to be, as strained and brief as a divorcing couple. Every Sunday morning, at 9.30 a.m., he'd simply pass me Jack's school bag and say the same thing: 'We've done his spellings homework.' Then regardless of whether we would, he always said: 'See you next Friday, Lisa,' before shutting the door in my face.

I became frustrated and angry. It was one thing to muck me around, but my heart bruised for Jack. His stammer began to get worse again and he started biting his nails on Thursdays, anxious, asking me if I thought that his dad would turn up tomorrow. He'd struggle to sleep and on Friday mornings, would be dark-eyed and edgy.

When he turned up on the Friday afternoon to collect Jack, my grandson's face was an unwavering beam of love for his father. Their time together was still great – when it happened. I hated weekends without Jack, but began to like them more than weekends *with* Jack – it was better to know that he was happy, than to have to deal with a disappointed little boy.

My hope for them waxed and waned depending on my son's ability to turn up; it never gained enough strength to became a full flame. Instead, sometimes it was little more than a flicker on a damp wick, sometimes it burnt much brighter, yet sometimes it seemed not to be alight at all.

If Jack's father had been an ex-husband, I would've been far less tolerant of the inconsistencies. I would've been in front of the court, demanding full custody. But not only could I not do that because I had no rights, I was prejudiced by wanting the best for my son. He was here, he had bought a flat within walking distance of his son's school, this must be what he wanted. He was still young – only twenty-four – and I reminded myself constantly to make allowances.

But when Jack's anxiety spread to Wednesday night and his teacher mentioned he seemed distracted and tired, I decided I had no choice but to take action.

It didn't take long to make a plan – it was a thin, raggedy little plan. Tissue thin, it wouldn't give me much, but it might be just enough to get a sense of my son's mind. If I could look in his flat, perhaps secure an invite in, that could be a start. If I could find a way to chat to him, I could find out why he sometimes didn't attend, and then perhaps I could help. It was clear that our relationship wasn't going to build up naturally. I would have to instigate it.

I couldn't let things limp along as they were. For Jack's sake.

thirty-nine:

– before –

The day I used my thin, ragged little plan to get a better idea of my son's life, was a spring day only a few months before we moved to Herefordshire. Of course, I didn't know that then and the cottage on the hill was unknown to me.

I hadn't slept well the night before – too much wine and not enough food. I always found it difficult to eat at the weekends without Jack to keep me company. Just the thought of him being with his father left me lonely – I'd have loved to have occasionally joined in with them, perhaps had a meal with them sometimes or accompany them on a trip to the park. That was my long-term goal still – that one day, my son would relent and allow me in a little. We'd never had an official falling-out. There was no one particular incident that led him to be cold and distant to me. Since he'd been an adult, no words were ever exchanged. If anything, I would've hoped that Jack being well cared for by me was a reason my son could be friendly to me one day.

I couldn't stand not knowing any longer what Jack's situation was like when he was with his father. Were Jack's bed and clothes clean? Was there food in the cupboards? If I was satisfied, perhaps I could relax a little – and I dearly wanted to because I couldn't change the situation.

Around five o'clock I left the house. In a bag I carried my son's favourite cake – carrot. I also had what they would know now was missing from Jack's school bag as I had purposefully removed it – his spelling book. My plan was to turn up before tea, when I knew they would be hungry, and offer the cake and then produce the spelling book and hope for an invite in. If he didn't allow me access, I would take the matter to Nick, I decided, but for now, to try was enough.

If my son relented and let me, it would give me the chance to have a look around and – in my wildest, craziest hopes – to have a conversation about him providing Jack with consistency. It was unlikely to work, but that was not a reason not to try.

Before I could change my mind, I'd grabbed my bag and my props. But as I took my coat from the hook, I hesitated. I felt a shiver, a sense of foreboding.

I paused. Was I sure I wanted to do this? Suddenly, before I could change my mind, I sent him a text, telling him I was coming round. He might not let me in, but there was no advantage to surprising him – I knew my son and understood he wouldn't answer the door if he didn't want to.

Standing there, coat in hand, I remembered him as a child, taking him to see my mother after giving up the buggy. I remember towing him by the hand, his every fibre resisting me every step of the way. He always resisted me with everything and this would be no different. But perhaps he would want the spelling book enough to answer the door. And then, if Jack saw the cake, perhaps that would be enough. Probably not, but I lived in hope that my son would open the door to his closed heart. Constant love had to be the answer.

But instead of feeling better, forewarning him only added to my sense of fear. What if he did let me in, what then?

Then, like an addict lifting the fag to my mouth even though I didn't want to, I took my coat down and pulled the door of my flat behind me.

forty:

– before –

I drove slowly round to his flat. I was nervous. It was dark; it was only five o'clock in the evening, and on a Saturday, normally the town would still be busy, but the heavy wind and rain meant nobody was around.

Gripping the wheel, I kept thinking through my plan. The key was to be relaxed, but the more I thought about seeing him, the more nervous I became.

My heart *wham-whammed* and I realised I was terrified. I didn't know why – it should be perfectly fine. I suddenly wished I could go home, but I thought of Jack's stammer getting worse and with Nick in Cheltenham, there was no one else to deal with my son. I wanted to leave, but his inconsistent behaviour couldn't go on unchecked. I needed to try and bridge the gap between us and to see what life was for my grandson when he wasn't with me.

As I trekked up the stairs, I clutched my bag; it felt like an optimistic joke that my son would want to sit and eat a bit of cake with me. Why he didn't I couldn't be sure, but the fact he wouldn't still hurt me greatly. But I carried the bag anyway, a talisman for Jack.

Reaching his front door, I found it ajar. I could see the hall light was off and checked around me, unsure. Of all the imagined scenarios I had been through, this wasn't one of them. It seemed strange it was unlocked and instantly I felt even more unsettled. I looked around – but he wasn't nearby. Shaking, I reached out, tentatively, as if I was putting my hand down a rabbit hole. I knocked once. There was something in the way the door moved that made me think he was gone.

Could it be that he'd left with Jack?

I could only wait a few seconds; I was so adrenalised, so *twitchy*, that I just couldn't think clearly. I couldn't *breathe*.

I knocked again; the noise of my knuckles rapping was louder than I'd expected. Even though my heart was pounding, I was thinking crazy thoughts: *He's left! Jack's been taken! He's hiding behind the door!*

But the door opened easily into the hall. 'Hello?' I said into the silence. I tried again, hating to hear the waver in my voice. 'I've texted!' I called out, adding that I had Jack's spelling bag. When no one answered, I knew I could never live with myself without finding if Jack was safe, so I stepped inside to my son's flat before I could change my mind.

forty-one:

- before -

I stood in the hall, dim with no lighting, still unsure. 'Hello?' I tried again, my voice a dry rasp, filled with uncertainty. There were five doors. The two on my right were shut, but one on my left was open and I could see into the unlit kitchen. There were no sounds of life in the flat – no washing machine, no TV or radio playing, nothing. Another door was ajar onto a darkened room, but I could see a cord switch hanging down: a bathroom.

The door at the end was closed, but light spilled from the gap at the bottom – the steady light of perhaps a side lamp, not the flickering light of a TV.

I took a deep breath. In my hand, I still clutched my bag. 'I've brought Jack's spelling book!' I repeated. Silence. 'Hello? I've just popped round!' My voice sounded too carnival bright. Danger seemed everywhere. I felt watched and couldn't shake the feeling that this was a trap.

To get to the door at the end – the sitting room? – I would have to pass the closed doors on my right. I could open them, but I didn't dare.

I hesitated, but decided to call out again.

And then I swear my heart stilled because in reply, beloved Jack's voice called back in a thin, reedy voice that at once told me all was not OK: 'G-g-g-granny?'

I wanted to rush to him, throw open the door and see him, but I didn't dare. In my mind's eye, I saw his father lounged out on a sofa, perhaps asleep with a can in his hand. If I rushed in . . . I could stand the violence, but I couldn't bear for little Jack to witness it. So instead I hung back.

'Hi!' My voice now no longer bright, but instead clearly fearful. 'I just wanted you to be able to do your homework . . . I wanted to give your book to your dad . . . is he there?'

Silence. Jack didn't reply but nor did my son. I expected him to rush to the door with a *What the fuck are you doing here?* But there was nothing. In some ways the nothing was worse. Like a scare you know is coming on the pier ghost train, but hasn't yet happened. I wanted this dread to be over.

'Jack?' I called again. 'Can you get your dad for me, please? I don't want to intrude,' I added for my son's benefit. See how thoughtful I am. *Don't hit me, I didn't want to intrude.*

Except I did.

And he would know that.

'He's not here.'

Again I was stumped. Not here? Not in the sitting room? I flinched, looking over my shoulder – was he about to come out of a bedroom?

'Where is he?'

'He's gone out.'

I threw open the sitting-room door. Inside was a main room, sofas and a TV on one side, and against the other wall, a small dining table with two chairs. But in the middle sat a monstrosity.

What had my son *done*?

Even as I stood there, I couldn't name him, couldn't call him Jack. I think to call him by his real name was to open up a window to our past selves – the way we had been when I was his mother and he was my son. But although I refused to call him Jack until he started calling me Mum again, I still loved him. I knew that. And I carried that love like a dirty secret, because he couldn't bear to hear about it.

No matter what he did to me, I have always loved him because he is my child. We always felt like one. We had spent so much of our lives together; I was so dependent on him, he was so dependent on me. I still hold dear the days when we were so close, when it was so blurred that I didn't know where he started and I finished. When being together was difficult but enough.

But it went wrong, so wrong.

It was wrong way, way before we had his son to consider and it was still wrong now.

His lounge was messy with fish-and-chip wrappers on the carpet, an upended ashtray, rope (why does he have *rope*?) and it *stank* – of poo and urine. But – but worse, worse, worse was the terror in the middle of the room.

Why had Jack never told me?

I struggled to fit this room to the rest of what I'd understood about Jack's life here. He continued to wear new, clean clothes back from his dad's. I always washed and ironed them and took them into school on a Friday afternoon to give back, but I rarely saw the same ones again. The flat always smelt fresh, when standing at the front door. Was that just air freshener as part of the facade?

Is this why my son always pulled the door to – so I couldn't see inside? Couldn't see the mess? Couldn't see the monstrosity?

There, in the centre of the room, was a horror: fashioned out of two kids' playpens, with one upended on the other and bound everywhere with Gaffer tape. And seeing that horror, perhaps my last glow of love finally, finally, finally dimmed to nothing.

Because even in the dimness, I could see the smallness of Jack trapped inside a cage.

forty-two:

– before –

With Jack in the cage and his father out of the flat, I knew I had a window of opportunity to rescue Jack. I was so relieved too, that I had trusted my instincts and come looking for my grandson. But I didn't know how long I had and I knew if he came back and found me, there was a very good chance he might kill me.

I remembered the violence with bile. I hated the physical pain, the shock, but most of all I loathed the shame. There was the shame that someone might see, either the attack itself (and over the years, people had witnessed the violence, often dropping their gaze and withdrawing into themselves in the subtlest of ways, with a tilt of the head or a turn of the shoulder before finally escaping, taking their embarrassment at watching the poor woman who clearly can't cope with her own horrendous child and leaving me in a puddle of my own disgrace), or the evidence of a previous attack.

There's no help for someone like me, a sufferer of domestic violence from their child. I realise for many women, they're too frightened – with good reason – to leave their abusive partners, but for me, I've always been even more trapped.

But Jack was not trapped – I would not allow him to suffer. There are laws on child abuse and I would ensure that Jack would never see him again.

'Jack,' I said, 'where has Daddy gone?'

'T-t-t to-to-to go –' he gulped, his way of coping with the struggle of getting his words out. He took a deep breath: 'T-t-t to-to-to . . .'

Normally I gave him all the time he needed, but I did what I never did and cut him off. 'Don't worry, darling!' I said in my best fake-happy voice. 'Tell me later!' There would be time to get the facts. *How often do you sit in here? Why does he say he puts you in here? Does he hit you? Why didn't you tell me? Does he always leave you alone? Is the flat always this filthy?*

The only thing that mattered now was for me to get him out as fast as I could. I tried to yank at the thick, black tape. It was bound round and round each corner of both playpens, binding them together. I struggled, infuriated, overcome, tears blurring my vision. Then through the bars I saw him, his small face tilted up towards me. Jack looked so innocent – so patient and unconcerned, those beautiful eyebrows finely drawn, lifted in a parenthesis of some question I hadn't raised – that I just stopped.

Just stopped.

I couldn't breathe.

Grief crushed my lungs and I couldn't inhale. I was overcome at how far my failures as a mother now extended. This scene of misery, of emotional deprivation, was my fault, and only my fault. I shouldn't have even had a child, I realised. I wasn't fit; I never had been. I was my father's daughter and as such I shouldn't have tried to be anything else. I was a drug addict and I was broken by life and then I'd brought a child into my mess, my life. And this was the result. The type of horror story that I would see on the news – but this was *my* horror story.

I gripped the plastic bars under my hand.

'Are you all right, Jack?' I managed, amazed at how utterly normal my voice sounded.

'Yes!' He reached round for something and held it up: *Bunny*. 'I-I-I-I've got Bunny with me. Sh-sh-she-she knew y-y-y-you would come tonight!'

I reached through the bars. The playpen on top was blue plastic and looked worn and battered. The one underneath, which Jack sat in with Bunny, a couple of cushions, a blanket and a sippy cup, was multicoloured. Although it worked well at keeping Jack in, I realised it would be easy for me to release him.

'I'm going to get you out, Jack. I'm going to get some scissors or –' *a knife* – 'or something.' I gave him a bright smile. 'I'm just going to go into the kitchen. Will you . . . be all right here?'

'I-I-I-I . . .'

Part of me wanted to listen to him, what he was trying to say, but there was no time. He was so calm, so relaxed, I knew it then as sure as I knew my own name, that he was used to his father putting him in there. It didn't concern him like it might a child who had never been there before.

Oh, Jack. Oh, my beautiful, beautiful Jack.

I ran into the kitchen.

forty-three:

– now –

The loud music has stopped and the opening doorway of the farmhouse throws a precious ingot of light onto the black lawn. For the briefest of moments, I feel like it's all going to be all right. But the figure starts to emerge, a silhouette against the bright light; and my eyes, as they struggle to adjust, pick out a stature that is both shorter and much slighter than I'd hoped. I was hoping for a big, burly farmer – someone who'd load me and his dogs straight into his Land Rover and drive me back to my cottage. But this isn't him.

I breathe in. 'Sorry to trouble you—'

'Go away.' A female voice, hard like jade.

'Oh!' I try to hide my surprise and aim for warm and reassuring. 'Look, I don't want to disturb you, but I just need some help. I've—'

'You have to leave. *Now.*' There's a cold authority behind this voice; a strong local accent, and also stubbornness. She's a young adult, maybe very early twenties, I think and one who sounds like she's used to getting her own way.

For a moment I'm stunned. I imagined many scenarios but not this. 'I don't mean you any harm if that's what you're worried about. I'm on my own.' She doesn't say anything. I look around and realise that I'd guessed right, it's clearly a working farm. Although not impossible, perhaps there are more – and hopefully more helpful – members of the family around somewhere. 'If your parents are in, would you ask them to come to the door?' For some reason I think of my grandmother and lift my chin a little. 'Please.'

My maternal grandmother told my mum to hold her head up high in the dock. She told my mum to be fearless – to meet each and every juror's eye when she told them what my father did to her. She kept a steady gaze as she told them about the nightly beatings – she never faltered. I saw that gleam of pride in my grandmother's eye when she told me, years later. We both knew by then that my mother was wrong to be so bold: she'd expected to be acquitted, but she wasn't. Looking unbeaten probably went against her. But I still saw my grandmother's look of pride and I wondered then, and I wonder now, what sparked it. My family's name was forever tarnished and my father's murder forever shaped my life in ways that neither she nor I would've wanted.

But, then, standing on this doorstep, I suddenly thought of something I hadn't considered before. Perhaps, when that knife slid stealthily, steadily, into my father's neck while he was sleeping, there might have been a bit of my grandmother who approved of my father's murder and would've chosen to have driven the knife in herself, perhaps even deeper, pinning him like a butterfly to his pillow as he slept.

My plea, or perhaps her curiosity, draws her out a little from the doorway. 'Oh!' she says when she sees me, then again: '*Oh!*'

I'm aware of what I must look like. I'm standing in socks, and I'm holding my hands up high either side of me, at right angles to my body just like a newborn keeps its hands up either side of its head as it sleeps. As I crossed the fields, it helped reduce the pounding in my wrists. Now, I realised, it looked as if I was showing her the damage, wrists up and turned towards her, as if wanting her to see the red, exposed flesh.

I lower my wrists and try for a smile. 'Sorry, I look a state, I know. I promise I'm a normal person, I've just been . . . in a car accident.' I don't want to scare her with the truth. The farmer needs the truth, but not her. 'My car rolled, my handbag is in the car so I haven't got my phone. I just need someone –' *someone my son can't attack* – 'who can help me get sorted.'

'No one is here. I can't help you.'

I feel a flicker of frustration. But I suppose it's remote out here, isolated. Perhaps she's been schooled to be defensive.

'What can I do? I can't just wander off like this.'

'Cleasong is north,' she says, gesturing with a curt nod of her head.

I blink, not believing that someone could be that cold. 'Really? You won't help me?'

'If you leave now, I'll call the police for you. I'll tell them you're on the Cleasong road.'

I decide I do not like this young woman. 'Please!' I take a step forward. 'Look, I've got a head injury. I don't want to cause you any trouble, I just . . .' I falter as she lifts something in her arms.

It's long and dark and dangerous and desirable: a shotgun. I know farms are susceptible to robbery – she is used to standing guard.

'I've already told you – there's no one here,' she says. 'Just go. The pub at Cleasong will help you.'

'Cleasong's four miles away!'

'Ask at the Red Lion. I work there – tell them Erica sent you.'

'You're Erica?'

'Erica who will shoot you – if she has to.'

I feel a flash of indignation: it never occurred to me that some-one could be so unkind to another in need. I've got my faults, but I would never ignore a cry for help. 'Look, I'm a woman on my own, hurt. I'm not in any shape to walk to Cleasong – I haven't even got shoes. If I passed out because of my head injury, nobody would find me until at least morning. Don't you think your parents would want you to help me?'

'They're practical people, just like I am. They'll understand. And in case you've got any funny ideas, don't think they'll be long, neither. They've got the vet out for a mare, but since he charges more than its bones are worth, they won't be lingering.' She stays in the doorway; she's savvy, she's in a place of safety. And like the expert she no doubt is, she's got the shotgun cocked over her arm. I wonder if it's loaded.

I decide that it probably is.

Around me the wind blows; it lifts her hair to her face but she doesn't move to control the strands. We stand motionless.

She drops her gaze first and seems to notice my shoeless feet for the first time. Her eyes widen a fraction, then narrow, showing her new thinking. 'How did you lose your shoes in a car accident? Don't seem that possible to me.'

I pause just a second too long – shock and pain and head injury and codeine making me slow – and I know that now I've blown it, as clearly I've run from something terrible. Her gaze moves thickly from my feet, to my wrists, to my head. She's figuring it out.

'Please.' I tried for firm, but of course it's obvious I'm near crying. I know she's not going to let me in and wait for her father. There's no help here. My mission has failed. I realise the truth: out here, in the night, no phone, no shoes, no map, it's an impossible task to save Jack now.

I rethink quickly and accept plan B. I realise I now have no choice, because I'd rather lose custody of Jack, if it means his safety. If I'm prosecuted for snatching him, then so be it. If there isn't to be any rescue by me, then it'll have to be the police. 'Can you please call the police then, if you won't let me in, please call the police, *please*.'

She raises an eyebrow and takes a step outside, without letting go of the gun. I can see her clearly now, her clear cheekbones, Ramones T-shirt and nose piercing. A line of disdain sits heavy on her forehead like she's used to defiance. 'You're talking shit.'

This is not what I thought she'd say. I take a deep breath. 'Look, I'll come clean. If you don't help me, there's a little boy's life at stake. My grandson's. He's only a mile from here –' I turn and point in the direction of my cottage – 'we only live just there. We're your neighbours. My feet are filthy because I've just run across the fields to get to you. My son is there, he's . . . a person who has done bad things. I totally accept responsibility for that, but he's got a son, Jack, who's gorgeous, only eight years old, and his dad, when he had him, was ... well, let's just say it's not a happy story. So I took him and brought him here and we've been living at that little cottage together for the last year, so happy. But tonight my son has found us and he attacked me and ... ' I look down at my wrists and hold them up to her, encouraged that she's angling her head to see. Do I see a softening in her face? Hope flickers. 'He knocked me out and I woke up on my kitchen floor about an hour ago. He's got Jack and –' I think of the closed bedroom curtains as I was leaving – 'and this is all a game to him and I hate the fact that he's dangerous but he is –' I think of Sunningdale and my mother – 'and I need help.' I push my wrists a little closer to her as if they evidence my point.

'He burnt you?'

'No, I had to do this. He tied me up and I had to get free. I used the gas cooker.'

Her top lip rises in a sneer: 'You did this to yourself on your gas cooker?'

I realise how ridiculous this sounds to her. 'When you've got a kid, you'll do anything for them. I can't let my son harm my grandson. I didn't want the police, because ...'

I want to jump over this bit, but she simply waits for me to explain.

'Because legally he belongs to my son, but it's me who's raised him since he was a baby. He's my child, too. And if you don't help me, he could die tonight.'

I'd hoped this last point would make her feel shamed into helping, but instead she says: 'He's not even *yours*? You took your son's boy? No wonder he knocked you out – I'd knock you out if I had a kid and you took it.' She shouts: 'Go away, you loon!' She's shutting the door.

'Please! The police! Will you call them?'

'Fuck off!'

I'm panicking. How can she not call the police for me? I don't have a plan C. I drop to my knees and hold my hands out to her, and I think I'm crying or begging or both, but she's still pulling away, and the rectangle of light thrown out is starved to a line and then that, too, is finally gone.

forty-four:

– *now* –

The farmer's front lawn is cold under my knees. I get up, shaking, confused. Somehow, I played this wrong. I know I will spend a long time going over the conversation in my mind, checking and rechecking what I said, analysing and reanalysing the mistakes I made. But I haven't got time to do that now. There is still a small boy in danger.

I need a plan C. Now.

I could go on to Cleasong like Erica said. I could call in at the Red Lion and ask them to call the police. I'm not sure I have any other option: my son will now be looking for me.

Reluctantly, I consider going on. I'm tired and the dark will slow me, as will the lack of shoes, but at a push – because for Jack I can just be heroic – I could get there in realistically fifty minutes. If the police come to the Red Lion immediately, that will take ten minutes, and then I'll have to tell them my story and then we will travel to the cottage – at best, that's another twenty minutes.

But maybe the Red Lion won't help me, maybe the police will be too busy on a Saturday night to respond quickly; maybe they'll try and resolve it in some unseen way. Even if they do arrive quickly and we get there, perhaps Jack might be retrieved easily and quickly . . . but maybe not.

I can't risk Jack's safety.

The breeze plays against my face and my thoughts flutter between possible ideas. The only one that resonates with any power is the idea of my getting hold of Erica's shotgun.

I think of how that would just change everything for me – for the better. I need it. With it, his power would tilt to me and then I'll have the control to take Jack back. It's the perfect solution – much better than getting the police involved. Simpler. He is the boy's father, after all. I have no legal rights.

It occurs to me, standing there at the farmhouse's shut front door, that perhaps I'm not the most vulnerable person when choosing between me and him. Of course, Jack is – indisputably – the most in need of protection. But it suddenly seems to me that perhaps I haven't finished my job of being a mother to my son. Yes, he's twenty-five and yes, he doesn't want me to parent him. But his anger makes him so vulnerable. And as his mother, I haven't stopped wanting to help him.

I hated my own mother being in prison and I would hate for my son to be there. The way he's going, perhaps it's inevitable. But if I could get Jack away from him, make Jack safe, and if I could find a way of making my son listen to me, perhaps I could – perhaps – still make a difference. I want to throw apologies at his feet. I want to beg forgiveness. I want to explain about myself, about my childhood, about my struggles. I want him to hear me.

I want him to know that I see him.

But none of that will happen if he gets a choice. The gun is perhaps the answer because it might force him to listen to me. A crazy, terrible answer, but perhaps the only one available. I still want to save him, despite what he has done. I still love him. I thought when I saw the cage that my love had finally died, but it seems not. It seems that it can withstand anything. My love for him is Teflon.

Still – *still* – I have to try to save him. Perhaps the gun offers a way to turn this around, perhaps there's only one plan that means I can still stand a chance of saving both my son and my grandson.

I look up at the farmhouse and realise I need to find a way to break in.

forty-five:

– before –

To rescue my grandson from the monstrosity, I realised I needed a weapon. Time was short and I had to get Jack out of this horror show of a flat.

I ripped open cupboards, pulled out drawers. The cupboards were almost empty of food – what did they eat? The kitchen was in reasonable shape so it only took seconds to find the knife drawer and choose the one I wanted.

Jack had turned his back to me, Bunny pressed up against his face.

I sawed up and down, seeing the black tape fray. After a minute, Jack turned his head and said: 'D-D-D-Daddy w-w-w-w-won't want you doing that,' but I didn't answer.

Instead, fragments of memories raced in my head. I thought of Nick kissing me under the mistletoe at Christmas, that very first time we were together over two decades ago, so young, so happy. I thought of being pregnant, my hands gripping the toilet bowl as I vomited. I saw my mum holding my baby when he was newborn, her face soft with a love I hadn't seen before and thinking: *Is that what you feel for me?* I saw tablets in blister packs, fat and promising. I saw the smooth paintwork, but with the hairs trapped forever in the paint. I saw Issy, Nadia and Nessa in our favourite café, laughing for a photo, all with their babies balanced on their laps as they posed. I saw the A & E nurse's face as she pulled away from examining the deep bite on my ear and telling me that it would need plastic surgery, trying to hide the concern in her eyes. I remember seeing my dad dead in bed, pale-faced, motionless; the smell of blood as it edged out, winking its lewd suggestion of the horror puddle beneath and the terror as I picked up the phone to call the police. And then the handcuffs on my mum as they led her away.

Then I saw what I'd missed: that the gaffer tape was wound differently in two corners, meaning it was hinged. I could just lift up the top playpen.

I saw a question in Jack's eyes that hadn't been there before. But what else could I do? I was a cornered animal, unable to do anything other than follow my own instincts. If I called the police and social services, they might leave him there with my son whilst they did assessments. I certainly couldn't guarantee they would place Jack with me rather than somewhere else, and even if they did, I would be obliged to stay at the same address like a sitting duck.

My son would come looking for us – that wouldn't work.

The trouble with love is that you can never walk away. And no one knows that better than my son because I never left him, even, perhaps, when I should have. But to save Jack, I would now need to do what I'd never been able to do before: I'd need to finally leave my son.

I lifted the top and reached in and slid my hands under Jack's armpits. I pulled him close to my chest and knew he was the most precious thing in the whole wide world. There was nothing I wouldn't do for him. I held him tight.

'Hold on to Bunny – we're leaving.'

No, you're not – you're not going anywhere. I so expected to hear his voice behind me, I swear I did. I felt like an actor in a movie, waiting for the madman to jump out from a shadowy hiding place and attack us.

Eyes wide, heart thumping, I turned round with Jack in my arms: but no one was there.

In the hall, I knew I should've run towards the front door as fast as I could, but I couldn't. Instead my legs remained immobile, keeping me in the dark with Jack on my hip and Bunny on his, waiting.

I could almost hear an imaginary audience screaming: *Get out! Why don't you run?!* But fear does strange things. Standing there, I became convinced – *convinced* – that my son was behind the furthest bedroom door, listening.

Perhaps, after getting my text, he'd laid a trap for me. Perhaps he knew I'd be nosey. Perhaps he was just waiting for predictable, neurotic, untrusting me to walk right into his flat and snoop around. And was I here, doing just as he predicted?

Impossible.

No – not impossible.

If he was going to come for me, I wanted him to do it now. I didn't want to have my back towards him as we ran for the door – if an attack was going to happen, I wanted to brace myself for it.

I felt something then. I shut my eyes as Jack nestled a sleepy head into my neck. I leaned my head gently back against the door and felt . . . *him*. It's true I missed him so much. It's so hard to even accept myself, but no matter what we had been through, he was still my son. I knew that when – if I was able to – I walked out that front door, I might never see him again. We had been adversaries for so long, but in that moment, I just felt him and his malevolent quiet through the door.

I felt the weight of sadness that I was leaving him alone for the first time. He had always been the one to leave – but I was taking that choice away from him now.

'Are we going home?' Jack whispered his question.

It was only later, when I replayed this scene over in my mind, as I had a habit to do, checking and rechecking all my decisions, that I realised he had whispered. I would've loved to have asked Jack – did you think he was behind that door, too? Did you whisper because you too thought he was listening?

But at the time I didn't answer, because as I stood there, I knew it couldn't be 'home' for us, ever again. I knew my life was about to pivot on a point and change completely, forever.

Mostly, what we do is the same old, same old. We go to the same place of work; do the same things; talk to the same people. We drive home the same way; eat the same thing for dinner; click on the same sites on our phones; watch the same things on TV. Go to bed at the same time and start again. Ad infinitum. I had been doing the same old for a long time.

But now it was going to change.

I didn't answer, because I *knew* he was listening behind the door. Does the mouse tell the cat his intentions? Because I knew this was now the start of an age-old game.

My son had always liked hunting. At fourteen, his school friend introduced him to the world of snares and rabbiting and although I refused to allow him to have a ferret, he bought one anyway; it fidgeted up and down his sleeves and was the first and only thing I ever saw him show public affection for – until he picked Jack up from school, that is. But I think he killed the ferret, because one day I noticed the hutch he kept it in was empty. 'Where's Arrow?' I'd asked him.

'Who?' He looked up from his computer game.

'Arrow, your *ferret*.'

He gave a little half-shrug, his eyes cool blue, innocent. 'Got out. Gone.'

By then, I'd started feeding Arrow because Jack often forgot. I'd learnt to ignore Arrow's lithe, snake-like body built for kill-ing and instead, enjoyed his black, bright eyes and smoothing his fur. He was cute and smart too – I could hide a raisin behind my ear as bait and he would come and search it out, wet-nosed and quick. 'Gone since when? I saw him yesterday.'

He ignored me, until I raised my voice in an I'm-not-going-away-until-you-bother-to-answer-me tone and then he gave another half-shrug. 'This morning. When you were out at work.'

I thought of Winston then, lovely Winston whose memory I had buried deep. I remembered his brown eyes and it seemed as if Winston and Arrow were friends, although by this time, my son was fifteen and Winston had been dead a decade.

'Have you looked for him?' I knew he hadn't; I could achingly see what his lack of interest meant, but I was annoyed, not just for Arrow who might be dead somewhere or worse, but what it meant about my child – what I already knew. I bugged him then, asking about Arrow until he shouted at me that he didn't 'fucking care, so why don't you get lost?' and I felt better to hear the truth, because standing there, watching him engrossed in his stupid game just made me sick. I finally faced up to what I'd always known but had run from: I finally accepted that I'd raised a psychopath.

Like grandfather, like grandson.

Oh, Daddy dear, you would be so proud.

And standing there, thinking about Winston and Arrow made me feel very, very anxious, not just because I knew that what had happened to Winston had happened to Arrow, but because I knew what had happened to my father and I feared the same for my son.

And now, all these years on, I was standing in his flat and perhaps I was now Arrow. I cared desperately about him, but my son had love for nothing and definitely not me. I couldn't leave Jack because the public affection was just a set of behaviours he wheeled out because he knew he should and it was just a way to get what he wanted. When he got tired of the demands of something else, he simply got rid. Selena, who had suddenly died of an overdose (*I'm not thinking about that, I'm not, I can't*), Winston, Arrow – and I couldn't risk Jack placing one demand too many on him.

But maybe this was a game he was in charge of. Perhaps to take Jack from the cage was me doing simply what he'd known I would and this was all a big, nasty amusement and he was hunting us now. Jack was the bait to draw me out and now we were in his snare. When I left, carrying Jack out of this flat, I knew the hunt would begin.

So I knew, as I turned away from that closed door, and walked down the hall towards the open door, that we weren't stepping to freedom, but towards something so much less clear.

forty-six:

- before -

Free from the flat, I ran with Jack in my arms. The wind whipped our hair; my footsteps echoed accusations.

By the time I reached my car, I'd already started to doubt my certainty that my son had laid a trap. Perhaps he wasn't there, behind the bedroom door, perhaps I would plough straight into him in the street.

We made it to the car. I eased Jack into his car seat, feeling strangely disassociated from the here and now. I just couldn't believe what had happened. I'd arrived looking to get a sense of their home, but had left with Jack. I had imagined many scenarios, but could never have imagined this one.

I started driving – anywhere and everywhere, simply taking turns without seeing them, just thinking, thinking. My son had always been scrupulously neat – not with his appearance, but with his belongings. Perhaps the only thing we shared was that we were, by nature, fastidious in our housework. We'd clashed when he was a teenager over just about everything, but we'd never had arguments about the state of his room, because, like me, he was almost neurotically tidy. So, why was he living in a mess now? Not just a mess, I corrected myself, he was living in filth. It just didn't make sense. I glanced up in the rear-view, where Jack was dozing off. 'Is Daddy always that untidy?' I asked before I could stop myself.

Jack's eyelids fluttered. 'Mmmm?'

'Daddy's flat was very messy. Is it always like that when you visit?'

'No.' No stutter I noticed.

I had to know. 'The poo . . .?'

'D-d-d-d-d –' He paused, silently blocking, then tried again. 'D-d-d-d-d –' Again he tried: 'Da-da-da-da-d-d –' but then his face crumpled to tears.

'Don't worry, Jack! You're so tired. Let's get you a treat!' Feeling terrible, I drove him to the nearest McDonald's drive-thru and bought him a Happy Meal, which placated him much too easily. I watched him after, when he was asleep, wondering if he would speak more about his experiences when he was fresher – his stutter was always worse for being tired.

I was exhausted too. Unsure of what else to do, I drove out of town to a Travelodge and checked us both in for the night, to give me time to think of my next move.

I tucked Jack into the double with Bunny, before I sat up in the tub chair, thinking. I wanted to make plans, to look forward, but all I could do was look back. The state of the flat and the feeling that he was lurking behind the door disturbed me.

My son had always been disturbing. Even from the start, it had gone wrong.

The sickness had been terrible. It'd hit hard before I'd even known I was pregnant. Nothing would shift it; sometimes, I couldn't even keep a sip of water down. Looking back, it was hard to appreciate just how bad it was, but I know at the time I actually wanted to die. I felt we were dying anyway, both of us, slowly failing together. Nobody could help us; the doctors admitted that because the anti-nausea drugs didn't work, all they could do was take me into hospital and put me on a drip. It was – without doubt – the worst time of my life. But despite it, as I withered, he grew strong.

But there was more. There was more and more and more. None of it was his fault. But nor was it mine. They denied it, but I believed the forceps damage was the reason that he screamed and screamed and screamed night after night, until he was five. Since then, I've read forceps can cause cranial problems, but the idea of cranial osteopathy was unheard of then.

The rain hit the windows of the hotel room like thrown shingle. It focused my thoughts to tomorrow and I thought: *Jack hasn't got his coat with him. It's still at his dad's.*

It was over, right then. I knew it. I wanted to say it aloud just to hear it, but not wanting to wake Jack, I just murmured it instead: 'You will never see your dad again, Jack. Whatever it takes. *I promise.*'

forty-seven:

– *before* –

I must've fallen asleep in that hotel tub chair, because when my phone rang, I woke, startled. In the first bleary seconds, I felt frightened and confused from my deep sleep, only aware of some trouble deeper than the stabbing in my crooked neck. But as I fumbled in the dark for my phone, I remembered what had happened. Glancing first at Jack to check the noise hadn't woken him, I then looked at the screen expecting the number to be my son.

It wasn't.

Two things struck me: the first that it was only 3.30 in the morning, and the second that it was my work calling me.

I knew then that things had got even worse.

As deputy matron, I was sometimes rota'd to be called during the week if one of the residents suddenly died, but at the weekend it was the weekend matron who was disturbed. If they were calling me on so early on a Sunday morning, then a catastrophe must have happened. And I just knew it was my son who had done the something catastrophic.

I took the call, listening to what I was told, and agreed to come immediately. Knowing I was again walking into a trap, but unable to do anything about it, I picked up the sleeping Jack and carried him out to the car, returning the hotel door card into the drop box on the way out. I knew we wouldn't be back.

I drove to my work, Jack thankfully still asleep in the back. Even a mile from work, I understood what my son had done in vengeance before I got there. The red glow in the sky told me.

I drove the last few minutes in shock. I couldn't process what might be happening. Dread sat like a rock in my stomach.

As I turned into the road, my worst fears were confirmed.

Sunningdale Nursing Home was a large, attractive building, usually calm in its sea of grounds. Elegant and refined, it was built as a Victorian convalescent home, on a gentle hill, enjoying an elevated position over its neighbours.

But there was no poise now. Ugly flames bit at the building, rising up out of the windows on the east side, with the nearby windows festering with anger. The night was alive with colour: red flames and blue flashing lights and orange street lamps ate into the black night, so it was clear to see that much of the east wing was now blackened and crumbling. This was a huge, huge fire. Crowds congregated on the road opposite, witnessing the horror. Two fire engines sat, one with its apparatus extended with water being hosed onto the building. A police car and three ambulances lined the road, one pulling away even as I arrived.

I pulled over as close as I could, getting slowly out of the car. There was so much I couldn't process; I needed someone to help me. I stood by my car and looked to see if there was anyone I knew. Although it was the middle of the night, the scale of the fire meant that the crowds were heavy. Lots of emergency-service workers busied around. I could see stretchers – and horror of horror – some with covered bodies. Shouts cut through the night and crying could be heard pitched above the murmurs of the captivated crowd.

I searched the faces for someone familiar, never daring to leave my car which cradled Jack.

Then, relief. I raised my hand at a figure by an ambulance, a heat blanket hugging her shoulders. 'Miriam!' I shouted until she noticed me. It was Miriam who'd called me – the weekend duty matron.

Miriam bolted straight for me. We didn't say anything at first, just looked at each other with wide, frightened eyes before we embraced, sharing our tears. After a few moments, I asked the question I dreaded: 'What happened?'

'The fire alarms sounded, but I don't know how it started.' Her voice came in the gaspy breaths of someone who'd been crying hard. 'We were in the sitting room and we got up straightaway –'

I noticed her eyes briefly averted from mine and I suspected that she, and whoever she was on night shift with, had been asleep when they were expected to be awake.

'– and we called the fire brigade and rushed around trying to wake the ground floor and we managed to get out six, but the fire was really bad – I don't know how it got bad so quickly – it was enormous, flames filled the room –'

'Who did you get out?'

She looked at me, a frightened child. 'Mrs Summers, Mrs Waite –' She continued and with each name it felt like a victory, but the list was too short.

She started crying again. I held her for a moment and then gently but firmly pulled her back so I could see her. 'Where was the fire? How did it start?'

'I don't know!' Her anguish was clear. 'The control panel said it was in the utility; we ran to it and I know you shouldn't open fire doors, but we peeped inside and the flames were at the ceiling! I've never seen anything like it!'

Was this a coincidence? Had I infuriated my son by taking his, and now this was revenge?

No. He might be angry, but this was too much. A dog killer did not maketh a murderer of the elderly.

Shame on me for even thinking the two things were connected.

I stared at the fire, the warmth sickeningly warming my skin. But despite my stance, I felt a screaming unease. The fire was so large; I was no expert, but I knew the home had a good fire alarm, good procedures. For it to get so bad, so soon, it seemed very possible an accelerant had been used. My face baked, both from the heat of the fire and the flush of possibly. I knew the utility room on the ground floor had a window that was often left open. I nagged and nagged the night staff to remember to close it in the evening, but I suspected it still got overlooked sometimes. The washing was hung in there; that and the dryers meant that it was always hot and humid, so the window was constantly left ajar and forgotten.

I searched through the faces in the crowds and amongst the shadows for my son. Could my fears be real? Was he standing here too, watching my darling residents, my passion, my career, my livelihood, burn?

My hand pressed against the roof of my car; perhaps he'd brought me here hoping that I'd leave Jack unattended for a moment, perhaps this was his way of drawing me close so he could snatch Jack back.

Perhaps he just wanted to see me suffer. *You set fire to my world; now I'll set fire to yours.*

But if that was true, if he was here, wherever he was, he'd hidden himself well. I gave up, my own brain on fire and turned back to the blazing building.

Miriam was still staring, horrified, and we viewed the death of the happy home together. The scale of the blaze, the immobility of our residents and the time of night, only really meant one thing. I felt desperate, wondering if I had caused this. 'Perhaps there's more news. Perhaps we should ask someone.'

With Miriam's help, I flagged over a police officer – reluctant to leave my car with Jack still asleep inside. The police officer briefly spoke to me, but could only confirm that the building was now empty of people. She took my contact details and asked me a few basic questions, but since I hadn't been in the building since Friday, I was of little interest.

I'm sure some decent stand-up citizens would've shared their concerns about their son being the arsonist, but despite loving those who'd died in the fire, I didn't even consider it – not least because I couldn't, quite, believe it.

After she'd gone, Miriam and I continued our watch over Sunningdale. We held hands as we witnessed the battle between the gallant fire brigade and the callous flames. I think, really, as we clutched each other, we both wanted to hold the residents' hands, but they were all gone, transported away in ambulances. We wanted to help, desperate to do something, but it seemed that the only thing left was to keep our beloved Sunningdale company as it burnt, so it didn't suffer alone.

So as Jack slept, we stood our watch, hands entwined, waiting out the night as the fire grumbled on, until the sun finally rose and the fire, like our hope, had finally died out.

forty-eight:

– now –

The countryside, which I've learnt never truly sleeps, is still strangely silent. Now that the woman at the farm, Erica, has slammed her front door against me, it feels like it's been watching our exchange and is now holding its breath: waiting. *What's your next move, Lisa?*

There's no sound of dogs; no sound of a Land Rover coming back from wherever the horses are; no sound of a whinny which might suggest proximity; no sounds of voices.

We are alone.

Circling the house, I find just what I need – a large window onto what is clearly the sitting room. The curtains are still open, giving me a clear view into the unlit room. Erica's not in there. I wonder where she is. I speculate whether she's called her parents, but decide probably not; after all, she's an adult with a shotgun and I am only an injured middle-aged woman on my own asking for help who's already been told to 'fuck off'. I stand on the periphery of the window waiting . . . watching, for a sign of movement, a sign of anything that might make me pause from what I'm about to do.

I've always been too spontaneous: Nick used to tell me so often. But I'm not planning on hanging around; I'll be gone just as soon as I find the plan B.

I look around for the right-sized rock – I want something with weight – but not too much and something with an edge. It doesn't take long to find one in a flower bed and I don't waste more time.

Against the bottom corner, I give a firm tap. I'm not really watching what I'm doing, instead my stare is intent on the hallway door beyond. But then I hear the sound of music starting back up – something punky played at full volume, coming from upstairs. I give a bolder tap, and when the glass doesn't break, I hit it again, bolder still.

This time I'm rewarded with a crack in the glass.

I follow the crack with my stone, grateful that it's only single glazing, *tap-tapping* to chase the crack further out. Within seconds, I – painfully but gamely – pull my sleeves over my hands and then push against the broken glass triangle. The putty is old and broken in places and it's surprisingly easy to wiggle out a large piece. I place the glass on the flower bed, and then reach in through the gap to unlatch the catch.

Not believing how easy or how quick it is, I'm opening the window and climbing into the house.

I stand on the carpet and don't move, not believing I am here. I get my bearings. The music is up so loud it floods the house.

The sitting room is large with dated furnishings, but I'm not taking in the details, I'm just looking around to see if I can see the gun. It occurs that she may have locked it away – I'm sure they have protocols for where they keep their gun and my heart sinks at the thought that it's under lock and key. But then I remember two things – one that Erica is upstairs listening to music, probably messaging her friends so is doubtless not too concerned about doing the right thing, and the other is that, while she's distracted, I can still look.

I step round the sofa and within seconds make a reasonable search of the room. But with the curtains still open and the light off, I think I can assume that she didn't come in here.

I'm scared when I step into the hallway, feeling heady and ready to bolt at the slightest movement from above. The light is at least still on. I know there could be more people in the house other than Erica, but apart from the music, the place has an empty stillness to it.

As I look up to the landing, the music seems to be coming from the room directly opposite the top of the stairs – if Erica opens that door, she'll see me.

I look down the corridor in one direction and can see it opens up to an unlit kitchen. In the other direction is the front door.

I can't believe it! The gun is propped up by the front door. I feel incredulous, grateful and stunned. With quiet feet – not that it's needed with the racket above – I move quickly through the hall.

Greedily, I grab the gun. In my hands, it's cold and heavy. Because of my son – irony of ironies – I know how to cock and load it. I check now and inside are the gold-ended cartridges. I shudder to think that Erica had pointed a loaded gun at me.

Her dad is going to kill her for her casualness, I think as I hold it. But I can't worry about that, not right now. I will return it just as soon as I can. This is not a steal, only a borrow.

The punk music suddenly gets much louder and I know what's happened even before I've turned round.

She's standing on the top landing, an empty glass in her hand. We stare at each other for a long, long moment.

I think I could tell her that it's only a borrow, or that I'll contact her father and explain, or even warn her not to follow me. I brace myself, ready, in case she throws the glass at me, but it's all she's got. And I have the gun.

But in the end, we just gaze at each other, until I turn and leave through the front door, no longer the hunted hare, but instead now the stoat, running out into the night.

forty-nine:

- before -

After the sun had risen and was throwing shadows across the
ruined bones of Sunningdale, and Miriam and I hugged what
we knew was probably our last goodbye, it was still early. I drove
to an American diner, a place I always took Jack as a treat, and
woke him gently and bought us both breakfast. I watched him
devour a stack of pancakes while I struggled to sip coffee. He
didn't ask why he slept in the car last night, and somewhere in
my grief, I realised that he should've.

The grief was hideous. Not just for the residents, but lurking
beneath was the knowledge that now I had no job, and worst,
worst of all, that my son might have crossed a terrible line.

Might. I had to remind myself of that.

Was it true? I didn't know but my brain was aching with the
deliberation.

I was frightened. If it was true, then I wanted an explanation,
a neat answer, to explain why he was the way he was, but all I
came up with was that I must've done something wrong; I don't
know what, but he – *this* – wasn't normal.

True or not, the memory of Jack trapped inside the makeshift cage meant that it was clear that we would need to get away from him.

Home would never feel safe.

The practicalities of money, fortunately, weren't something I had to worry about. I'd always worked hard and I earned pretty good money, with no one to spend it on save Jack. I also still had some of my inheritance, so I thanked God that at least I didn't have to suddenly worry about cash flow. Jack and I could live frugally for years on what I had put by.

Jack looked so happy, chatting, without stuttering, loving his pancakes; it was a curious juxtaposition to the vile deeds of my son.

Before we had said goodbye, Miriam and I had called the local hospital and although the staff were careful, we gleaned enough to know that the death toll was bad, very bad. I had then called the matron and she'd filled the gaps. Many years ago, I'd had the chance of promotion and could've been Sunningdale's matron, but it was when Jack was just a baby and it was clear my son would need a lot of support in raising him, so I'd declined.

Now I had never been gladder of that decision.

Matron knew I'd be going away, and the ability to just leave now, mid-disaster, felt more precious than gold. She had my number if she needed it – but I suspect she had bigger concerns than me and I wouldn't be hearing from her for a while. The home was evacuated permanently with the residents allocated to other homes – no one would be able to return. Sunningdale was gone; my job was gone.

I started to think about the practicalities of the day ahead. I needed a shower, clean clothes etc. and decided we would go to my mum's. It was near and I'd be able to say goodbye, but I also wanted to tell her what had happened. I wanted the reassurances about him that she always gave. She would tell me I was bonkers and her shining faith in him would ameliorate my anxieties.

Well, that's how it'd been in the past; I wasn't sure it could work like that now, not after the horror of those covered bodies on the stretchers and the wide-open grief in Miriam's eyes mirroring my own.

I kept checking my watch; my mother was not an early riser. 'After years of getting up for the bell, dear, I think I've earned a lie-in or two, don't you think?' But now it was 9.30 and we'd finished breakfast, and although it would still be too early for her to accept visitors, I couldn't wait anymore. I paid and we left.

As I got Jack back in the car, he asked: 'Where are we going?'

With a crushing sense of sadness, I realised we weren't *going* anywhere: we were running *from*. Instead I said: 'To see Nana.'

He was so pleased and so was I: my mum would help us. She wasn't afraid of anyone. Not even him. I thought of the light-hearted way she discussed him and thought: *particularly not him*.

It didn't take long to get to my mother's home. After she was finally released from prison, she had been allocated a small flat in a sheltered housing block by the local authority. She'd been quietly amused to be offered sheltered housing, declaring herself too young at sixty, but it'd turned out to be a good thing for her. She had been released on licence and the sheltered option had helped keep the probation service happy.

I found a space in the car park and turned off the engine. I suddenly felt a flicker of disquiet – what if he'd come here looking for us? The car park suddenly felt too secluded, the low morning sun catching on the shrubs and trees, casting long, dark shadows. I stared into them, watching for any flicker of movement. 'Let's go in and see Nana,' I finally said, feeling irrational but spooked.

Jack picked up his bunny and I opened my door. I slid one foot out and stopped. My hand gripped the door handle. *He's here.* The thought was so sure and clear that I felt it with an absolute certainty: *He is here.*

fifty:

– before –

I froze, half in and half out of the car. The morning air pressed like a cold cloth against my face. The light was too bright for my stress-addled brain, and I felt afraid. I believed that my son was waiting for me, somewhere out of sight, watching me, knowing – somehow – that I would come here now.

Jack had opened the car seat and was climbing down.

Get back into the car! I wanted to shout. But I didn't; I couldn't. I could hear Jack's little footsteps on the tarmac. I squeezed my eyes shut, my heart seemingly squeezing too as I expected my son's voice to shout: *Gotcha!*

But instead Jack just knocked on the window. 'No sleeps for you, Granny!'

The feeling of paranoia was so strong. I'd got used to living with it over the years, exacerbated by the codeine, of course. But the paranoia started when I began to perceive that my son was different and wanted to cover his behaviour up. I suspect that many parents with children who bite, or with children who hit, or with children who cry more than others, will know what it's like to try to hide how much of a problem their child's behaviour is. But for most people, the behaviour passes. Eventually time steps in and handles the problem by moving them on a stage.

But that never happened for me. He just kept getting worse. And with it, so did my neurosis. In some ways, codeine stepped in for me; it gave me the ability to change when Jack couldn't. Wrapped in a warm blanket, I didn't worry so much what other people thought, I was able to live in the moment more, stop overplanning. Where some might indulge in too much wine, I found the codeine was better for me – it gave me more control, it was harder to detect and easier to stay at a certain point of equilibrium.

I don't think I had ever missed it more than I did in that car park, with the charred bones of Sunningdale behind me and an uncertain future ahead of me.

Despite being clean, though, the paranoia was back with me then, playing with my mind, making me uncertain as to where my fear started and stopped being real.

I stretched out for Jack's small hand waiting patiently for mine. So warm; so small. So gentle. I closed my hand over his and let him pull me out of the car. How could it be that this child could give me the strength to stand again?

It felt brave to fight the questions in my mind, to only walk towards the building – not run – when it felt that a sniper's sight was silently moving with me, watching me.

Jack tugged on my hand, seemingly keener to get inside than me.

The sheltered housing block my mother lived in had two entrances; the car park entrance was to the side and the smaller of the two. The door was half-glazed, so after I'd pressed the silver button of the intercom, I leaned into it, glad to press my forehead against the cool glass; it felt like a soothing hand against the fever in my mind.

The hallway was empty.

I pressed again. Somehow, even the sound of the intercom ringing somewhere inside the walls, inside my mother's cosy flat, made me feel better – like an umbilical cord, it connected me to where I wanted to be.

I refused to glance over my shoulders. It still felt like he was here, but he couldn't be – could he? The fever increased in my head and I realised I was asking the wrong question: why *wouldn't* he be here now?

I rang the bell again, suddenly impatient to be in. I wanted to be amongst my mother's overfilled flat with too many throws, too many plants. The place stank of incense which I suspected she used to cloak the smell of pot, a habit no doubt she'd acquired in prison. I guessed Mrs Dale and she got stoned every night – Mrs April Dale, another ex-lifer my mother knew from her time in Holloway, lover of talking edgy politics and You-Tube conspiracy theories of global control and now my mother's neighbour. Probation must've settled loads of ex-offenders in this block. I wondered what the neighbours would think, if they knew.

Sometimes my mother and Mrs Dale were so tight, it irritated me. I wished my mum had made some new friends, people who were less 'prison' than April was. Now she was out, it seemed a shame that she was keeping the same habits and the same company. I wanted something different for her. A couple of times I'd tried taking my mother to one side to complain about April, asking her to send her home so as not to influence little Jack. But then there would usually be something like a scream of laughter and we'd peep round the corner and see April doing something irritatingly brilliant like playing cards with him, once chasing him with a beautiful orangutan hand puppet she must have brought for him, or reading to him in an attentive way.

And then I would typically just feel mean and childish and would promise myself that I wouldn't do it again until the next time. My mother told me that I just didn't 'like sharing' – that I never had. It made me feel like crying, because all I'd ever done was share her. The fact that April would've spent more time with my mother than I ever had, and that now she was her neighbour she got to spend every day with her, just felt like a massive injustice.

I pressed the intercom again and heard it ring – I felt desperate to see my mum. Right now, even April would be welcome.

No answer.

I felt skittish. It wasn't unusual for my mother not to hear the bell ... *but still.* My mother barely answered it on the first or second ring. She said she was always too busy to hear it but the truth was I think she might've been getting a little deaf and was too vain to admit it.

I don't know what my mother was like before prison – I was only eight when she went in – but since she'd come out, she seemed very resistant to any kind of coercion. I suppose it was all those years of being told when to get up, when to turn your lights out, when to eat, what to wear, but now it was like dealing with an impossible teenager. Part of me indulged it – thought it funny, even – but now, standing in the cold, I knew *I would never tolerate again* her just not answering the door when the bell was rung. It was just so impossible – *she* was just so impossible.

How could she leave me out here, frightened, when I needed her?

I pressed the intercom button again: hard. It started to ring again in my mother's flat, the noise expanding in the silence, into . . . where was she?

Anger was subsiding back again, beaten away by something more powerful. It was folding in like a sandcastle against the tide; overwhelmed by waves of panic. I wanted to fling myself against the glass and bang the door. *Let us in!* I wanted to shout. *Mum!*

How I have yelled and cried for her across the years. And she never answered, she never could. But I couldn't yell for her now – I had to think of little Jack.

Instead I breathed out really slowly, concentrating on my breathing the way the counsellor showed me a zillion years ago. *Centre yourself, Lisa*, I remember her saying.

Breathe.

I dropped a smile to Jack standing patiently at my side. His other hand was clasped round Bunny.

'Is N-N-Nana not in?' he asked in a smaller-than-normal voice.

I noticed on his cheek a new shadow. Perhaps it was nothing; perhaps it was a bruise that I'd somehow missed. My smile became so wide I felt that it would shatter into a million little pieces. 'You know what she's like!' I said, hating my diamond voice.

The buzzer had stopped ringing, and without hesitation I pressed it again and again.

The fear was rising and gathering in strength and I was starting to reach and grasp for other ideas – any ideas that would lift me from this nightmare. I could go, get back in the car. I could leave and go . . . where? I was thinking through my options when I saw my mother's door open. Relief suddenly soared high, then instantly dipped low when I realised it was April Dale. She stepped into the hallway, still dressed in her dressing gown.

I hammered on the glass. 'Mrs Dale!'

She didn't notice me. She was looking down the hall as if looking for something. Her back was still turned to me and I realised that she could turn and go back into her flat and never see me.

I hammered again. 'April!'

She continued to stand in the hall and I wondered what she was doing – why was she just staring down an empty corridor? Why hadn't she heard my incessant buzzing to the flat if she was in there? Why didn't she react to my banging now?

I rapped on the door, hurting my knuckles, feeling the rising swell of anxiety forming into something else.

But still April didn't turn.

There was something in the way she held her body; some stiffening. For someone who usually moved a little too slowly on account of the arthritis that she constantly complained about, she was just too . . . poised. On a woman her age it seemed . . . *too* alert.

Too . . . waiting for something. What was she waiting for? She turned back to my mother's flat.

I'm almost ashamed to say that I had already started to shrink away. I wanted to help her, I wanted to see if my mum was OK, but I had Jack. He was only seven years old and he needed me to get him somewhere safe. My anxiety was rising into something bigger – a dangerous, rising swell.

Just as I took a step back, her body started to turn. I saw it as if it was in slow motion. Her shoulders swung round, but her head was the last to turn as if reluctant to stop staring at my mother's open door.

I couldn't breathe – I wanted to retreat even further, but as I started to pull away, Jack stood his ground. I tried to pull on his hand so she wouldn't see us; she wouldn't open the door to us and tell her what was on her mind.

Because I think I already knew and I did not want to hear it.

And then I noticed something I'd seen and not noticed, but now I saw it, it seemed so frightening: she only had one slipper on. Cold fear washed over me as I understood then that this woman was not herself, and then I finally saw her face. Her mouth was ajar and her mouth was formless, soft, slack.

Finally, finally, she saw me through the glass; her hands pressed against her cheeks and she shook her head, her eyes never leaving mine.

Sandcastles flattened, formless, and mountains became washed under seas, as my panic became a tsunami and finally over-whelmed everything.

fifty-one:

– before –

April didn't greet me at the door or acknowledge Jack, she simply opened it and we followed her into the corridor. I held his hand and shuffled my own feet as I stood staring at hers. One was encased in a pale pink slipper mule and the other was bare. Brown and wrinkled, her foot suggested that she'd spent every summer since she'd been released tanning herself. It felt wrong to see it when the other was covered: too intimate.

I realised that that slipperless foot told me something else about that night, something about how suddenly she'd left her flat. (*Or Mum's. Maybe she left it in there!*) I knew I should look up, re-establish eye contact. But I could only stare at her foot because I wanted to be the child; I wanted to hold someone else's hand, someone bigger and stronger than me, someone who would take the lead. When I looked up, I'd have to be what I was supposed to be – the strong one – and take charge over whatever in my mother's flat had caused April to feel so scared.

Perhaps she read my mind, because she took my hand in her own. It was warm and dry. 'Lisa . . . your mum. I think . . . you should go in.' Her tone was gentle, before it changed, becoming charged with imperative: 'But not with the boy! He must stay with me.'

I wanted to snatch my hand back. I felt a sudden, almost absurd in its depth, stab of annoyance: *of course* I was going to go in. It was why I was here.

'Now, before I call the P-O-L-I-C-E, shall I take Jack to mine and give him a biscuit?' She had already dropped my hand and taken his before she finished her sentence. At the word 'biscuit', Jack had left my side and headed to April's so familiar, many times visited, flat. She always laid pink wafers and Bourbons in a daisy pattern whenever Jack visited.

But she paused. With a sudden snake movement, her hand whipped out and grabbed my arm. 'I didn't leave the door open, Lisa – it was already wide open . . . anyone could've got in.' And then she was gone.

I was left standing in the hall on my own, with no other option but to go inside.

fifty-two:

– before –

I didn't want to go into my mother's flat, not because of April, not because my mum hadn't answered the intercom and not because I thought my son might be ranging around looking for revenge. The reason I felt sick as my fingertips touched the wooden door and paused was because my mum never left her door open. She was funny about it. Insistent, even. I would've thought after spending so many years in prison, she would've loved an open door, but she didn't. She liked a shut door.

Always.

I knocked it gently. 'Mum?' I called in. The drop of dread hit my stomach, before I pushed the door slowly open and took a step inside the small, dark hallway. Somewhere inside, my mind screamed: *Don't go in, don't go in!*

But I had to, so I did.

fifty-three:

– now –

As I run across the field back to Jack, I dodge stones and dips, my breath cold in my lungs. As I run, I cradle the gun. It's a struggle to hold – I'm afraid of it, but I'm glad of it. I can't help but hold it and not think of Mungo, my son's one-time best friend.

I don't want to think of Mungo, because he was so much part of my family for a while and because it ended so sadly. So I don't think of him, and instead think of Nick because that's easier, and because it was due to Nick's intervention into Jack's schooling that Mungo even came into Jack's life in the first place.

Jack's schooling was always an issue. Over the years, I'd had to call on Nick for some of the bigger issues and he was always there in the background, always willing to helicopter in to help with our son when I needed him. He always paid maintenance – more than he should have really, and never late. He phoned every week and took an interest in Jack's life.

When it went wrong at yet another school, it was Nick who forgot his socialist beliefs first and arranged for our boy to sit a scholarship exam for a prestigious private school. When he passed, it was Nick who paid for the gap in fees that the scholarship didn't cover, as well as the uniform, the travel and all the little extras that added up to a lot.

Jack went to that school for two years and complained bitterly about it every day. From the age of twelve until he was fourteen, he was out of the house from 7.00 in the morning until 7.00 at night and when he came home he was angry, truculent and even more uncommunicative than ever.

I didn't want him to leave, partly because of the possibility of opportunity it gave him, but mostly because I felt he underestimated the change it would be to join a bigger school mid-year. Nick's hunch that he was above-average smart had been confirmed when we got his scores from his entrance exam – he was incredibly bright. Unusually so. I expect Nick also felt a secret swell of pride – I know I did. I thought that he'd inherited it from my side of the family – my father was a doctor of literature and there had been rumbles that he'd be made a professor shortly before he died.

It came to a point when I decided that I had to go up to the school and find out what was making my son so miserable. It was either change whatever it was or change his school. He wouldn't let me – he told me I was only a nurse so not posh enough and I'd embarrass him – but I persisted. When I picked up the phone to make an appointment with the school, he physically attacked me, taking the handset out of my hand and wrapping the cord around my neck. He was out of control, yes, but I detected something else, some deeper shame or fear or desperation, so reluctantly, it was one of the times I got Nick involved.

Nick – to his credit – drove straight down from Gloucestershire and the two of them went off somewhere and although I was nervous, they both came back in a good mood. Jack gave me a bunch of flowers and Nick stood there while Jack apologised. Nick then said that, if it was all right with me, Jack would like to leave his private school and apply to go to the nearest comp that would have him. I was surprised, but I also knew Nick well enough to hear the rivets in his voice, meaning that his request was just a show of decency – the decision had already been made and Nick was really asking if I'd respect that. Jack would be leaving with immediate effect.

Nick took leave from his job, checked into a hotel and stayed for the week it took to get it sorted out. By the time he left, Jack was going out the door in a new uniform.

I never found out what had gone on. Fear of what might've happened actually made me ill and so I begged Jack to tell me, but he wouldn't. Nick wouldn't tell me either, until I'd threatened to go to the school. He said he'd promised not to, but after a particularly tearful phone call, he relented and said he promised that Jack hadn't been expelled for the third time, but it was still an urgent situation to get him out. What did that mean? I pressed. Nick said that he had virtually no relationship with his son, so couldn't I just let them have this? So I never found out what had happened and instead put my mind to supporting Jack in the best way I could.

Holding this gun makes me think of my son but it also makes me think of Mungo, because Mungo and my son were connected by a shotgun. As I run, there's little to focus on but the past. I can see where I'm heading because of the black swell of the hill against the indigo sky, but the feel of the stock in my hands reminds me of the thin, friendly boy, with his shock of black curls, looking at me from the chair in my son's room, as he held the stock of his shotgun like a pet.

After Jack went to the local comp, the only friend he made was Mungo. It was Mungo who introduced him to hunting; it was Mungo who introduced him to ferrets and guns. Mungo used to visit every day, always very grateful for the cups of tea with three sugars I made him. I'd see him with Jack, showing him how to make nooses for snares and showing him articles in his endless hunting magazines.

When Jack was fifteen he bought a second-hand shotgun; I went bonkers, but he said he'd just joined a shooting club. I don't know where the club was, how he found out about it or how he got there, but the gun was carried around in a bag on the rare occasions it wasn't in his hands – oh, how easily Arrow was replaced as the thing to be caressed!

At first, I hated him having the gun. It was the year after the brutal, high-profile murder of young school children in America; watching the news reports chilled me. When he got it, I remember I lived with a deep, deep sense of panic and unease.

I try not to think of Mungo; even instead trying to think of the rawness in my wrists. But it's Mungo who charmed me enough once, wanting to include me in their gun cleaning, and then later, asking me to drive them to where they used to practise. Even my son was a little friendly to me about it – I remember once he even put his arms around me as he tried to help me hold it right. He showed me how to press the stock against my cheek to get a good cheek weld and develop a decent gun mount, as well as aim and fire.

Sometimes, after a few months of him having it, I would even take them to buy cartridges. I didn't like it, but by the time he was sixteen, I think we were done fighting.

I try to ignore the past and instead concentrate on running on the uneven ground in the dark with a loaded shotgun – the last thing I need is an accident.

Each discordant step feels like it could just bump the gun out of my arms; every memory seems to bump in my head with a new understanding.

The fog seems to have dropped without me seeing it. Afraid, I stop. Looking up before, I could see the stars, but now I can see nothing above and nothing around me. I can see no edge of the field, it's only grey.

I wonder if Mungo died in the fog. At the time – there, I'm thinking about him again now – I thought Mungo had killed himself. That's what the coroner decided. When he was seventeen, he was found hanging from a tree in the nearby woods. On his phone, there were lots of hits on websites related to suicide in the days preceding his death. Despite his family arguing against it, saying that he'd lost his phone the week before his death, the police thought it was suicide and told the inquest that they'd found his phone in his pocket.

Fog has its own smell, damp and heavy. It turns and twists, mesmerising like mystic hands, warning me not to go back into the past.

It's impenetrable now, and I wonder how it could've fallen so swiftly within minutes. Because I've been thinking about Mungo, thinking things I've kept blocked for years, I realise I've just been plunging on towards the cottage, not noticing my vision was fading in the fog. Now I grasp that I have to stop or I could get lost.

I stop running, turning and looking for something I can fix my bearings on. But as I gaze into the night, I remember something I didn't think about before. Perhaps I was too stoned on codeine, perhaps I was too busy with life and work, perhaps I just didn't want to face it, but now, in the crazy way the brain works, I realise what I have missed. Devastated at his death, wanting to support my son, I attended the inquest with Jack.

Mungo must've had very few friends, because there was only one other teenager present – a sallow-skinned girl, thin, with straight blonde hair, she sat just behind Mungo's parents. I only noticed her, and then barely, when she turned to look at Jack; she mouthed something at him I didn't catch. But it wasn't her who really caught my attention, but instead my son, because in response he did something I rarely saw him do – and standing in this damp, fog-smothered field, I remember it now with goosebumps – he smiled back at her.

And Selena, Mungo's girlfriend, the following week became Jack's girlfriend.

fifty-four:

– before –

I didn't move in my mother's tiny hall: I stood so still I daren't even breathe. I was listening. I think I stood there for two minutes before I realised what my behaviour meant: I was acting like she was dead.

To contradict myself, I called out: 'Mum? Are you there?' My voice was too loud in the small space. It was like déjà vu from yesterday evening. What I found then, in my son's empty flat, was terrible. Now, the silence seemed to foreshadow another something awful to come.

The door to the living room on my left was open. The door to the bathroom in front of me was ajar. I pushed it open; inside it was empty.

The door on the right was her bedroom. It was shut. I opened my mouth to speak again but I didn't like that she hadn't answered me. The silence in the flat felt . . . oppressive.

And not like my mum.

She always had noise somewhere. The radio, the TV, something. I'd find the TV on and say: 'Are you watching this?' And she'd glance at the screen and say: 'No, I don't know what it is.'

'Can I turn it off then?'

'I like the noise,' she'd tell me, shaking her head. She was a woman of noise: singing, tapping, talking.

She *is* a woman of noise, I told myself.

But already I believed the past tense.

Already I *knew*.

I put off going into the bedroom; instead I pushed open the half-open door to the living room. It was a long, bright room with a kitchenette, opening up to the lounge with its French doors onto the shared gardens. The room was empty; the doors shut, curtains pulled. I snapped the light on. The radio was off; the TV was off.

What had happened here? I thought of the expression on Mrs Dale's face – '*Anyone could've got in*' – before I accepted that the answer was behind door number three.

And that was the bedroom.

As I reached for the door handle, I noticed that my hand was shaking violently.

fifty-five:

– *now* –

Away from the farmhouse, I am lost. Now I turn in the field like a weathervane trying to find my north. The fog hugs the ground, smothering me. I have no stars, no wind, no lights, not even from the farmhouse. My ears strain for the sounds of something – anything like a road that might help me place myself.

Nothing.

I want to cry out: to rage. I want to scream. But I can't.

How could I lose my way?

I wish my mother was here.

I think I even whisper her name in the dark. I think I call to her through the fog.

She doesn't answer.

fifty-six:

- before -

'Mum? Are you in?' I was back in my mother's tiny hall, my steps mouse small and timid to her bedroom door. I leaned in close, knuckles murmuring a knock against the door. My held breath finally exhaled against the wood, warming only my face. In the stillness, only silence whispered back.

She did not answer.

I went to try again but the words dried in my mouth.

I didn't want to think back, my thoughts bridging time between then and before. But I did, because I thought of the times I used to hide outside my parents' bedroom, when my father was still alive.

Despite the years, my thoughts were blurred, but I still knew that when I opened the bedroom door I wouldn't see my mother with the knife in her hand, the blood on the sheets, my father struggling to sit up – but only for a moment because the air went out of him like a punctured balloon, leaving him sinking back down onto the bed. I ran from the room and did what my mother had taught me to do when he was attacking her: *Ring nine, nine, nine and tell the operator: I need the police*. She'd taught me to give my age: *eight*. And my address: *3 The Greenfields*.

It felt like the right thing to do.

When I did it before, they would always come and give him a telling-off and then it was quiet for a while, before it started again.

It always started again.

And that's how I thought it would be that time. I thought that it was bad but that it would go back to normal for a while and then it would start again.

But it didn't.

The police came and they didn't just give a telling-off, this time there was handcuffs and my mother shouting and being led away and this time my father didn't shout back. This time he just lay on the bed with his eyes open staring at the ceiling and he was finally, finally quiet.

I wanted to ring 999 again, because standing outside my mother's door, it was too quiet. My fingertips reached out and pressed against the cool wood and I tried to brace myself as it opened, because I knew the world was going to stop again.

And as I peered in, much of my mother's bedroom looked just as it should.

The beige carpet and brown curtains that came with the flat had never been replaced. But everything else, all the additions, were my mother's. Purple silk scarves pinned to the ceiling to create a boudoir. Incense dripping ash into painted, clay receptacles. Artwork loud and brash, created by friends I've met before and don't care to meet again.

The light was on but the garishness clashes with the silence.

But I was thinking about the wrong thing. As much as I wanted to think that the room was much the same as it always was, I knew it wasn't. There was a big difference. Huge. I already knew the room was wrong, so wrong and I was simply delaying the inevitable of accepting that.

Because I had found her.

fifty-seven:

– before –

My mother was face down on the bed. I could see no sign of a struggle, but I remembered April – *'I didn't leave the door open, Lisa – it was already wide open'* – looking frightened in the hall. Did she know something about what happened here? Was my son here before me? Or was it just the fright . . .? Yes, of course, that's all it was. It would be shocking to anyone, the discovery of their friend dead.

I stared at my mother's body; she was fully clothed. She had jeans on, socks, and her favourite ivy-coloured cardigan that belts like a dressing gown. She always called it a housecoat and I knew what she meant – in colder months she would come in, take her real coat off, and put the long, thick cardigan straight on. I don't think I've seen her wear anything else in the evening. She was never a wearer of ballgowns but if she were, then I think she would've just popped that over the top. It looked dreadful: tired and worn, a hole laddering one elbow, a dropped hem and a missing pocket all meant that it begged to be binned.

It was not fit to be seen by anyone except her very nearest and dearest.

My brain was sluggish with shock; it ruminated on this essential fact like it was important. It was that the housecoat screamed out to me, its tired, synthetic voice rising shrill above the silence of my mother's bedroom.

It was its very ugliness that made it so important. My mother was not a vain woman, but she had her standards. She wouldn't wear make-up, but she would always brush her hair if she knew someone she didn't know was coming to the flat. And she most certainly, definitely wouldn't wear her cardigan in front of even a delivery driver.

And yet she was wearing it now.

Whoever she let in, she knew well enough not to take her cardigan off for. Someone who had already been buzzed in from the front door.

I know it was him. I know it was her grandson. After I took Jack, he must've either come here first or gone straight to Sunningdale before coming here. She let him in and then . . .

Did I really believe that? My son, the arsonist murderer?

– *The door was open wide* –

I reached out, and with a butterfly touch my fingertips landed on her skin above her sock, below her rucked-up trousers. I had to know and the warmth of her body instantly told me what I didn't want to understand – she was alive very, very recently. I didn't need a pathologist's graph of heat loss from a body – I've worked around more dead bodies than most after a career in elderly nursing, and certainly enough to know that my mother was alive within the last hour or so.

Despite – or perhaps because of this discovery – my thoughts wound back over the years. Standing there, I was surprised that of all the people I should think of in that moment, I thought of Issy. I thought of her in the café, clutching at my hand which I tried to withdraw but failed, because her grip was like my manners – too strong. I thought of her trying to be a good friend, trying to get me to leave Nick: '*We've seen the bruises.*'

I thought about how it would've been if I had left Nick then, just like Issy wanted. Was that the moment I should've acted – the defining moment that was the trail of breadcrumbs in the forest and the only path out of the nightmare? When I finally left the busy café, was I rejecting the only route to safety, the one that meant that my mother would not be dead now? Or if I'd found a way to keep Nick in my life, would our son be a very different man? Or was it, that no matter what I did, all paths in this nightmare would've led to the same terrible conclusion – that he'd still have grown into what he'd become: the man who killed my mother.

And did I truly believe he had done this? I looked around the undisturbed room. The only motive in killing her was, what, to inflict pain on me?

'*We've seen the bruises.*'

Although I hated that he named his son after himself, when it was clear in the immediate weeks after he was born that Jack's mother, Selena, was going to be a truly dreadful mum, their sharing the same name made it easier for me to move in and take over. It felt natural to hold the little baby in my arms and call him Jack – they even looked the same. It was like I had gone back in time. I felt that I could push the pram onto North Road in Brighton, straight to our favourite café, and find the rest of the NCT gang. That I only had to walk the same route, push the door open and I would find them there, fleshed-out ghosts of my past, drinking coffee, and they would raise their hands in greeting: 'Lisa, over here!'

Of course, they were long gone. Their own kids would now all be in their mid-twenties, grown up and elsewhere, birds on the wing.

But it felt glorious to hold baby Jack to my face and breathe in his newborn smell and remember what had been before. I loved the idea that it felt possible to go back. He became a door which made me feel I could just open and return to where I had been before it all went wrong. For it to feel possible felt just so freeing, so empowering, it became intoxicating. I even thought I might get another dog. I wouldn't have called him Winston, that would've been so . . . gauche, but I liked the idea that I *could* do.

When Selena died suddenly, it felt tragic for Jack – but like I was now Jack's proper mum.

I reach out and touch my mother's foot; my finger grazing her heel.

Of course, my mother never liked the bond I had with Jack. She said I was living in a bygone fantasy. She said only ghosts, ghouls and fools lived in the past. She said that survivors looked to the future and that was where I should set my sights.

But I couldn't. My son was just as awful as a father, and Jack was simply just so good! He was so different to his father at that age, endlessly smiling and sleeping like he was on a timetable. I couldn't take her advice to butt out: 'Mind your own, Lisa. You've got a new role now. Find it, embrace it. In it, you will find all that you need.'

My mother was often full of shite too.

'Sorry,' I whispered, still only looking at her foot. I smoothed the bedspread from around her. 'I wish . . .' I said, my voice a whisper in the silence, *I wish I had smiled at you more. I wish I had taken you to lunch sometimes. I wish we had watched comedy films together – even just one.*

I'm sorry I called the police.

I am so sorry about that.

I'm sorry she had to spend so long in prison for me.

I'm sorry I killed my father and I'm sorry I didn't speak up for her. I was only eight and I thought I was doing the right thing. I thought he was going to kill her that night, but he didn't. Instead he fell into a drunken stupor, but I was frightened about what he would do when he woke up. I'd heard his threats. I wanted to save my mummy.

'Mummy,' I say softly, my hand still on her foot. What a terrible daughter I've been. Trying to save her – but in the end, not saving her at all.

And now I have to be sorry about this. I'm sorry she let in my son and I'm sorry I made such a bad job of him, that he wanted to do this because of me.

She always defended him. 'He's not that bad,' she would tell me when I raged about him and then ignore what I had to say. 'He's just a bit troubled; he'll grow out of it.' Even when he got

Selena pregnant when he was only eighteen, she was the first to stick up for him: 'The baby will be a blessing, you wait.'

When I complained that he'd called Jack after himself, my mum laughed and told me that if he was self-indulgent then he only got it from me. And when I refused to listen, she put her hand up and said: 'I liked the name Jack when you picked it for your son and I like it now he's picked it for his. Besides, I'm now so senile –' she said, when she was nothing of the sort – 'that I wish everyone was called Jack'.

Then, when Selena was found dead of an overdose, I'd started to speculate about things I didn't want to ever think. She cut it short. 'Lisa, you've always been hysterical. It's my fault: you had a difficult start to life.' When I'd dared to pursue it even tentatively, sharing my darkest fears, it was the only time I saw her get angry. Even when she came in, her nose bleeding and her eye swollen, and found me with the blooded knife in my hand, kneeling over my sleeping-but-now-dead father, she wasn't angry. She was cold and calculated – she took the knife. Wiped it. Firmly gripped it in her hand, fingertips pressed with hope.

'Don't you ever . . .' she hissed: 'Tell. Anyone. About. This. *Ever.*'

I don't think I was the only one who passed on personality traits to my child.

Then another time, after I'd had another row with my son about Jack, she didn't take my side. This time she didn't make things better. This time, she gripped me by the shoulders, hissing again: 'Selena was a drug addict. Has it ever occurred to you *why* your son might have pursued a relationship with a drug addict?' She shook me to evidence the point. 'You need to stop persecuting him. *He's* the victim.'

I withdrew my hand. I'm sorry that she had to see the truth for herself. I'm sorry she had to see that I was right. I'm many things, but I've never wanted to be right – the opposite – I would've so much preferred to be wrong about it all.

Without thinking, I went to the bathroom cabinet, where I knew she kept a medicine box. Inside – I know because an addict is always checking these things out, even if they are clean – were the DF118s my mother had for her sore back. She didn't take them because she said they made her constipated. I seized them and then went back to her.

I stared at her body. Her hair: grey, too long for a woman of her age, was still barely ruffled, something I noticed as mine was so easily knotted. With practised fingers, I pressed against the blister pack and popped out four 30-mg tablets, popping them straight into my mouth.

I didn't think of Jack. I didn't think of myself. I thought only of my dead mother. I could see the lines on the soles of her feet, like lines on a map travelling out from here, to be anywhere but here. She was leaving me again.

Again, I wasn't ready for it – hadn't foreseen it.

I dry-swallowed. It struck me that my mother must have taken good care of her feet: they were smooth, her heels rounded and un-calloused. She walked a lot – she loved to walk every-where since she'd been released from prison, yet they were the pink feet of someone who rubbed moisturiser on them nightly. It surprised me, this unexpected self-interest.

It occurred to me then, that perhaps I didn't know my mother like I thought I did. One tablet had caught in my throat and I swallowed until it was gone.

I paused for a moment longer, trying to catch the thought that followed my not fully knowing my mother, but it was already away before it had had a chance to form and arrive. Like a starling, it slipped into a thousand, a tumbling flock of thoughts and ideas that I should've grasped and yet, somehow, have failed to understand, and took flight from me.

Perhaps the thought was not to take the codeine, but if it was, it was too late.

I gave another dry gulp, just to be sure. Then I turned the gold sixpence necklace around my neck – the one she'd given me all those years before – put the pills in my pocket and left.

I couldn't risk leaving Jack alone for a minute longer.

fifty-eight:

– before –

I pushed my way into April Dale's flat. It was the same drab landscape of beige and vanilla, only accentuated by landscapes in gilt frames and dark wood furniture.

April had seated Jack on her sofa and, although there was no daisy display, she'd given him a pink wafer. The thought of its oversweet crisp dryness made me gag. But he was chewing it with delicate nibbles, slowly, in case he wasn't given another one.

When I came in, he watched me silently with his beautiful eyes. Was he thinking about the cage? April came and joined me in the identical small hallway as my mother's. I glanced at her bedroom door; I was glad it was shut.

'My mother is dead,' I said, realising how blunt I sounded only after I had said it. She sighed heavily. 'I need you to call the police,' I asked, 'but only after we've gone. I can't . . . be here, it's not . . .' I cut a glance at Jack, who was licking his empty fingers with thoughtful, neat licks. 'You should bolt your door after we go,' I said, still not looking at her.

She pressed her hand against the wall, as if to steady herself, then said: 'If you like, I won't say I've seen you – if it's simpler?'

I could still feel the imprints of the capsules in my throat. I swallowed. My mother was dead. It didn't feel like this was even happening to me. 'Thank you. I think . . . Jack and I have to . . . go.' I turned to look at her. Her glasses were thick, her cheek-bones showing that she was still a handsome woman. 'I can't risk them holding us back.'

April regarded me from behind the dense lenses with watery eyes. 'Leave now then, dear, if you need to.' She patted my hand. 'I'll tell them that I found the . . . your mother.'

'Would you do that for me?'

She looked surprised. 'Of course.' A thought occurred to her. 'Wait – I have something that you should have.' She headed into the kitchenette and took a tin off the top shelf of the cupboard. She pressed it into my hands. 'Your mother never wanted to keep all her eggs in one basket,' she said. She thought it made sense if she kept some emergency money with me. She didn't trust banks and seemed to think there was a reason that I should look after this for her.' She pushed the tin at me. 'It's quite a lot.'

I pulled the lid off; inside was a thick roll, bigger than my fist, of twenty-pound notes. I stared at April: 'No, I can't . . .'

'But dear, if not you, then who?'

I left the tin on the kitchen side when Jack and I left.

But the money, I took.

fifty-nine:

– now –

Stuck in the fog, it's impossible to know how to go on. But still stuck for directions, I hear a car in the distance – by its speed, I realise it must be on the Cleasong road. From that, I know I can turn until it's on my left. But I am still not completely sure, as I know if I'm only a few degrees out, I risk plunging right past my hill. Only a year ago, I wouldn't believe I could be this lost in the dark, that the countryside could be so empty of light, but I can't see anything, perhaps only a paler stone here and there, puncturing the sea of dark mud. *Help me, Mum.* My hand squeezing my gold coin necklace.

The ridges, my mum whispers. *Lisa, remember the ridges.*

Where the field has been ploughed, it rises and falls in orderly rows. I know that when I came into this field, I was going up-down with every step. I carefully ease my direction a few more degrees to the left. I am now going the right way. Now I might be able to find my way back home.

My feet are so cold, they are completely numb. I start half running again. 'I am coming for you, Jack,' I whisper into the night, 'and now I can protect you.'

He doesn't answer, but now it's the drugs in the tin in the larder that whisper back to me; they use Mungo's voice, as they say: *Hurry, Mrs L, hurry. We miss you.*

sixty:

– before –

After April Dale gave me the money, I only went back briefly to take a small framed photo of my mother and me when I was a baby, a packet of Amitriptyline my mother took for sciatica, and a jumper that smelt of her. I stood briefly above her body and before I left, I kissed her shoulder. I'd only returned to her flat for three minutes, but leaving was the hardest thing I have ever had to do.

I shut the door, feeling the weight of regret. Regret for not arranging her funeral, for not staying for it, for not packing her things away. But I also knew I had no choice: I had saved Jack from a life of abuse – a cage! – and the job was not yet done.

The only comfort was that I knew she wouldn't mind one bit; my mother was the most pragmatic person I ever met. And as I picked up Jack, it was almost like I could hear her whisper her blessing in my ear.

As we stepped out into the corridor, Jack put his arms around me and pressed his face against my neck. I didn't want to, but I couldn't help but jog towards the exit. My feet were quiet against the carpet tiles, my soundless stealth somehow disconcerting.

I gripped him hard, almost wanting him to speak. But he didn't ask why we weren't seeing Nana, and there was part of me that was worried about that. Sometimes, Jack didn't ask the questions that other children would.

He must have asked April, I told myself as I pushed against the door, but if he had, what she said to him in return I still don't know, because I never saw her again.

It occurred to me as I plunged out of the door into the now raining car park, aware that *he* could be anywhere – squatted between parked cars; crouched behind bushes; silent in shadows – that my mother was dead, but all I thought about was Jack's silence. Perhaps it was the shock and cognitive overload; perhaps it was the early effects of the strong painkillers I'd just necked; perhaps it was because if I thought of my mum then I'd collapse in this car park and not get up again. But whatever the reason, as I ran from my mother's, all I could think of is that I'd found Jack in a cage *and he hadn't mentioned it.* I know his stutter really affected his confidence, but still . . . We'd run from his father's where he was supposed to be, stayed in a hotel, driven to his Nana's, arrived but left without him seeing her and run again – but he still doesn't ask me a single question.

Not one.

He loved seeing my mum – perhaps even more than I did. While he was only seven he was intelligent enough – academically able, the school had said. But *was* he? Could I be sure when he didn't seem to react in the way that I thought he should?

Wasn't there something just a teeny bit wrong? More than his severe stutter?

We reached the car. I lowered Jack to the ground and searched my coat pockets for my keys. He clung around my waist as I did, like a sailor gripping the mast in a relentless storm.

I wanted to grasp him by the shoulders, to pull him away and stare into his sweet face to demand: *Why don't you ask me what's going on? Or ask for sweets or moan for your own way or anything else tired seven-year-olds ask for?*

I thought again about sallow-skinned Selena, staring dead-eyed at me.

'See?' my mother had said once after my Jack and Selena left, 'you don't give your son any credit. Jack's only still a teenager, but as soon as he's found out his girlfriend is pregnant, he's done the right thing by the girl in a heartbeat. I'm proud of him and so should you be.'

I got what she was saying – she was saying that I was never satisfied. That everything my son did was wrong. Perhaps she had a point: now that his son was quiet and compliant, I still wasn't happy.

Anxious to stop replaying old criticisms from my mother, I clicked the button on the fob – and then we were in the safety of the car. Jack scrabbled for his car seat and with a swift dexterity, he did up his own seat belt. Then, as if in response to my silent questions, he put Bunny over his face and seemed to fall instantly asleep.

I stared at him in the rear-view mirror longer than I should. He didn't move. I think the wind must have gusted, because a Coke can clattered along the car park, bringing me back to what I should really be thinking about.

I flicked the car's central-locking system, locking the outside out.

I felt sick. Unshed tears burnt in my eyes as I pulled out of the car park. I knew I needed to make a decision about what to do next quickly; I was going under with both grief and the medication I'd taken and I wanted to make a good decision whilst I still could. My gaze flicked up to the rear-view, not to look at Jack but at the road behind me. It was clear. Good; my driving could get a little hazy when I was on tablets.

I wanted to pull over. I wanted to scream and cry. *My mother is dead! My mother is dead!* My. Mother. Is. *Dead.*

I wanted to see her; I wanted to go home – back to when I was a child. I wanted to go back to her flat and hold her body close. I wanted to collapse into a chair, after taking some really good shit, before pulling a rug over me and thinking of nothing but my mother, and scream and cry until the bliss of the drugs had taken effect and I could finally pass out into nothingness.

But I couldn't. I needed to take my life in a firm grip for Jack.

I realised I was never going home again. All my things! I have never been a material person, but . . . I loved my book collection . . . For a moment I glimpsed everything I'd lost: my son for good; my workplace and the people there I knew; my home and belongings; my mother and also my dearly-held sobriety. Even my safety.

All gone.

My mother the greatest loss of all. Shock felt strange, almost as if everything was happening through a television screen – I could see it but couldn't touch it.

But I knew I didn't, yet, understand the true weight of it.

I gripped the steering wheel: I had to use my shock whilst I could. Before I got buried under the landslide of grief coming my way, whilst it was still only a deep rumble, a vision I could see but not yet fully feel on me, I needed to concentrate on Jack. If we were caught, I'd lose him. I couldn't lose him: Jack was my air. I'd suffocate without him.

But where could we go?

sixty-one:

– now –

I follow the ridges in the field, careful to step in the right place. I don't care about my feet anymore – only that I don't lose my way again. I am focused: Jack is the only thing that matters. He's a magnet and I am the metal particle, drawn onwards, onwards.

I'm not sure how long I've been limping, running shoeless, in the dark Herefordshire countryside, because I've got no watch, no way of marking time. I think about my breathing; it keeps me calm. Managing my emotions has been something that has helped me over the years, and it helps me now.

This side of the hedge, the electric fences are clearer and both times are low enough for me to step over, before negotiating the hedge. Now I know they're there, it's all so much easier.

I push on.

Finally, I can see it, lights above ground – my cottage on its hill. The fog has lifted enough now for me to know that I'm home.

I hug the gun a little closer.

The journey to safety has been so long; I am ready to finish it.

I don't waste time trying to find a gap in the hedge; instead I turn my back to it and press against it. At first it doesn't yield ... but then it does. The twigs drag against me. They pull at my hair. They scrape against my face. My feet struggle to find a way through over the ridge of earth. This no longer bothers me so I push harder.

And then I'm out the other side with a sudden thump and I stumble to regain my balance. I'm in my garden. I am back home.

I start the gentle climb up. I ask myself, as I fix my eyes on the cottage, if I'm ready for what I will have to do. I think of Jack – tender, innocent, in desperate need of safety.

I think of Selena too, again. She keeps returning to me now. Within eight months of Mungo's death, Jack was born.

I was very fond of Mungo. For a little bit, just before he died, he'd started to come round and have a cup of tea with me when Jack was out; it made me think that he was just as pleased in my company as he was my son's. When he used to chat to me, it'd started to feel like the mother-son relationship I'd never had, but Jack came home one day and it was so evident that he didn't like it, Mungo never lingered again and then he was dead.

I think that after his death, I shut down a bit. I thought of him, his body hanging, alone in the woods and I couldn't bear that he hadn't talked to me about how he felt. He'd always seemed so bright, so sparky, I couldn't assimilate the version I saw of him every day, and his bouncy: 'How's it going, Mrs L?' to standing on a log and then kicking it away.

They found him full of barbiturates as well and I had a sneaking suspicion they might've been mine. I kept rigorous notes of what I had and when I took them, not just from the habit of being a nurse, but because it was the equivalent of drinking expensive wine out of a tasteful glass – it made my addiction feel just a little bit more classy, more measured and therefore just a little bit easier to live with. There were gaps in my records – times I assumed I'd just forgotten to note . . . but maybe not.

It seems those gaps could've been something else.

I adjust my path – I don't want to keep going this way as I will hit the driveway at the front of the property. Instead I know that if I walk round the periphery a little, I will be able to approach the cottage from the back and will – if I hide my approach through the rhododendron bushes – be able to get really close to the back door.

And then what?

Then I think of him. Jack – my Jack. My son. He was once so beautiful. He too was once so tender and innocent.

Something in me twists. The pain is so raw that it's not something I can carry. It bends me. I miss him more than I would miss breath if it were taken from me. I miss him so much – Nick always said I was too attached.

Becoming a mother was hard for me. Perhaps, because I hadn't had one when I was growing up, perhaps I just didn't know what to do well enough. Perhaps I'm not clever enough to work it out. I tried. I bought books and wrote down sleep cycles and hand-mashed food, but it was just too much. Even when he was growing inside me, I suspected I was just not up to being a mother. Someone once famously said: *No man is an island*. Well, for me that's wrong. Since I was eight, I've always felt alone and adrift. And when an island that has always felt like an island gets joined to the main coast, it loses its identity forever. I guess that's OK if you want that, I'm just not sure I knew how to change.

But I did love him. I did still love my son so very much.

More than perhaps I realised at the time. At the time I worried about the wrong things: the mess; the noise; the lack of control.

But it all changed. The wind picks up and it's cold against my cheeks. I realise that I'm crying.

Perhaps that's why I hold *his* son so close. Perhaps that's why I breathe in *his* skin as he sleeps. Perhaps that's why I graze my nose across *his* cheeks. Because I think of his daddy when he was young. Because I wish I had done that with him. Because none of us can truly go back and change the things we got wrong, but when baby Jack was born, so like his father before him, and when Selena died leaving my son needing me for the first time since he was a child, himself now bewildered and overwhelmed with the responsibility of being a lone parent, it was perfect for all of us for me to step in and take over the main parenting role. After all, some mothers are the same age as me when they have their babies. As I pushed his pram, everyone just assumed I *was* his biological mum and – somehow, between the wanting and the needing, it became an almost truth.

And he needs a mother: I am his mother now because Selena is gone. I think of her as I stare at the cottage that contains her partner, my son, and her child – now my child.

I forget how it was that she came round one day, when Jack was at work. He'd got a job doing something he wouldn't discuss, but was making good money. Perhaps she was lonely – perhaps she knew I knew how it felt but after that initial time, she'd started to come round every day. I was happy to encourage her; it gave me access to beautiful Jack. I'd put a chair in the garden for her and I would hold Jack while she smoked. She smoked a lot. She'd watch me through the kitchen window. I always thought she cut a lonely figure, sitting there, watching me from the outside, looking in. I tried talking to her, but unlike Mungo, she was reluctant to engage in conversation. She didn't want to talk about anything, she just wanted to watch me look after the baby and smoke, silently, the cigarette always so twitchy in her hand.

The closest we came to having a meaningful discussion was once when she was watching me feed him baby food. I'd been making new recipes – not in the 'I need to be perfect' way that I had done for my son, but more relaxed, enjoying using butternut squash and other veg I didn't have easy access to when my Jack was a baby. I marvelled at how easy it was, uncertain as to why I had found it so stressful the first time round. It wasn't as if I didn't have a baby to look after – Selena came round at nine in the morning and stayed until five. But as I made the food and then spooned it into his beautiful mouth, it was good for me to laugh at my previous self, to see me as I was and how out of proportion I'd got things.

The person it may not have been good for, was Selena. She graduated from sitting in my garden, to sleeping on my couch during the day. She was the silent, ever-present shadow in the house, a ghost – there, but not really there. I thought it was because she was up during the night breastfeeding, but she became sleepier the older Jack got. She got thinner in front of me and slipped further away from the living, day after day.

Perhaps it was drug abuse. Perhaps . . . something else.

As I stand looking at the cottage, carrying a gun that might make her son an orphan tonight, I realise there's sinning not just by action, but also by omission. I might not have really known much about her, but I could sense that Selena was unhappy and I didn't do anything about it. I had lived with my son and I knew – better than anyone – what he was like and I didn't check in with her. I had the power, perhaps, to change her situation and I did nothing. We didn't talk but that wasn't all it was, it was also that I didn't want to risk her not bringing Jack to see me anymore. And now she was dead.

The coroner ruled that she'd overdosed after injecting oxycodone after a long history of heroin abuse. I think of the long sleeves she used to always wear, even when it was warm. The coroner noted she'd switched to oxycodone, but there were no details available as to why. At the time, I wondered if she'd lost her usual supply, and desperate, stolen them from my own internet-ordered hoard.

I think of Mungo in the woods. I think of Winston. Images of so many awful things flash through my mind. I feel a huge, overwhelming sense of sorrow infect me. With it is an understanding more terrible. Something I had stubbornly ignored.

But now I think of it, I can no longer ignore it: they both died of drugs which I keep myself. This can't be a coincidence.

The hardest thing I have ever had to do, is to accept my son for what he is.

I have an aching in my chest that means I accept him now. I recognise what I think he might've done. But the trouble with accepting his past, also means recognising what he is still capable of.

I look at the cottage and know I am about to go inside. I know, in there, the only thing that stands against Jack's safety is my own son.

My finger finds the trigger.

sixty-two:

– now –

I know I've only got to cross the lawn and that will be the end of the journey. As soon as I break cover of the rhododendrons, I'll be at risk of being seen.

He will be waiting for me. He has set the trap.

I bathed him as he sat in the kitchen sink. I loved him then and I love him now. I suspect I might falter.

I remind myself that, in the middle of us, there's a child who needs me to be brave. My finger caresses the trigger like a lover's touch, as I think of Jack's light freckles on the same too-cute nose his dad had when he was the same age. I think of his dad at that age. I shut my eyes briefly, head swimming with head injury and Ativan and Valium, remembering, reimagining.

He grabs my sleeve in the park as he wants to go on a swing, his lovely face turned up to me like a sunflower to the sun, and says: 'Mummy?' The colour, the grass smells and the pull of his hand, makes it feel like I'm there again. But this is different – the same but different. It occurs to me suddenly: 'Jack, can I ask you a question?'

He raises a quizzical eyebrow and gives a little shrug.

'What should I do, Jack, to save your son from you?'

His smooth forehead creases and he tilts his head like a quizzical dog. 'I don't understand what you mean, Mummy?'

I don't understand it either: but it feels right. I try again: 'If Daddy was chasing us, say he was super cross with us, what would you want me to do?'

'Get away, of course.'

'But say that we couldn't. Say I had to choose between you, a little kid or Daddy, who I also love? I'm stuck because I love you both. It feels like I have to choose between you. I don't want to – I love you both.'

Jack wrinkles his nose. 'You need to do your best.'

'But what if that means a fight?'

He shrugs. 'Just do your best, Mummy. That's what you always tell me. Your best is your best and no one can ask for more,' and he runs for the swings.

I open my eyes. To be back, standing in this dark garden, outside the cottage that is twenty years after the park I used to take my son to, is just too strange. I was there – I swear it. It was daylight and now it's night again. I blink, swaying in the cold wind. It might be my head injury, but even as I try to tell myself it is, I know that it's not the first time that I've had these . . . space-outs.

Not for the first time, I promise myself that I will give up the painkillers. I have to get a grip on it, I vow. After this, I tell myself, I will be clean again.

Before I change my mind, I start to run.

It takes seconds to cross the lawn. The door is half-glazed and as I draw nearer, the opaque glass shows there's a figure standing behind the door. It's tall, broad: it's him. He might see me.

He's been waiting. I must not falter.

My heart is whamming in my chest. I'm going to throw up.

Before I can reach it, the door is starting to open. The light is spilling out. I blink, the light is so bright. I raise the gun up. I'm not yet holding it right; I'm panicking. I need to bring it up and press it into my shoulder – I remember Mungo helping me do this – but my hands are suddenly shaking so much. The gun is against my open burns and they are screaming, screaming; the pain is overwhelming.

My breathing is short and shallow. I can't kill him. I just *won't* – no matter what. I know it – I've *always* known it, it's just been crazy bravado – instead he will kill me. I don't mind dying but what about Jack?

There's no answer to this, I understand. What happens is out of my hands. I still run towards the door, but the gun is already sagging in my grip. I don't want it. With an overwhelming sense of relief, I place it on the ground.

I will do what I've always done, I will do my best, but I won't hurt my son. Because I can't.

The door is opening more and it's just as it was with Erica; I can't see him properly because it's so bright in the kitchen and he's a silhouette. My eyes hurt as they strain against the sudden light.

Then I manage to focus. I blink, once, twice.

The man is standing in the back doorway with a look of disgust on his face.

But it's not *his* face. It's not my son.

I've got this wrong – all wrong.

Staggering back, I think:

It's.

Not.

Jack.

sixty-three:

– before –

I know why my son, aged only five, killed our beloved dog Winston. Why he hit him with the broom and snapped his back. It's because of what he heard his father say the day before.

By this time, any hopes that starting school would help improve Jack's behaviour were already sunk. He was currently suspended and I was dearly hoping that, as the letter confirming his expulsion hadn't yet arrived, the school might relent and he'd be allowed back for one final chance.

I dearly hoped, but I didn't believe it. Cutting an earlobe off another child because you want 'to know if it would snip easily', was not the action of a treasured student.

I'd not worked during his suspension, but the day before Winston died, I had. The agency called and they were desperate and promised to pay double time, so I'd agreed and Irene had kindly offered to have Jack for the day.

I'd just got in from work. I'd said hello to Jack, offered him a snack and come into the kitchen to cut up an apple for him, when Nick uncharacteristically put a cup of tea in front of me. When he spoke, his voice was strange – a harsh whisper. 'Lisa, listen to me. We've got to talk. We've said this before, but I'm saying it properly, *properly* now, and I want you to understand what I'm about to say. I want you to *hear* me.'

'Honey, what?'

'There's something badly wrong with Jack.'

I thought about the teacher telling me that they had to command Jack to give back the snipped earlobe. 'Wrong with him? I think we know that already—'

'*No.*' He glanced at the door, his voice a low, urgent husk: 'I mean, I'm now *frightened.*'

My knife paused mid-air. 'What do you mean?'

'It's not normal the way he attacks everyone all the time. We always said he'd grow out of it; we just thought he was a late developer. We've always made excuses to each other, but we have to face up that he's no tantrumming toddler now.'

'I'm hardly going to argue with that, am I? But we always said that—'

'I know what we always *said.* But he's not growing out of it. Nothing we have done has ever worked. So, I don't think we should just *talk* anymore, I think we need to *do.* We need to face that he's not getting better, but getting worse. Much worse.' He passed a hand over his face. 'Mum's had enough. She refuses to look after him on her own anymore.'

I couldn't breathe. This felt different. When I cried about Jack, Nick always tried to cheer me up. When Nick raged about Jack's behaviour, I always tried to calm him down. Between us, to try and cope, we each interchangeably played different roles of anger and sadness and optimism and even humour.

But neither of us had ever admitted to being frightened.

Fear meant lack of safety and lack of safety meant . . . a whole new level.

And what Nick didn't know was that today I couldn't counter his argument. Today I had to agree.

I felt cheated because I really wanted Nick to reassure me today, tell me that everything was going to work out fine, because every time I went to our hall to see if the letter had been delivered, my own nerves became increasingly torn.

I couldn't believe it was happening again. I'd had to move Jack from nursery to nursery, but as the paying customer, change always felt like an option. School was different. If he failed in his first few weeks, what did that suggest about the likelihood of success for his next school? And what if he failed the next school after that?

My fear started to get ahead of me and I'd stared at the empty doormat as I'd let myself in from work and had a nightmare image of being forced to homeschool him. If his lovely school wanted to kick him out in his first year and his own grandmother, Irene, didn't want to look after him, what did that suggest about the future? I could see a reality where I'd have to give up work and all that meant. (No more drugs pilfering! No more independence money!) Worse, the thought of trying to homeschool Jack all day and then look after him in the evenings made me feel fraught.

I looked forward to Mondays like some people longed for the weekend.

How had these two things happened on the same day?

Because he's getting worse. The line on the trajectory was still going down: sharply. Where would it stop?

I suddenly felt Nick's terror: I'd been fooling myself that this was under control. We looked at each other. *He's going to keep getting worse until . . .*

When?

'He's going to kill someone one day,' Nick said, answering my unspoken question.

For a moment I didn't say anything. But I dismissed it as soon as I found my voice: 'Now you're just being dramatic.' Repelled at the spoken fear, I turned back to the counter. I picked up the knife and started chopping. I didn't want to think about that. I didn't want to think this was going to go on for years. I didn't want to think where this could end. How would I cope?

I still had my back to Nick, the tea next to me on the counter untouched. I could tell from his voice, and the scrape of the chair, that he'd sat down at the table. He was here to stay.

I carried on chopping again, but slowly. I'd nearly run out of apple. I tried to think. Finally, I asked: 'What did he do to Irene?'

'He bit her.'

'That's bad,' I said, actually shuddering with relief that it wasn't worse.

'Lisa, stop chopping that bloody apple into a pulp and turn around.'

The apple was mush now. I put the knife down and pressed my hands flat against the worktop. I couldn't do this, I wasn't ready. A bit of me even wanted Jack to come in so that I didn't have to have this conversation.

There was a gasping sound, and then Nick said something in a voice so unlike his, my bladder twitched. When I turned round, I saw he was crying.

I held on to the countertop, so unsure, so shocked. I wanted to do the right thing and comfort him but it was so strange – so alien – to see this big, strong man cry, that I stood motionless, so unsure. Just how bad was the attack on his mother?

'She had to go to hospital, Lese. Didn't you wonder why I was home from work with him?'

In truth, I hadn't. All I could think about when I came home from work was checking the doormat for the letter, and after I saw it was empty, could only think about checking the space by the toaster where we put the picked-up letters, and when I saw that was also empty, I finally relaxed a fraction, took 2 mg of diazepam, and then said hello to my son and made him a snack. There was no space in my head for anything else other than the letter, Valium and Jack.

'What did he do?' Defeated, I sank to the chair opposite him.

'He bit her on the cheek.'

'He bit her . . . on the cheek?'

Nick's jaw tightened. 'Yes, Lisa. Wake up, will you? You're always in such a fog. He bit her so badly on the cheek that she had to have stitches. It's going to leave a scar. She's a mess. She loves him but she doesn't want to look after him on her own, anymore. The hospital were giving me right funny looks and I had to get him out of there really quick in case they got a social worker involved or something. I kept telling them he hadn't done it before, I even –' he put his face in his hands and his shoulders shook – 'I even lied and told one of the doctors that my mum is too sharp with him and that it must've been her fault.' His shoulders shook, then he looked up, eyes wide with panic. 'She doesn't know that! Don't tell her!'

'No, Nick, I won't tell her.' I didn't know what else to say. I was so struck by how sad Nick was – was he always sad?

I think it had been a long time since we'd talked about anything meaningful. I realised that recently we hadn't even tried to cheer each other up – it'd started to feel too false to try. Instead I took my feelings to my therapist and to the sympathetic ears of codeine and Valium. I definitely couldn't remember thinking about Nick's feelings in any substantial way. Jack took everything meaningful from both of us.

Nick reached out across the table, palms open. It'd been so long, it took me a moment to realise he wanted to hold my hands.

He pulled them towards him and cried over them. Eventually, he let go and sat up. He dragged his sleeve across his eyes. 'What are we going to do, Lisa?'

'Do?'

He flushed red. 'Of course! He's out of control!'

I shook my head a little – only a little, more from confusion than denial. I didn't understand the question: *What* was *there to do?* We'd both tried the doctors and got nowhere. Nick didn't know I had tried private counselling for Jack so couldn't even share the disappointment that it hadn't worked. After months with my own therapist, I hadn't managed more than agreeing to pack a go-bag in case I needed to leave. But even that was challenged now, because how could I leave him with Nick? Nick had a job and any fantasy that Irene would just slip in and fill my empty place was now dead.

Although I hadn't even been close to fleeing, the fact that it was no longer a possibility felt suffocating.

'Lisa, don't shake your head like this isn't happening. I know you bury your head in the sand, but you've got to see: it's worse than we thought. She had a hole in her cheek, Lisa. It's obvious there's something massively, hugely, fucking wrong with Jack and I want us to try to get professional help again. Something specialist. We mustn't give up this time, we've got to make a fuss. Take it all the way down the line and get him something secure.'

'Something secure?' I could hear the horror screeching nails down glass in my voice. 'What do you mean . . . secure?'

Nick swallowed but he kept his gaze steadily on mine. 'Somewhere where he can't do anything . . . worse.'

I didn't move, didn't breathe.

'We've lost control.' He gave a dry laugh. 'Who am I kidding? We never even had it.' He shook his head. 'Lisa, he *took the flesh out of her cheek*.'

I thought of Nick's lovely mum and felt my heart bruise for her.

'And what about him breaking your rib?' he continued. 'And the kid he put in hospital with concussion in his last week at nursery, before he left? Now the earlobe in school? I'm so scared of what he's going to be like when he's bigger. Lisa, I worry he's going to kill someone –' he struggled against his now openly flowing tears – 'I'm worried he's going to kill *you*.'

My voice was a whisper: 'When were you thinking?'

'I want to make a call today. *Now.* To social services. I shouldn't have lied at the hospital – I just panicked. I wanted to talk to you first. Then all the way home, I kept thinking that moment was my golden opportunity to admit the truth. I was furious with myself: I thought I'd blown it, missed my chance. But, Lese, we don't have to miss it – I could ring now and explain.'

I shook my head: *no.*

I knew the damage of what it was like to grow up without parents. He was our son. We couldn't just send him back: *No, sorry, parenthood just isn't what we'd thought.*

We were trapped, I knew that, but I thought we were both trapped together. I didn't know that within three days that would change abruptly and for good.

Nick didn't know it either, because he kept going. Even when he might've stopped, he kept pushing the point. 'Lese, please stop shaking your head. Think about what I'm saying. We need to come clean – we need to admit we aren't coping. We will still visit and love him every day, but we tell them the truth. I rang my mum before you got home and I've discussed it with her. She's agreed to talk to them, tell them what happened. I've told her everything about Jack.'

He pressed his hand to his chest and looked almost happy. 'I can't tell you how good it feels to have told her the truth. She's horrified for us but fully supports us. She thinks it's best to seek help too. Particularly in light of what's happened at his school – she says they might get in touch with social services anyway. Don't you think it's best that we tell them before they do?'

He took my hand, squeezed it. 'We love him but we have to accept that we're not the best people to look after him. It's not working. There has to be a breaking point – let's do it while you're still alive.' He kissed my hand. 'It might not need to be permanent. Perhaps there's somewhere that can cure him.'

That's when we noticed Jack standing in the doorway.

Everything then got very . . . smudged, but I don't remember the details. Just the noise. The stinking, spiky cacophony of noise in our kitchen.

And then the duvet . . . but after the pills.

Always the pills.

sixty-four:

- before -

The day Winston died was the end of us.

It was deeply disturbing when Jack killed Winston. He said he didn't do it, but when Nick came home and found the dog's body in the hall, Jack playing Lego in his room, and the bloodied broom hidden under the sofa, it was clear what'd happened. The yelling got me out of bed.

I'd been in the flat, but I never heard anything, because I'd had the duvet over my head, my earplugs in and a large dose of fentanyl in my blood. In my defence, there was a reason I was hiding. I'd been very upset because the letter from Jack's school had finally arrived. With shaking fingers, I'd opened it and read that the permanent exclusion had been agreed and was finalised. I'd phoned the local authority, listened to our remaining education options, and my anxiety had gone sky-wards. I just didn't even want to look at Jack. But thinking of earlobes, I did remove the scissors – and then after a moment's thought took the knives too and hid them in my room. Duvet up, I'd cried myself to sleep.

The next thing I knew was the shouting.

Then after I lost it with Nick and beat him with the broom handle, and the neighbours knocked on the door and threatened to call the police, and I apologised to Nick, and Nick apologised to Jack for hitting him, and I cleaned up Jack's split lip, we then sent him to his room.

Nick couldn't understand this: 'The dog is dead and you were in *bed*?'

'Because of this,' I said and showed him the letter.

He read it. 'Shit, Lisa,' was all he said. He sank to the bed next to me, rereading the letter, whilst I sat crying, head in hands.

It had been a horrible shock. Biting cheeks and snipping ear-lobes was one thing – but killing was new. Now Nick was hitting Jack and I was beating Nick. It had all gone so very toxic.

Eventually, he put down the letter and started to pace up and down our room – which was ridiculous given that the room wasn't very big. I couldn't bear to look at him. He loved that dog. We both did.

Losing Winston just killed us.

'So tell me again what happened after I left for work this morning?'

My hands flung up in despair: 'This isn't some police interview, Nick! I'm not the guilty one here.'

'Aren't you?' he raged. 'Are you sure about that? Because something has gone wrong – badly wrong. I told you yesterday he needed locking up.'

'Don't mention that secure place again – look what happened because of that! He heard you say that and that's why he killed Winston!'

Nick stared at me, only then comprehending what I'd understood straightaway. There was a clear sequential line running through this, starting with Irene's bitten cheek.

'We can't go back to how it was now, you realise that, don't you? That thought has occurred in your spongy, drug-addled brain?'

He'd never called out my drug abuse before. 'Don't be rude!' I cried. 'Just don't be rude to me!'

'Why not, Lisa? You were at home. It was on your watch. If someone got clubbed to death in the next-door room to me at work, I think my boss would want to know what I'd been doing whilst it'd been going on.' His voice dropped to a new, flinty tone that I hadn't heard before: 'My boss might sack me if I was asleep on the job.'

My head jerked in a way that I suspected gave me away. My shame made me angry: 'You're only getting at me because you were the one who said you wanted Jack sent away. This was a revenge attack against you. And, for the record, you're not my boss.'

'No, I'm not. But if I was, we wouldn't be in this mess, because we would've called social services yesterday. I shouldn't have listened to you. I'm disgusted – him killing Winston and you zonked out in bed in the middle of the day.' His voice was cold. He stopped pacing and looked at me a long time. His handsome face was thinner, I realised, and his jaw had tightened his cheekbones to new, drawn angles. He looked ill. 'And let's face it, if I was your boss, you'd have been sacked a long time ago.'

I stared at him, chilled. I wasn't sure what he was saying. It wasn't clear, but nothing was. It occurred to me that Jack could be listening to all of this, but I realised for the first time that I didn't care. We always tried so hard to keep our arguments away from him, particularly when they were about him, but after today, we were way past that. Perhaps it was better that Jack heard what we thought anyway.

We stared at each other for a long moment.

We didn't really look into each other's eyes anymore. Who wanted to see what was there? But now we did. I think we stared to see if what the other one was thinking the same.

Nick blinked first.

After he slammed out of the room, I found an unconcerned Jack playing Lego again in his bedroom. He very compliantly let me bath him and feed him cheese on toast, which he ate in his room, whilst I read to him, to keep him out of Nick's way. I put him to bed early, expecting a fuss, but he was placid. I would've taken raging if it'd meant there was any sign that he engaged with the idea that killing our family's dog was wrong, but I didn't get that.

I remember smoothing his Peter Rabbit covers around him, with him just lying there staring at me, and me pretending not to notice, instead adjusting the teddies around his bed as if those simple actions made me a good mother. Made me the mother that I'd had at the start of my life. I wanted to be good, but I knew I wasn't. I had beaten my husband with the broom, not just because he'd crossed a line with Jack and I was frightened, but because I was so upset about the dog that if I hadn't hit Nick, I think I would've hit Jack instead. I don't think I've ever felt as sad as I did then. That sort of crashing heartbreak which threatens to drag you under and hold you there, suffocating until you can't breathe anymore.

I smoothed his covers again, waiting for some sort of acknowledgement that Jack was sorry. I needed to hear his regret, see his tears, so I could reach for him and comfort him. I wanted him to be sorry so I could feel relieved. I also wanted him to feel bad because then there would be recognition for Winston. And if I'm honest, I needed him to be sorry so there would be a sneaking chance that he would learn his lesson and not do anything like this again.

I wanted to be able to take his regret to Nick and spread it at his feet like a golden blanket, an offering to make it just a fraction better. *Your son is truly sorry.* But Jack just looked at me. I wanted a line, some dialogue that would happen in a movie – something significant – but I got nothing.

I remember that I bent over and kissed Jack's forehead. I remember feeling unsure – so unsure. Everyone I knew seemed to know instinctively how to treat their children, like they'd been to parenting college and had lessons. Like someone wise had given them advice on how to behave when this or that happens. But if there was a parenting college, no one had sent me the invite. And so I didn't know if I should rage at Jack for what he had done, or be caring and nurturing because he was so clearly somehow broken. I just didn't know what to do with him. And it felt like I wouldn't be able to count on Nick for much longer.

In the end I just said: 'We will have to talk about what you did to Winston another day. I'm afraid it's too serious not to talk about it.'

'What I did?' he asked me, small hands gripping the top of his duvet.

'Yes,' I said, angrier now at the angelic look of innocence on his face, 'yes, what you did to Winston.'

'But Mummy, I didn't do anything. You did, Mummy. You hit Winston with the broom and his back went crack.' He blinked. 'Don't you remember?'

sixty-five:

- now -

I'm standing on my own back doorstep, blinking. The man is still holding the door, but as he steps forward, his face becomes clearer. I only see more plainly what I already know.

He's nearly six foot; he has a heavy beard and broad shoulders. I can't see the colour of his eyes, but I can see the look of contempt in them. I feel skittish, nervous.

Nick has never hated me, but judging by his stare, I fear he might hate me now.

sixty-six:

– now –

'Lisa,' Nick says, standing at the door, looking out at me. 'What are you doing?'

I hear his disdain and feel weak and weary to the point of dying. I don't think I can take any more of this day. I haven't got the strength in me to hide my feelings for him. 'What are *you* doing here, Nick?'

'I'm not talking to you whilst you're near that thing,' he says, pointing at the gun now lying on the lawn. 'And where the hell did you get it, anyway?' He looks me up and down. 'Shit, Lisa, you look like you've been pulled through a hedge backwards.'

Perhaps he's trying to be funny. 'You're wrong – I push myself forwards through them,' I say, meaning to sound sharp. Instead I just sound like I'm about to cry.

'Where did you get a *shotgun*?'

'I just borrowed it,' I tell him.

He rolls his eyes. 'You are not bringing that thing in this house with my son and grandson in here.'

I want to tell him that I wasn't going to – that I'd already changed my mind – but suddenly I'm too exhausted to even speak. I don't move.

He knows me so well that he adds to his point. 'Lisa. If you don't move away from that gun, I will call the local police myself. I should do it anyway. Unless, of course, you've got a licence for it?'

I am just too tired to talk about the gun. I'm still stunned he's here.

'Even if you have,' he adds, eyes narrowing, 'I'm guessing you don't want the police here. I'm guessing you're still avoiding them at all costs, after what you've done?'

I leave the gun where it is and walk towards the door. We are now close enough to touch. *Oh, baby, how I still miss you. Don't ever think that I don't. I told you I would never give you up, and I haven't.*

But I don't stay that. Instead I ask: 'Why are you here?' I'm slow to process but I'm amazed to find I'm both pleased to see him but also frightened. I don't know what this means.

He drops his hand away from the door and stands aside to allow me entry to my own kitchen. 'Jack asked me to come.'

'Jack?' I'm distracted by the moan of relief as my hurt, tired, beaten-up feet step onto the cool kitchen tiles. For a moment, I imagined Jack finding my mobile and somehow managing to call Nick. But of course, it was ridiculous – he doesn't have his number.

He knows me so well, he's followed my train of thought. '*Your* son. Your *son* who is called Jack.'

'Excuse me,' I say, overwhelmed by too many mixed emotions, and stumble into the pantry. I retrieve my pills and swallow only one. I want far more, but don't dare. Just as I'm rethinking this, I glance up to see Nick standing in the doorway looking at me.

Shame stings: the chunky kid caught with her hand in the cookie jar. 'Only one. My feet hurt. My head hurts. My wrists are burnt. You have no idea what I've been through tonight – what he has done to me.'

Nick puts up a hand as if to say: *Tell me no more*, and disappears back into the kitchen.

I feel anger flare up. 'Look at me!' I shout to the half-closed pantry door. I feel unintentionally comedic, the Hammer House film villain, as I limp towards it.

The door recoils under my touch and smacks back against its hinges. 'Look at me!' I repeat, wanting him to hear the point. 'Look at what he has done to me!'

Nick is now sitting at the table, an empty tumbler in front of him and my bottle of whisky. I want to shout at him, but I need to get to Jack. I need to save him – that's all that counts.

I stumble through the kitchen door and just make it into the hallway when Nick reclaims me by the scruff of my fleece, pulling me, like a naughty child, back into the kitchen. We struggle, a silent dance that I never, not at any point, come close to winning. Even though I'm already resigned, it seems I can't help but just try one more time. He holds his own. He is like his son – determined and strong.

Finally, when I know I've given up, I rest my head against his chest and wrap my arms around him, just like I used to.

Holding him is like slipping on old trainers. I want to cry against him but I don't. He holds me back, though, and for several minutes I simply rest.

'Lese? You OK?' he says finally, when he's probably thought of Anne-Marie. He pulls me away a little and looks at me. 'Seriously, what's happened to you? Where have you *been*?'

I glance down at my filthy clothes, the deep, red welts on my wrists, the mud that clings to my legs and feet. Suddenly, I'm annoyed that he seen me looking like this – that this is what I look like when he hasn't seen me for so long. I'm irritated that I even still care. 'Jack did this to me,' is all I manage. Then: 'But is Jack – little Jack – is *he* OK?'

'Our son did all this?' Nick gestures to the mud, the scratches, the burns.

'Well . . . no, but yes. I'll explain – but *please* tell me first, is Jack all right?'

'He's fine, I promise. He thinks you went to visit a friend. He's still awake, though. Too excited. Jack's with him now. You're going to sit down and rest, and then I think you need a bath.'

I sob again; I'm frightened at what will happen next, but I'm so exhausted. Emotions rise and I can't stem my tears as they flow. I sob, feeling the overwhelming surge of feelings that I can't tease apart. I'm just too tired.

Nick has placed his arm around me again. 'Lisa, don't worry,' he says at some point and I feel his surety flow through me. His arm is welcome, a bough I can shelter under. I want more: I want him to lift me up and put his arms around me, just like he used to.

Instead he lowers me into a chair. Then he pours me a stiff drink and slides it over like a bartender in an old Western. I catch it and try not to smile. With stiff movements that make him seem older than I remember, he gets up and goes to the larder. He comes back and gives me the green first-aid kit.

I drink the whisky: it's sour enough to give me a shiver. I look at the green kit and then at him. 'How did you know where it was?'

'About the third thing I did when I got here was look for your tablets. I found some under your bed, but I know you well enough that you only keep a stash there for emergencies. So I carried on looking.' His head jerked in the direction of the larder. 'And clever me, I thought that looked about the right place for your main stockpile.' He looks sad when he says: 'You don't change, Lisa.'

Nothing about me has changed, least of all how I feel about you. I finish my drink. 'Not true. I only started using again after my mother's death. I had been clean for years.' When Nick didn't say anything, I changed the subject. 'When are you going to let me see Jack?'

'Do you want to?' His dark eyebrows knit together and a hand rubs his face briefly, in a habit I'd forgotten that I'd even known about. 'I mean, is that a good idea right now? You've both had a bad night with each other – we don't want any more rows.'

'Not *that* Jack,' I said, hearing my own disgust in my voice as I carefully peel my socks from my feet. 'Little Jack.'

I study Nick properly for the first time, ignoring the *thwang-thwang* in my feet and wrists and head, ignoring the need for another dose of something that I'm not prepared to take in front of him, and am surprised at just how different he looks. I haven't seen him for the best part of two years. In that time, he's changed and now looks noticeably older. Not bad old – good old, really – but his eyelids have grown heavy and white now graces his beard.

'Lisa, I do want you to go up, but only when you've tidied yourself up enough to look half-reasonable – *and* after we have a chat.'

I don't like the way he says this. 'Look at what he's done to me!' I'm not talking about the beautiful boy upstairs now, but Nick knows this.

He stares at me. I thought he wasn't going to speak, but in the end, he does. 'Our Jack says you did that to yourself.'

I'm confused. My head *thwangs* again, heavier now. '*What?*' I can hear my own incredulity. 'How could I do this to myself?'

'Well, I suppose all of the mud and scratches and your feet – you need to tell me why you've been outside without your shoes, by the way – is because you've been wandering around the countryside in the dark. Now look,' he says, no doubt seeing my rising fury, 'I'm not an idiot. I know what our son is like. I'm under no illusions that he's a saint, please be clear on that right now. We'll thrash all of this out together – I'm here for little Jack only, not to take sides – but it's better you know what our Jack is saying before you two meet. So,' he holds his hands up, 'don't bite my head off, but what he says is, is that *you* attacked *him*.'

I have no words.

'He says that when he turned up and asked for Little Jack, you attacked him with a rolling pin.'

'Unbelievable.' I reach for the bottle myself. 'Lies – as usual. He tied me up, you know.'

'I know.' He puts something on the table. I'm not looking at it, instead I keep on staring at Nick's face. For some reason I don't want to look on the table, I don't want to see what it is.

'He said he didn't know what else to do to stop you from raging. He wanted to keep you in one place until I got here. Believe it or not, I only live an hour from here. Sometimes I go shopping in Hereford. Can you imagine? We could have bumped into each other.'

I feel like saying something sarcastic, but I don't. Instead I just stare at him, willing for him to continue.

'But he felt bad when he saw what you'd done, trying to free yourself. The burns. That's when he called me.' His eyes flicker to my wrists. 'He was upset both for you and that he'd had to turn off the gas.'

I don't breathe. Instead, I think of him standing over me while I was unconscious. Where was little Jack when this was going on?

And: didn't I turn off the gas? I want to remember that I did, but I don't. With a rising nausea, I realise that what Nick is saying is possibly true.

Nick reaches out and lightly rests his hand on my arm. I almost lean into it.

'Like I say, I remember how awful Jack could be when he was little, but Lisa, he did cut you free. And – because I asked him to until I got here – he did keep out of your way as soon as he was sure you were regaining consciousness. That's true, isn't it, that he stayed upstairs with Jack?'

I don't speak because I can't agree with this, even though this is the truth.

Instead, I look at the table: I can't help it. Now, I want to know what has been placed in front of me.

sixty-seven:

– now –

I drop my gaze to the tabletop to see what it is that Nick has put in front of me.

It's the cable tie. It's been cut. I thought I had burnt it off. It's a little bit charred, but I can see the neat edge of a cut from a blade. It is unquestionable.

For the first time, I feel just a tiny – so tiny – flicker of doubt.

It seems like years ago I had tried to free myself, but glancing at the clock, I can see that only three hours have passed.

I reach out and touch it, turning the strip of plastic under my fingers. I couldn't really see it, so how can I be sure? Although it looks the same, it could so easily be a lie.

Because *he* lies, I remind myself.

I hold onto this now, gripping this fact like a buoyancy aid because it's all I have to guarantee my sanity. That and Jack. 'When can I go up and see Jack?' I persist, not wanting to think about the neat edge of the cable tie and what it might mean.

Nick rubs one finger around the rim of his glass. 'I don't know, Lisa. It might be better if we all waited until morning now. Perhaps it would be better if you were fresher and—'

'No! Why?'

Nick eases away as if my voice is a blast to be avoided. 'Jack hasn't seen his son in a year – because of you. Don't you think he's entitled to a little time?'

'No. He doesn't deserve anything after the way he treated him.'

Nick shakes his head as if he's weary of this conversation already. 'You need to go to sleep, Lisa. It'll all look better in the morning. I've made up the couch for you.'

'You've made up the couch for *me*?' I can't believe it. Nick has been back two minutes and is already taking control of my home. How is it that I have been evicted out of my own bed?

'I'm sorry, Lisa, I think it's safer if you sleep downstairs. Our Jack and I are going to camp out in your room. In the morning . . .'

'In the morning?'

At least he has the decency to drop his gaze to his glass. 'In the morning, Jack's going to contact social services. He wants to tell them that he plans to take Jack back full-time. He says . . .'

'He says *what*?'

'Lisa.' He sighs like a dying man's final fight. 'He wants to make what you've done, official. He wants it recorded in case you ever try anything again. But he's being reasonable – he says, if you let them go without any trouble, then he won't file the complaint with the police. You don't want that: kidnap carries a heavy custodial sentence.'

I stare at Nick. Our eyes lock together across the table, across the years, across the wasteland of our disappointment. This is all we have now between us – an unspoken but shared sadness for how it turned out. Our hopes, our dreams: our *baby*.

Nick's a good man and always was, and it's to my shame that I let anyone else think otherwise. Even now, after all these years, I'm amazed I can see the memory of my love for him so clearly.

'I'm sorry that this has happened when, before all this, you were so great for little Jack. I know you think of him as your own,' he says as he takes my hand.

Nick means this to be kind, but I shake him away. 'After all we went thorough together, I can't believe you'd help him to take my Jack from me.'

'But he's not—' He doesn't finish, looking quickly away, but I hear it anyway: *He's not your Jack.*

My hand grips my glass, but it's empty. I pause before pouring any more into it, but then I think: *Fuck it.* I know I'm not going anywhere tonight. My body is shot; I've got a stolen shotgun lying outside the back door; for all I know the police or the farmer are looking for a crazy woman who broke into a farmhouse to steal it; my feet are so damaged I couldn't even put Crocs on; a head injury; a burnt, drugged self; I've done enough visits to prisons to know I never want to be in one and now Nick's presence bringing my old pain into even sharper focus.

It's game over.

I'm not sure I've got more fight in me anyway – not when I see that neatly cut cable tie. I wish I could place the memory of it coming off my hands. I was so sure I burnt it off, but maybe I never did. I can't remember.

I catch Nick looking at me as I look at it. I know he knows what I'm thinking. Angry, I give him a jab back. 'Did Anne-Marie let you out tonight then?'

'Don't, Lisa.'

'Don't?' I'm a raging lion. No. I'm a *cornered* raging lion. I hate not being able to remember about the cable tie. And I hate that another woman has succeeded with my husband where I failed. I met her once: insipid, thick, just too nice. Gawky-looking too. But apparently better at marriage than I am. And worst of all: she is a better mother than me. If we've had children with the same man and her children are normal, what does that suggest about me? I can't bear it. 'Don't *what*?' I challenge.

He shakes his head as if he was expecting this mention of Anne-Marie.

'Where is she?'

'At home with the girls.' His voice is careful, considered.

The girls. Feel the burn, Lisa, feel it deep. Girls who probably play piano, dance, and pass their tests like they were born to do nothing else but be perfect and easy and straightforward and nice and, and, and – *normal.*

I bet they are normal.

I bet they've never snapped their pet's back under a Woolworths broom handle.

Winston.

He's a lifetime away but suddenly I see him, panting his smile, the drool falling from his velveteen, flobby mouth as he gazes at me with loving eyes.

'Don't do this, Leese.'

Nick is covering his eyes, but it just makes me angry. I want to thump the table but my wrists won't let me. 'You've traitored Winston's memory.'

Nick barely flinches. 'I loved that dog, too, but it was twenty years ago. It *has* to be water under the bridge.' He squares up to me in his seat and sighs. 'Lisa, I'll tell you again: I'm not here to side with him. But just because someone is an awful, violent, challenging child, does not mean they are not entitled to raise their own son, if they so wish.'

'But you know how dangerous he is.'

'Yes, agreed, he *was* utterly dreadful – *but*. I'm telling you this and you have to accept it: as an adult he is squeaky clean. This kid is his and therefore if he wants to raise him, he can. You don't have to like it and maybe there's even a bit of me that's . . . a little anxious about it too, but the facts are the facts. The law is on his side.'

'*He killed him.*' I swipe at my glass and it smashes to the floor, a punctuation mark to my anger. I feel unreasonable; melodramatic; off-key, but . . . . I still trust my instincts.

Nick doesn't move. I sit watching him, only hearing the sound of my rapid breathing. I wait. I want Nick to react. He may have fully forgotten what he was like, but I haven't. And with Jack upstairs with him, it's never been more important for him to remember.

When he doesn't say anything, I decide to prod again. 'I loved that dog.'

'Did you?' He says it so quietly, I'm not sure he has even said it.

But the way he looks at me . . . in my hands now is the cut cable tie – why am I holding this of all things? I turn it between sweating fingers, seeing again the neat edges, not burnt at all – not as I remembered.

sixty-eight:

– now –

I feel the throb of my burns; I turn over my wrists and stare at them. I appraise them in the light; they are not as bad as I thought. Perhaps I didn't hold them over the flames as long as it felt like. Maybe time constricts and expands. The blue light of my burns starts to thrum in time with my head. I can feel a scratching of wanting to unlock some memory – something perhaps gone, long gone . . .

. . . or perhaps it was never there.

Nick has been gone so long, our quarrels too antique to have life, but it still feels vital that I'm understood. 'Don't you remember,' I say, wanting to steer the conversation towards what I want to talk about – not this, never this – 'how difficult Jack was when he was young?'

Nick nods, again rubbing his face to show how tired he is. 'Of course I do. Who could forget?'

'The violence? You haven't forgotten?' For one awful moment, I think he's going to deny it. I think he's going to say that it was all my imagination.

'I remember, Lisa. I couldn't forget something like that.' He looks at the smashed glass on the floor and then at me, before he gets up to fetch a glass of water. 'He was a very, very difficult child.'

I pause, nearly lose courage, but still want to know. 'Your girls, they're not . . .?'

He turns off the tap and looks at his glass filled with water as if the answer is there. Of course he understands what the implication of this question is to me.

'They're fine,' he says finally. He puts the water in front of me.

I remember looking out of an upstairs window, listening to Nick smashing our plates and knowing it was over. Perhaps it wasn't just my DNA. 'And your marriage?' *Do you smash plates? Does she smash glasses?*

'Anne-Marie is good to me.' He's found the dustpan and brush. I watch him sweep up the broken glass, which is now a metaphor for my heart. It takes time to sweep in the grout, and he covers the whole floor very carefully – it keeps him too busy to look at me. I watch him, this man, my husband for many years, but not now, now someone else's. She's lucky I think, Anne-Marie. 'So, she treats you nicely?'

His foot triggers the bin lid and he tips the glass in. 'Yes, she does. She's very kind.'

'Was I kind?' This matters suddenly, even after all these years, it matters more than anything.

He looks up, but looks away too quickly. 'You did the best you could.' He reverted to staring into the bin.

'What does that mean?' Fear flutters crow wings inside my chest. 'You don't think I was a good wife?'

'It was hard for you.' He releases the bin lid and it *clangs* shut, punctuating his statement. 'Jack was hard, even right at the beginning, even when he was tiny. It was a terrible labour – it was all just . . .'

Terrible?

'. . . from the start, just so hard.' He fills the kettle. 'We should have something hot. Tea. No more booze for you.'

'Can I have something else for the pain?' I hesitate. 'A bit more from the larder?'

'You don't need to ask me.' He laughs, but not meanly. I like the way his eyes crinkle now; it suits him. 'You never used to ask my permission.'

'My head hurts.' I sound like I'm grumbling. I'm surprised when Nick gets up and goes to the larder. He comes back with a light dose of Valium.

'How did you know these were what I wanted?'

'They always left you in the best mood.'

I swallow them. 'I didn't know that you . . . noticed what I took.'

Nick sighs and briefly closes his eyes. 'Lisa.' He pauses. 'There were times . . . there were lots of times when you . . . just weren't there.'

I open my mouth to argue: I was always there. But of course, he doesn't mean that. I know what he means. I feel my throat thicken.

Maybe he feels it too because he rests his palm lightly on my arm. 'You did your best. I know you did your best and I never doubted that, not once.'

I open my mouth to respond, but I don't know what to respond to.

He increases his pressure on my arm, just enough for me to know he's about to say something. 'You didn't grow up with a family. You didn't know what it would look like.'

'Are you saying this, all this, is because of *me*? Jack's behaviour is because of *me*?'

Nick looks puzzled, his eyebrows drawing together. 'Don't you think that? Isn't that what you thought went wrong between us?'

'No! He was born . . .' I yank my arm away from his touch. I want to say he was born *wrong*, but that sounds brutal. 'He just came out that way. He was just . . . angry.'

Nick doesn't say anything, but he pours himself another drink. Just for himself. Up until now, Nick has been quiet, kind, but when he speaks his voice comes like a punch. '*You* were so angry, Lisa.'

'Me?' Why are we still talking about me?

'Yes, you were – always.' He holds his chin up like he's a defiant child. 'Nothing would stop your anger. You would be angry over anything, everything. All the time. Only that,' he said, jabbing a finger at the larder, 'would keep you quiet.'

I shake my head, bewildered. 'I'm not an angry person; in fact I'm the least angry person I know.'

Nick is rubbing his finger around the rim of the glass again; he never used to have this habit and I decide I don't like it; it's irritating and a clear excuse not to look at me. Then he surprises me by both looking at me and speaking. 'Lisa, your mother was taken to prison when you were eight after she killed your abusive father. You were the same age as little Jack is now – I can't imagine how awful that was for you. So, of course you're angry. Just because you don't shout and throw things, doesn't mean you didn't show it. You just showed it in a different way, a *withheld* way. You were always so . . . remote. It was as if . . .' He turns his head, his mouth pursed, clearly trying to reach the right word. ' . . . as if you were *careful* of being too close to us.'

I can't even breathe. It occurs to me that I might die tonight; I might have a heart attack. I am overwhelmed. It then occurs that actually I might *want* to die, just here and now, I could just expire. Nick will look after Jack; he's a kind man and I know he can be trusted.

'So, although I know you loved Winston, what I mean is you were always *cool* with him.' He took my arm briefly. 'I hope I'm saying it right. I don't want to offend. And I certainly don't want to blame you. Jack was bloody *awful* – and you got the brunt of it, for sure. I worked long hours – we needed the money and I was too bloody ambitious. It was all our fault, all of us in different ways.'

If my heart were simply to stop beating, I could be with my mum. I really want my mum, right now.

I press my hands against the surface of the table and I'm glad that it hurts my burns. 'He killed my mother.'

Nick sits up and looks startled. He runs his hand through his silvering hair. 'What? What do you mean, Leese?'

'I think he murdered my mother. Don't you understand? If I was angry, it was because I didn't know how to handle a boy capable of such things. I knew what he was like – I always did, but you – you . . .' I feel angry now I'm making the accusation. *See?* a thought whispers – *he's right, you are so angry.*

But I dismiss this: of course it's right to be angry in such circumstances. It would be wrong *not* to be. Instead I plough on, feeling myself warm to this. Enough is enough. 'You, Nick, were always out working.'

Nick holds up a hand, tries to interrupt, but I won't have it. 'You!' I continue hotly. 'It's all right for you to be bloody contrite about it now, but the reality was that I was stuck at home with him every day, day in, day out, on my own, doing it all. Only one day off from him a week and that was thanks to your mother! At best it was boring, and at worst, I knew I was dealing with a psychopath! Don't shake your head at me: he frightened me, even then!'

He tries to interrupt me again, even standing now. But I answer him by rising out of my own chair. '*You* got to be busy and virtuous,' I continue, jabbing my finger at him, 'but *I* was isolated because I was going through this big thing with our son and I couldn't tell anyone. I've always been on my own – all my life. And having a family wasn't like I thought it would be. I blame myself, of course I do, but I also blame you,' I say as I jab again, 'and I blame him,' I say, pointing upstairs, crying now. 'He just shut me out, even from the beginning. He wouldn't even breastfeed! Do you remember?'

Nick nods slowly, never dropping his eye contact with me. I can tell he's remembering.

'Do you remember the pinching of the other children at nursery? The biting? Can you remember the manager ending up asking him to leave? And the next one and the one after that?' I rub my hand against my eyes, as if by forcing them to shut, I can no longer see – no longer remember.

But I do remember and it hurts.

'But how is it that after a few years of being with the lovely Anne-Marie you get to remember a different version, one that blames me and exonerates *him*?' I jab a finger in the direction of upstairs. 'Of course, if you don't have to blame your own flesh and blood, you don't have to bear any responsibility. How bloody convenient.'

His eyes widen a fraction and I know my dart has hit the bullseye.

I'm hot now with rage, and the heat makes me braver than anyone. 'Yes, I know I'm a pill addict, but when you're raising a child that's dangerous and no one is around to hold you at night, do you blame me for blurring the edges of my reality? I was still there every day, doing the laundry, serving the breakfast, making his bed. Then he kills my mother like a brat breaking a toy and yet *I'm* branded the angry one?' My voice drops to a new low pitch I haven't used before. 'And I haven't even told you about the fire I think he started that and killed fourteen people I loved from work – yes, I'm not *sure* he did – but in my heart, I believe he did. And since I *always* loved him, *never* treated him badly, *always* did my best – I am not responsible for that. So yes, I'm angry. *I'm. So. Bloody. Angry.* And that's OK. So, if you don't mind – and even if you do, I'm going to get my boy.'

sixty-nine:

– now –

Nick holds his hands palms out to show he means me no harm. 'Lisa,' he says, using his best taming-the-tigers voice.

He stares at me for a long time.

I realise I'm holding my breath, waiting.

Waiting.

Save me from myself, Nick, I think savagely, desperately. *Perhaps you were the only one who ever could.* I love this man still, I suddenly think, both savagely and with sorrow. I love him and I have missed him and I have to stay silent about it. I suddenly feel the extent of how much I have missed him, through my addled, pain-filled, opiate-soaked brain. I want to step into his arms and press my face against his neck and inhale the smell of him. I don't want to have to fight with our son anymore and I don't want to try to save anyone anymore. I am tired and in him I could find rest.

I don't want to do this, I realise. I don't want to keep running. I don't want to keep looking over my shoulder. I want to live somewhere where there are people; I want to drink a decent coffee; where I can get a dog and talk to other dog owners in the park; where Jack can go back to school. I want to smell the sea again. I want these things. These are normal things.

I think I even want a man. I can't have this one anymore; there are too many feelings between us that aren't just love. There's too much disappointment, too much hurt for us to find a way back to each other. And he already has another – *better* – family. But I realise that I do want to love another man again. I want to be able to rest my head on someone's shoulder again. I want to move to slow music with someone; I want to cook a curry for someone who wants to eat it. I want to go to bed with someone who makes me laugh; who thinks I'm interesting . . . sexy even. Golly, I want to find the depths of another who isn't just me. I really, really want these things.

I can't have any more of this: this isolation.

I'm an island and I have been all of my life. Growing up first with my maternal grandmother – and then when she died, my father's sister – and my mother in prison, I never knew anyone who had the same experiences as I did. No one who knew what it's like to look at your father dying with the blood pumping out of him, out of his neck, and –

– what it is to hold the knife. But holding the knife wasn't the problem. It's what I did *before* then that was the problem. That is what I can never truly, fully accept. It took anger, it took fear, it took force and it took for him to be asleep first. It took for me to feel it was the right thing.

Even after, to feel the mass of it and the weight of the shock at what happened is all just stuff, awful stuff around what I did that blew my life and the lives of my family apart. It was so messy: it was such a surprise.

I remember looking up and seeing my surprise mirrored on my mother's face. Her shock and horror reflecting my own. I'd seen my father threaten my mother with a knife so many times – saw him rest the point on her neck for a game. But now he was gone and it seemed so clear, no more complicated than a simple equation: three minus one equals better.

Seeing her face, though, I knew I'd got it wrong.

Secrets like that can hold you back. They hold you back from developing real friendship. They hold you back from having a happy marriage. They hold you back from trusting your own child.

seventy:

– now –

Nick says: 'Lisa.'

His voice is really soft. I stop looking at the knife and instead look at him. He is still standing there with his palms up. I've been gone a while, I realise. Somewhere else; some other foggy world in my brain.

'Nick?' I speak so he knows I am with him.

'Lisa.' His voice is calm, but clear.

'I'm listening.' He always liked me to tell him that I was listening. I used to be irritated: I thought it was to do with his job; it was the cop in him that demanded I stay focused. Now ... now I'm not so sure. Maybe Nick helped me more than I gave him credit for. I'm just not sure about so much.

'*Lisa.*' His craggy face is serious. 'Jack didn't kill your mother.'

'How do you know? You weren't there, I was.'

'Because I saw the autopsy report.' His breath leaves his body like the longest sigh. 'Lisa, she died of natural causes. She had a massive heart attack – no one can fake that. I should know, shouldn't I? As a copper? Her doctor confirmed she'd had high blood pressure for years. And she was smoking pot – did you know that?'

I sink into the kitchen chair, never once taking my eyes off Nick. I knew about her blood pressure because I found her pills, but I still can't believe it's true, I just can't. I tell him this and Nick patiently repeats what he's told me. He adds medical jargon as a way of adding authenticity but I still don't believe our son wasn't involved.

'But why? Why would you rather think that your mother has been murdered, than just accept that she died of one of the most common causes of death, in this country?'

'Because of her neighbour for a start! April Dale was clear that she thought someone had broken in . . .' Was she? Even as I say it, I'm rethinking the scene.

She didn't say that.

Nick speaks at my silence. 'Mrs Dale told me that your mother had come round in the morning needing milk. She hadn't brought anything to pour it into, so Mrs Dale offered to tip some into a mug for her. She said your mum was flustered and pale, and just wanted to borrow the whole thing and said she'd bring it straight back—'

'Flustered because he was there!'

'Or because her heart was already in trouble. Your mum didn't come back. Mrs Dale got caught up in a long phone conversation and afterwards she wanted a cup of tea herself and so Mrs Dale went to retrieve her milk and that's when she found your mother dead on her bed.'

Nick just looks at me, waiting for some reaction, or perhaps is just being kind and giving me time to process it. 'Lisa, Mrs Dale said that when she found you mum's body, she came out into the hall. She was about to ring for an ambulance, when she saw you standing by the door, so she let you in first. The rest you know.'

He sits back as if satisfied with this version of events. But this can't be right – it can't be. 'She gave me the cash my mum kept for emergencies.'

'Yes. She was flustered and told me it felt wrong to keep it in her flat with your mum being gone. But it wasn't a statement of not expecting to see you again: she was confused when you weren't at the funeral,' he says. 'She asked me and Jack as—'

'*He* went to my mother's funeral?'

'Of course. It was his grandmother's funeral – why wouldn't he?'

The pain is terrible – he was there and I wasn't. I'm so confused. I shut my eyes briefly and try to remember what happened. He was there, I know he was there, at my mother's. I just need facts to convince Nick.

To stay convinced myself.

No. *No.* I am convinced.

'I couldn't tell her why you weren't there – we knew you'd run with Jack but we thought it was just for a few days. We thought you'd been overcome with grief but would be back for the funeral. We phoned you, texted you; it all went to your voicemail. And don't think I didn't tried to trace you: I know you binned your phone. You went off-grid.' He lets go of me and sits next to me and takes the knife out of my hand. I let him. 'We were both very upset.'

'You and Mrs Dale?'

Nick's forehead creases with annoyance and he presses his fingers against his temples. '*Jack*. Goodness, Lisa, if I'd stayed with you, you'd have driven me to drink.'

I want to say something biting but I'm thinking about my mum's funeral; I want to know what Mrs Dale said about me not being there, but all I can do right now is try to imagine my son upset.

I can't imagine it. Instead, I remember him being upset about his Peter Rabbit money-box. Thinking of the tears, the snot, the absolute rage, I remember what he did. I also remember what Nick did, his standing by and watching our son attack me for too long before he finally stepped in and stopped it. He later apologised: he'd called me names and was furious himself, but he knew he was in the wrong.

I forgave him, though, because I shouldn't have broken it. Neither of us always got everything right.

'We thought you'd be there, Lisa, and you weren't.'

I don't need to look at him to hear his surprise and disappointment.

'We thought you would turn up and Jack would be dressed in a little black suit and you'd apologise—'

'Apologise! Apologise? For saving Jack?'

'What did you have to save him from?' Nick's hand is flat against the table, but I notice that its tightening to a fist. 'What? He had a place in a great school; he lived mostly with you but also saw your mum and his dad every week. Jack had been the most settled he'd been in years, he had a job and was finally doing okay, he'd managed to rent a lovely flat, but you ruined it—'

'How do you know the flat was lovely?'

'I viewed it with him and then gave him the deposit.'

'*You*?'

'Yes. Who else was going to help him?'

My mouth is incredibly dry. 'Why didn't you come and see me, if you were in the area?'

Nick rubs his face; I know he's tired. 'Sorry.' He shrugs a little. 'I should've done. Planned to, even. But we were buzzing around, so busy with getting furniture, prices for carpets and things, and Amelia – my daughter – had a dance thing one time and flu another and I had to get back, you know, long drive back and all.' He shrugged again. 'I meant to, though. Wanted to.' He pats my hand, the dry gesture that should only be reserved for maiden aunts.

'Well, what about when I rang you? I rang to tell you that Jack had turned up, wanting Jack at the weekends, and you never said you knew about it!'

He covers his face briefly. 'My mistake. When you rang, I was literally keys in hand, about to go shopping, Anne-Marie was in a tizz about guests we had due and I felt bad, back-footed because Jack had asked that I ring you and I didn't . . . I forgot, things were busy. I did ask you to call me back. I wanted to explain properly, but you didn't call back. It was easier for me to let it go.'

'All that plotting with him.' I shake my head, bewildered. 'I'm so shocked that you'd help him set up round the corner from me and not find a space in your life to clue me in.'

'Don't get angry. I realise I was wrong. Truth is, Leese, I just put it off. I knew you'd go mental about it and . . . I just put it off. Too long, I know. I am sorry.'

I didn't know what to say to him. I just felt overwhelmingly heartbroken. I thought of us kissing by the bus stop, that first time; his hands in my hair, the urgency of his mouth. I thought of us lying in bed, making sure that every bit of our bodies were touching whilst we stared into each other's eyes. And now, even when he was in the neighbourhood seeing our son, there was nothing left for me . . . no wanting to see me. I felt ridiculous for thinking it, but I realised for the first time that Nick wasn't even a little bit in love with me anymore.

Not even a little bit. It seemed so incomprehensible, when I felt like I did, that we'd had so much love and – for him at least – it had drained to nothing.

I sit there, trying to breathe. The drugs have dug in deep now; I can survive anything. And it feels good: now I'm on the safe ground of righteousness because Nick let me down. No one could pass that off as a medical misunderstanding; this was not me getting it wrong. I realise it's time to dig in: I want Jack back.

It was me that lifted him to safety. 'Nick, no more of this. The facts are plain. He was keeping him in a *cage*. The flat was disgusting, poo on the floor, mess everywhere.' I lifted my chin. 'I want an apology for saying I ruined our son's little set-up. Then I want you to come upstairs and help me rescue Jack.'

But Nick doesn't ask after the cage. I thought he would; I thought his eyes would widen and he'd interrupt and say: *What cage, Lisa? Jack didn't mention that.* And then I would tell him, and Nick would become angry and say: *You did right, Lisa. I understand now! Let's go and tell Jack now that you must have the boy and we'll fight him all the way. Together!*

But he doesn't say any of that.

Instead all he does is look at me with a sourness, a seriousness, as if he's tasted old milk. 'You got it so bloody wrong.' He shakes his head, slowly.

I swallow against the dry in my throat: this is not going the way I thought it would. I'm confused why this is about me when I did not put anyone in a cage. My belly feels funny; perhaps I was the only one who ate something old, something sour. Why is it that he looks so angry with me?

His hand balls to a fist. 'You silly, *silly* ... I'm sorry, Lisa, but *really*. You've ruined so many lives. For what? A drugged-out mind's misunderstanding. You didn't know, did you? You didn't know the facts and you jumped to one hell of a conclusion, all on your own. But that's you, isn't it? Always running in your own lane, no thought for anyone else.' He shakes his head again, goes to say something, but stops himself. 'You didn't know,' he finally says, but this time, he just sounds so sad.

The cold has slid from my stomach down to my bladder. I want to wee. I am frightened about what he is going to say. I thought I was on safe ground, finally. I don't want to hear I was wrong again.

I don't want to know, so very, very much.

seventy-one:

– now –

'The puppy, Lisa. You didn't know about Lennie, did you?' I don't answer but he bangs his hand against the table. 'The *puppy*, Lisa. Lennie. You didn't know, did you?'

I find my head shaking. No, I don't know what he's talking about. I don't know who Lennie is. I'm a little transfixed by the anger in Nick's voice. He looks like a caricature of himself. If he was a cartoon, he would be drawn with a pink face and puffs of steam leaving his ears. I'm properly stoned, I realise, sorry, not sorry.

'Say it,' he says, slamming his fist on the table. 'Say you don't know what I'm talking about.'

I focus, now a little scared. 'I don't know what you're talking about.'

'He got a puppy, Lisa.' His eyes are cold, hard and intent upon my own. Clearly I'm supposed to understand something that I'm not catching. What is the significance of this?

He uses my words back at me: 'The *significance*, Lisa, is that that was what the cage was for. I helped him make it. He had Jack's old baby playpen and someone he knew suggested he tape the two together, so that's what we did. Yes, he should've planned better, yes, he shouldn't have fallen for a sob story down the pub and come back with a puppy, but golly, it was so cute. Still is.'

He rubs his face. When he speaks, he sounds sad again. Suddenly I wish for angry. 'He wanted to make a real home for Jack. That's why he agreed to get a pet. He didn't tell you because he thought you'd lecture him about a dog being in a flat, but he thought . . .' He picks up his empty glass and refills it with water. Then he looks at me a long time. 'Tomorrow, you need to go to hospital.'

I feel a crawl of fear: perhaps he doesn't mean a normal hospital, perhaps he means something else. Something with doors that buzz and treatment plans for substance misuse and people who expect you to talk about your problems.

'Why are you not asking me about the puppy?' He gives an angry huff of breath. 'Damn you, Lisa, you were always so fixed, so unreachable. Do you not understand what I'm saying? Jack was only in the cage because he insisted on keeping it warm for Lennie. You know what little kids are like when they get an idea in their heads.'

I blink; my eyeballs are so dry, it hurts to move the eyelids. Puppy? I'm hearing him properly now. I'm seeing the flat. I'm seeing the ripped, torn material; the newspaper spread on the floor; the ripped sofa; the old rope; the poo. It's not living the dream, but . . . but perhaps that was the sign of a puppy playing. I think of the kitchen – clean and tidy. The hallway that always smelt fresh.

I remember Jack, looking at me calmly. I thought it meant something else . . . but perhaps he simply was calm?

'Where was your son when I found Jack in the cage? And where was this puppy?'

'My son?' He gives a dry laugh. 'What, where was *our* son when you found Jack in the cage?' He stares at me with real pity. 'He'd popped round to the neighbour's flat to get some loo roll. The puppy had pooed in the flat. Very *sensibly* –' he clearly takes pleasure in emphasising this word – 'he was glad Jack agreed to stay in the cage so that he couldn't go near the poo.'

'Then why was I able to come in, look around for a while, if our son was just next door getting loo roll? That would only take a couple of minutes.' I'm looking for holes in this story. I know I sound desperate; I am. Because I'm visualising the flat and I'm seeing it differently now. I'm remembering how easy it was to break open the makeshift cage – how I'd tried to cut it open before realising it was hinged. Easy to open. Not a cage for Jack but a dog crate. I feel a dull, cold, dropping sensation in my stomach.

'The first neighbour didn't answer and the second one, their disabled mother had fallen and they needed Jack's help getting her up off the floor.'

'Then where was the puppy?' My voice is a plaintive cry. 'Why was the puppy not in there?'

'Because our Jack is not a complete div – he didn't want to leave a new puppy unsupervised with Jack.'

I think of Winston: was Jack scared for the puppy or for the boy?

Nick is continuing. 'So he picks the puppy up and nips next door to get the loo roll. He only meant to be gone for a minute. And I know what you're going to say – he shouldn't have left Jack, not even for a moment, and what parent can say that they haven't taken the same risks themselves?' His eyes are fierce: I daren't take the challenge.

'A puppy?' is all I can say.

'Yes, Lisa. You ruined young Jack's life because of a puppy. You ripped him from his father's life because of a puppy. You didn't attend your own mother's funeral and you stopped me from seeing my grandson, you've brought him out here in the middle of nowhere, and Jack says you've stopped Jack from going to school, *all because of a puppy*!'

He stands up. 'I hope you're proud of yourself.'

seventy-two:

– now –

A puppy. Can this be true? I don't know what to say. I'm weak, I'm hurting and all I can think of is the gun lying on the lawn. I remember Erica's face as she looked down on me from the landing, in silent condemnation. How could this be all my fault?

'What about the fire?' I finally manage, weakly. Perhaps I've been reading everything wrong. Is that possible?

But I do want to know about the fire. It's all I've got now.

'The fire? At your work?'

I can only nod to say: *Yes, that is what I mean.* I wonder if Nick will judge me harshly if I go to the larder and get a little something else. Just another 2 mg of diazepam will do it. Just a little something else to take this growing horror away.

For the first time I see a shadow of doubt cross Nick's features. He was always confident with me, but less confident in his decision-making. He changed though as he matured, I suppose it was what helped him progress in his career. I don't like to think about how maybe both things happened when he was no longer around Jack and me.

'The fire started in the laundry room.'

'I know that, Nick. I kept in touch with work. My colleague sent me the fire report. An accelerant was used. The window was left open and it was poured through.'

'That could've been by anyone.'

'Or our son.'

'I know through work that the owner of the nursing home was dodgy. They'd overextended themselves, setting up home after home after home. They had big debts. It could've been connected to that. Or something else entirely. No one even looked at Jack for the arson – why would they? It's not always about you, Lisa.'

'Someone did it. And you don't know that he didn't.'

He presses his temples with this fingertips. 'But we *don't* know . . . and we have to be cautious.'

I think of Mungo and Selena and feel panic. 'So what's all this leading to? Telling me I'm wrong about everything. Sitting here, laying out evidence after evidence, that I'm terrible and what, our son is just a victim of me? Because of my childhood, I'm just delusional about my mother, the fire, the dog, I get what you're saying. I don't believe it, but what I want to know, is what's next? You said you wouldn't take sides, yet you clearly are. You say that Jack is going with his father tomorrow and I'm just going to wait it out in my own home, tucked up like a guest on the sofa. So what's this leading up to?' I feel a jelly-fish whip of anger. 'Let's have it now, Nick. You've done your copper thing. Broken down my alibi, so let's just get to the point now, shall we.

'What's the message you're delivering?'

He spreads his hands out against the wooden knots and whorls of the table. He stares at them as if they are going to save him from something. 'Lisa, in the morning it will be time to say goodbye to Jack. I'm sorry. They are both going to leave. Jack doesn't want you to know where. He's taking little Jack with him and he doesn't want you to see little Jack ever again. I'm sorry. I realise this is hard. I can't do anything about it – I want you to know that I did speak up for you. But ultimately, I'm here to make sure there's no ugliness in front of the child. That wouldn't be good for anyone.'

Nick has the decency to get up and put the kettle on so he doesn't have to witness my drowning panic.

Grief is instant. I start crying. Eventually I ask: 'Why won't you help me?'

But Nick mishears me, perhaps because of my tears or perhaps because of his guilt, because he answers a different question: 'I tried! Before we were over, I really tried. I tried to discipline him, intervene . . . but you wouldn't let me.'

'You didn't, you didn't!'

'I did, Lisa. I wanted him to go somewhere better for him than us – a kids' home or something. I didn't know what else to do – I didn't know how to make a difference.' His voice rises to a retch. It hurts me to hear this powerful man so fractured. 'If I could've changed things, I would've. But you wanted to manage by yourself. You would hide from me how bad it was – you would hide it from everyone.'

'I was ashamed!' I shout back, crying harder now. 'I was *embarrassed*.'

'You shouldn't have been in front of me.' He rubs his temples, like he's in pain.

'Maybe not, but it wasn't just that – I had to protect him from the world. And from himself. I couldn't let him go into a unit. What sort of mother would I have been who did that?'

'A sane one?' His face drops. 'Sorry, Lese, sorry I said that. He's turned out well. You did the right thing. I couldn't see it at the time, but you were right. And I want you to see now that you were. He's different now. He's matured. And that is all credit to you.'

'But what if it isn't? What if you only think he got better because you're looking at him from a distance? '

'I think he's changed, Lisa.' He strokes my hair. 'It's been a long time.'

'But how do you *know*?'

He rubs at his temples again; I bet he wishes he was sitting on the sofa next to Anne-Marie instead of having this conversation with me. But that thought doesn't make me feel bitter – I don't blame him. I wouldn't want to talk to me either.

I just wish that I knew who I could've been if I hadn't done what I had done. My eight-year-old self made a flash decision and it's still shaping my life. I don't even remember making it. I understand why I killed my father, but who I could've been if I hadn't, I will never know. Who my parents could've been, what would've become of our family, I will also never know. There's a lot of sadness in that. That's a sadness that was between my mother and me – she never told and I never told. Even to the end, she protected me.

I think in life, all the love songs and all the poetry are about wanting that connection with that special someone who understands us – truly understands the bones and blood of us. Friends, lovers, even children, see us for who we are and it's a real self. But it's that special connection that is one in a million: it's the love that, if we are lucky, we have once in a lifetime, that tortures.

I could never have that connection.

Oh yes, you're a handsome man, we could fall in love, get through all that shit that everyone gets through – but not have the same thing in common. We like the same songs, we love the same literature but we don't both know what it is to watch a sharp knife held against the skin of our father's neck and see it pressed hard enough so it didn't just cut, but cut deep enough to end life.

No one knows how I feel and I can't tell them about the memories that shadow me. So I can't share who I am.

Oh yes, we went through similar things, didn't we? We know what it is to watch how quickly the blood pumps out of an open wound (shockingly so) and how the eyes do open. He was asleep: but he didn't stay asleep. Despite the suddenness of his death, he was afforded one last waking moment. I alone saw his eyes open and meet mine. I alone saw his stare: his shock, anger, fear.

Then the hurt of betrayal.

About how the hands don't reach for the knife-bearer, but instead clutch at their own throat, blood pushing through the fingers. And then there was no grip.

It's a memory that keeps me alone; an archipelago of one. No one knows about the road I have taken. The person I might have been, I will never know.

Instead, I am left with me. And I don't think about what I have done, I really don't. It's just . . . sometimes, if I was careless and I looked directly into my son's eyes, I knew I could really see my father. How funny he has come back to get me, not through dreams but through my own body. It's like standing in a cave and shouting, and now my own scream has come back, bouncing off the stone walls of time, finding its way back to me.

I press my hands against my forehead. I think I'm going to have to stop the echo.

'I'm going to accept it, Nick.' I say it and it surprises me – I can see by his widening eyes that it's surprised him too. 'I still think,' I add carefully, 'that he's not the best parent for Jack. But I can't fight it. I've got no rights. Besides, perhaps I'm not much better.'

'Oh, Lisa,' he says and squeezes my arm. 'Obviously, I don't really know little Jack as well as I probably should, but it's been great catching up with him tonight and he's a lovely boy. Bright, sweet, you've clearly done a great job. *Again*. You've done a great job *again*.'

I ignore the flattery. 'You promise me though, Nick, if you're supporting this, you have to keep in touch with Jack. I bet his dad won't let me, but you have to speak with him on Skype or something *at least* once a week if they don't live near you and be careful to watch for signs that he's happy. Or unhappy.' Even as I say it, my heart breaks because I understand just how impossible a task that is. Nick doesn't even really know him.

But finally I see that there's nothing I can do.

I debate just how I might fall apart tonight, when Nick's phone rings. It's her: his wife, I think. Anne-Marie.

He answers it. 'Oh, hi!' He sounds surprised. He glances at me, before subtly turning his body away from me. 'Yes, we are done here.' I watch him closely. He seems relaxed; I can tell by his shoulders, his easy movements away from the table. He doesn't want me to hear this conversation.

'Oh!' he says, instantly changing. He looks at me now. 'Why?' His voice is a bark, and he frowns. 'Where?' He sounds cross. What has she done?

'I'm coming. Don't go anywhere. No! Now. *Now.* I said so, didn't I? I won't be long.'

He stares at his phone as if it has let him down. 'Fuck,' he says.

He looks at me like he's trying to move rusty cogs in his jaw. What has she demanded? I wonder.

'It's our Jack.' His breath comes jagged, panting, and I know at once he's nervous.

My breath freezes: I don't move. I can see in his face, the drawn eyebrows themselves a question mark, that something isn't as he expected it. He's nervous: and that makes me nervous. Suddenly, the thought that something has happened to my son is the worst thing in the world.

'He's not here.'

'What do you mean, he's not here? He's upstairs with little Jack.'

'No. He was but . . . he's just said he's not here *now*.' Nick is already looking around the kitchen. 'I've got to find my car keys. Something's wrong.'

'He can't have left . . .' But I realise he could've done. Right out of the front door. No, I would've heard the creaking of the stairs. I bet he went out of the bedroom window.

'Where is he now?' My voice is so high and clipped it doesn't even sound like me. 'What did he say?'

'He's just down the lane. Something . . . I don't know. He says he had to get out of here.'

He stops looking around the kitchen and instead stares with an intensity at me instead. 'You go upstairs and check on Little Jack and I'll go and find our son.'

I hold on to the table, gripping the pine tight under my fingertips. 'What do you think's happened?'

He shakes his head, his bewilderment clear. 'I don't know, Lisa. I thought . . .' He bites his bottom lip. 'Go. I'll get my keys, I've just put them down somewhere . . . but go now. Stay here with Jack. Wait until you hear from me? Check that . . .'

. . . *he's OK.*

He doesn't have to say it aloud. I understand it. I see it: I see doubt and concern in his eyes. He's been so sure he's had all the answers, but now . . . now he's not so sure.

'Go *now*.'

seventy-three:

– now –

I'm no longer thinking; instead I take the stairs two at a time. I'm at the top of the landing within seconds. The floorboards complain under my feet as I cross to Jack's bedroom in a heartbeat. My hand is on the door handle before I take a breath.

My bladder is cold; my lungs are fire. I don't know what I'll find.

It occurs that there's a simple reason why my son has fled the property and left Jack here. My hand, on the door handle to Jack's bedroom, drops like a dead bird.

I remember the blood; so much blood.

Will I open the door and find that here? Will this be what structures my life? Blood and death at the start; blood and death at the end? Because if he's hurt or taken Jack, it would be the end. I would only go down and find my stash and slip them silently down my throat, until they were all gone, until I was gone. I wouldn't waste my time seeking justice – I watched my mother lose twenty-two Christmases with me at the request of Her Majesty's sense of justice, before she was finally released. I'll not waste my time.

I grip the handle and open the door.

The room is hot. It's dark, but the curtains are now open again. The flickering light from the grate reminds me of Sunningdale burning. Jack is in bed, a small hump of perfection under the duvet. So small, it's as if he's not even really there.

I cross the room. I need to know.

I stand above the shape in the duvet, my hand hesitating as I reach out. I realise so much, and I embrace my addiction and all that it's caused, if only, only, that this anxiety is also true. I make a deal with God. *Please, God, I'll accept my faults, if Jack is safe – please. I'll be better if I can just be wrong about this.*

My fingertips touch the top of the cover and just before I pull it back, I realise that I haven't seen him move – it's motionless, this lump, the same as if it's just a childhood trick with a pillow, the oldest in the book. I know Jack's no longer here: he's already gone.

I lift the covers.

seventy-four:

– now –

I can't believe it: Jack is here, curled foetus-like, in his pyjamas, around his favourite bunny. Is he all right?

I reach out, knowing my hand is shaking, and hear the front door slam and think: Nick has found his keys.

I touch Jack's shoulder and . . . he's breathing. *Thank you, God. Thank you, God. Thank you, God.*

I hear Nick's feet on the drive. I lean close, breathing Jack's still almost-baby smell. I want to gaze at him, drink him in, soak in his safety and nearness.

I hear the squelch of Nick's car alarm answering the key fob.

I cross to the little lead-latticed window and quickly unlatch it, pushing it open just as the car door slams. I want to call down to him and let him know Jack is fine, but he's too fast. His lights turn on, and with a roar, he's away.

He doesn't normally drive fast – he's worried. Something our son has said has upset him. I gaze into the darkness, watching his red tail lights until they suddenly vanish as he turns a corner.

I wait, expecting . . . I'm not sure what. I enjoy the feeling of the night air on my face and wait for something to change – the phone to ring, the sound of Nick's car returning. Where is my son? But the minutes pass and nothing. I continue to wait, tired, exhausted, unable to go and do anything. I'm very hungry and my wrists need attention, but all that can wait. My brain is mush with the spent emotion of my evening. I'm trying to figure it all out.

This can't be the end – there can't be all of *this* and now . . . nothing.

Somewhere, abruptly, a firework goes up into the night sky. It's early – it's not the fifth of November for nearly two weeks. The colours are bold, brilliant. The *pop-pop-pop* is loud and I lean out to shut the window against the noise in case it wakes Jack. As the burst of light catches the glass, I can see that the heat in the room has caused condensation to mist on it.

And there it is: in the light of the fireworks and the damp of the condensation, is the answer to my questions. Written in the opaque damp is a short message to me.

One letter in each diamond.

IMSTILLHERE

seventy-five:

– now –

He's sitting at the kitchen table, my son. His back is to me, his shoulders broad in a leather jacket that looks expensive. His hair is very short – I never think of him with short hair, it looks neat, tidy. He turns his head: 'Lisa! And here you are!' He sounds friendly, but I don't trust it. He doesn't look at me, not properly. I think some people could spend years in the company of my son and not realise that he only pretends to look at you – that he does all the right actions without actually making eye contact. But I see it because I see *him*.

He smiles at me over the top of a glass – just like his dad, he's drinking my whisky. 'Glad you're not crouching in the stairway now. Must've been uncomfortable for you, earlier, hiding like that from me as I went to the bathroom. Sorry about that – I heard you coming up the stairs – but when you've gotta pee, you've gotta pee.'

I pause in the doorway, shocked. I can't breathe. But not from surprise that he saw me before, cowering and afraid and yet said nothing – that's just so Jack – but because what shines through is love: I've missed him so much.

My son.

Love is amazing: how it endures even through the duress of such wanton destruction. It seems even fire doesn't turn it to ash, but instead melds into something tougher, more enduring. I could've never believed it possible. I think of my mum, what she would say if she knew I still loved my son despite what he did to her, what he did to the residents of Sunningdale. Regardless of what Nick says, I still believe my truth. And I believe that she would just love him anyway – my mother was full of love. She loved being his Nana.

'Why didn't you say something if you saw me there?'

'None of my business if you want to creep round your own home. Besides, I was being a good boy. Dad told me to leave you alone, so I did.' He pats the table as if he wants me to sit. 'I'd would've poured you a glass, but it's not your poison, is it, Lisa?'

I keep my hand on the door; my escape hatch. Like I could leave if I wanted to.

'Come on, come and sit down.' He grins. 'No point hanging around like you're going to leg it across the fields again. Although ten out of ten for effort that you did it in your socks.' He looks me up and down. 'No offence, but you look like you need a rest, now.'

'What did you do with my shoes?'

'They're just neat and tidy in the bottom of your wardrobe. No drama.'

I pull the chair back; it scrapes loudly against the slate tiles and without thinking, I glance upstairs, always on the lookout for waking Jack.

He wrinkles a lip: 'Don't worry about him – he couldn't wake if I exploded a bomb.'

Suddenly I understand: 'What did you do to him?'

His face turns towards me suddenly – again that pretence of face and near eye contact without the real thing: 'Only what you did to me.'

I press my fingertips against the wood grain as if it will suppress the scream building in me: 'How dare you. What did you use?'

'Relax Lisa, nothing of yours. But cut the indignant crap: you used to drug me all the time.'

'I didn't – how can you say such things?'

'Now, now Lisa. Is that really true? Or is that just one of the lies you tell yourself so you don't have to engage with what a shit mother you've been?' His handsome face twists to a sneer. 'To *me* anyway. Of course you're Mother of the Year to *Jack*.'

There's too much to react to; I just blink, exhausted.

'Would you,' he says, mimicking my voice now, 'like your Sleepy now, dear? It's soooo yummy!'

It sounds grotesque coming from him.

'It was only a child's antihistamine, I gave you,' I tell him. 'It was just a difficult situation and I admit, I struggled to cope. If I didn't give it to you, you would become really difficult visiting Nana. You were very challenging.'

'Well, if you will take a little kid into a terrifying prison, what do you expect?.'

'It was Nana! She wanted to see you and we had no idea when or even if, she was ever going to get out, so what was I supposed to do? Leave you at home on your own? Your father never changed his shifts or his golf or anything else he wanted to do, for me.'

He laughs.

Something in me simply shatters. I jump up out of my chair and grip my son by his shoulders. I want to shake him, punish him, but it's like shaking a boulder. I want to hit him and kiss him and hurt him and love him. I still – regardless of what Nick's told me – think he killed her, but it seems that what I feel for him is indestructible. It's hard; it's confusing; it's painful. I collapse into a boxing clinch; leaning and struggling against him. 'Did you kill her?' I finally gasp into his shoulder. 'I have to know. Please, please tell me the truth.'

I have spent the whole of the last year mourning – I don't think I will *ever* get over the loss of her.

He lets me rest for a minute but then takes me by my elbows and says: 'I didn't kill Nana on purpose, if that's what you're so pissed off about.'

I am crying and crying and crying now and I just don't think I can get my voice back. I'm not sure how long this goes on, but then I do finally sit down. 'Tell me what happened,' I finally say.

He shrugs – urgh – I hate even that casual movement of his, as if my mother's death is a casual thing.

'I went to see her and she smelt smoke and petrol on me and asked me why. When I told her, she went mad and had a heart attack. Not my fault.'

'You told her about Sunningdale?'

'She asked.'

I want to ask about Sunningdale: *Why? How?* I want to ask about Jack. But most of all, I want to know about my mum. 'Did she suffer?'

'It looked painful.'

I start crying again. 'Did you help her?'

'I don't know how to do CPR.'

'So you just watched her die?'

'Look, Lisa, Nana was always good to me. She walked herself into that grave by having a go at me, but I didn't want her to die.'

'Then why were you there?'

He shrugged: 'I thought you would turn up with Jack. I expect you did, but I wasn't going to hang around with her being dead.'

'And Sunningdale? Why?'

He lights a cigarette and shakes his head. 'You know why.'

'No, I don't know *why* you would do that. I actually have no idea.'

'Because you took Jack.' He blows the smoke out slowly. 'You pissed me off, so I thought I'd piss you off.'

I feel I could lose it. Properly lose my mind. I see their faces: Gladys Silsbury; Rose Nuttel; Maureen Squires. Dead. Killed by him. 'You were in the crowds that night, weren't you? You were watching me as the place burned?' How my voice sounds so even, I will never know.

He reaches around and locates a saucer. He flicks his ash neatly into it. I should've guessed when I saw his flat that there was a particular reason for the mess – of course there was a puppy. My son has always been meticulous with his things.

'When I saw your face, mother dearest, it was worth it.'

At his confirmation, I realise I can't give up on Jack upstairs – I have to try to get him away from this man. I press my feet against the floor to steady myself. I have to focus on saving my grandson. This is a dangerous situation and I need to be clever about it. 'Thank you for telling me. And about Nana too.' I'm satisfied with how calm I sound. It gives me the strength to continue. 'She would be glad you've been honest with me. I think I will have that drink, now, please,' I say, buying for time. I drink my water and substitute it for a double of whisky. I wonder where he put my phone. 'Top-up?' I ask him, holding the bottle up. I want him to see I'm shaking – he always liked it when I was scared and I know it'll put him at ease.

His mouth flickers with a rare smile, says, 'Lisa, you always crack me up,' but he drains his glass and holds it out for me to fill.

I know I shouldn't be drinking with him, but I don't care. Yes, I need to buy time to plan what I'm going to do next, but it's more than that. Deep in my marrow I think I might not see him again after tonight. Something in the way it has all come together makes me feel this wildness, this craziness, cannot continue.

The thought gives me courage to drag my gaze over his face: he has suffered a broken nose, I think, since I've seen him, but perhaps he's filled out a little too; and I'm glad – he looks better for it. He's gained a maturity I've not seen before. I want to ask him about his job, about his life, but he wouldn't tell me if I did. I want to put my hand over his large knuckled one – I so want to touch him and tell him I love him. My baby, my sweet, difficult, tormented baby.

'I do wish you wouldn't keep crying, Lisa.'

I swipe away the tears, not even aware that I had started again. 'Who says I'm crying?' I try to smile through the ache in my throat and the diamonds in my eyes. Despite the initial horror, it actually feels like a relief to have the truth from him. And to realise I'm not mad. But it's even more than that: I've missed him so much. It's almost as if this time without him was just marking time until this moment.

Even when he was a little boy, after he killed Winston, I would try to hold him, worried that one day he'd pick a fight he wouldn't win, and that I'd find out, many years after the event, that he died in a terrible way. But here he is and it hasn't happened. Not yet.

Sitting across from him, I want to speed this up so he's gone far away from Jack, but at the same time, I want to revel in his company, be close to him while I still can, before we say a final goodbye.

I remind myself to stick to my new game-plan-that-isn't-yet-a-plan. I need to start with finding my phone. I change the way I'm sitting, hoping to spot it, but suspect it's in my wardrobe with my shoes. 'You rang your dad – he tore out of here worried about you.'

He only raises an eyebrow as if he's learnt something new. 'You want something – I could always tell when you want something, Lisa.'

'I do want something.' *Oh, so very much.* 'Tell me the truth, please, because I have to know. I know I've disappointed you, but tell me that you do know, because it's so very important to me, that you know—'

'Spit it out.'

'I just want to know if you knew that I always lo—'

'Loved me?'

He draws on his cigarette and blows out slowly. 'I don't know why you have to assume that everything is about you. Bit of a narcissist, aren't you, Lisa?'

'No!'

'Ha! Always so easy to wind up.' He drums his fingers briefly against the table and checks the wall clock. 'Is that the right time?'

'Yes.' I wonder why he wants to know: I wish I knew how this will end. Perhaps I asked this question because he reaches out and grips my wrist. Hard. Oh, how quickly we revert to the old days. I think I might even tell him he's hurting me, just to reminisce. That's all it would be because it certainly wouldn't make him stop – it never did.

Then I look at his hand, consider what he's just said, think of the speed in which Nick sped off. 'What did you do, Jack? Where is your dad?'

He lets go of me. 'He's on an errand.'

Now that he's here, I've got the perfect opportunity to talk to him. To buy time until I can figure something out – some way of saving Jack from him – but also because I suspect I might never get another opportunity to try to get answers for the thousand questions I have about my son. 'Now it's just us, maybe we could talk a little more. Perhaps we could be honest about a few more things.'

'Like what?'

'I just want to know where we all went wrong for us.'

'Do you mean why I'm different?'

I'm surprised – I've never heard him acknowledge that he's different before. I wasn't even sure that he knew. I'm not sure if it's a trap. I play safe and raise one eyebrow: 'Different from . . .?'

'Oh, don't pretend. Or is this your way of being tactful?'

I don't say anything.

'Let me help you out. You're wondering why I just don't really care about anyone? You're wondering if it's something you've done. Oh!' he says, raising his voice to mimic me again. 'Oh! Are you all right? Poor little Jack! Poor baby! But don't mind me while I –' his face twists in fury and his voice drops an octave – 'while I drift into a drug-induced haze for a few hours and leave you all alone with nothing to do and no one to play with!'

I hold my breath. I'm scared of him, but I'm even more scared of the truth being reviewed like this. I thought I wanted honesty.

'But you don't want to hear that, do you? I'll tell you instead that it was fine; you were fine. It was all fine. I just don't care. I never have.'

I'm so overwhelmed, stunned that he knows there's something wrong with him; gobsmacked that he knows I care about him; sickeningly ashamed that my drug abuse affected him when I'd been so careful to kid myself they were only 'naps'. 'I know you don't care about *me* . . .' Pathetically I pause, hoping – still – that he'll frown and say: *No, I care about you, Mum.* When he doesn't, I feel almost amused that I am *still* so sad about this.

Then it occurs: 'But you must care about one person – you must care about your son. Otherwise, why did you try to kill me to get him back?' I say, checking over my shoulder to check he's not standing in the doorway, listening.

'I didn't try to kill you – if I'd wanted to, I would've. If you got a whack on the head, though, that's your fault – you deserved it, stealing him from me.' He gives me a sly look. 'But don't believe that guff I fed Dad. I was one step ahead of you the whole time. That day you took Jack, I got your text saying you were coming round. I was expecting you. Let's be honest, it was only a matter of time before you'd weaken and come snooping, but I knew, even before I got your message, that you were coming on *that* day. That's why I set you up with the whole Jack-in-the-puppy-cage thing.'

I stunned with the truth. That I was right all along. 'How did you know?'

'Simple. Jack was adamant that he'd put his spelling book in his bag. He's a very sensible lad, so I believed him. If he said he did, then he did.' His grin deepened. 'Which means you had to have removed it from his bag as you followed us after school, back to mine. And you would've only done that for one reason.'

I'm speechless. Finally, I say: 'You *were* behind your bedroom door.'

He laughs a little and lights another cigarette from the dying embers of his first.

'But why let me take him if you didn't want me to?'

'Because I did want you to. I never wanted Jack. I just wanted to piss you off.'

'No,' I say slowly. 'That's not true. You make it sound like you don't care about your own son.'

'Can't think where I get that from.'

I ignore the dig. 'No, I just don't believe it. I've watched you both together; all those times I've followed you home from the school pick-up, hand-in-hand. I've seen the way you both look at each other. You don't just fake that.' I stare into his face, wanting – needing – to see something. Some hint that I'm right. When I don't see anything, I push again. 'All that effort of getting a flat near the school, reeling Jack in, he's only young, you wouldn't do that. You might want to hurt me, but you're not so cruel you'd do that to a little boy, your own son.'

He just smokes and watches me.

'And all that you told Dad, you just said all that stuff to what, piss me off?'

'And him. He's no better. He abandoned us, I seem to remember, when I was only five.'

'But what are you saying? I just don't get it.' I press my fingertips against my growing headache. 'Are you saying this is just one big dig at me? That doesn't fit. If you didn't care about Jack, if you knew I was going to come to the flat and take him, if you set me up to do it, it doesn't mean you'd be so angry you'd murder elderly folk in their beds.'

'Just because I knew you *would* take Jack, doesn't mean you *should've* taken Jack. You always let me down Lisa, you always have. That's why I'm pissed off.'

'You are so . . . cold.'

'Just. Like. You.'

'*No*. I am nothing like you. I accept I've struggled. I accept I may have had a little postnatal depression. I hold my hands up that I didn't always get it right with you, but I was never cold with you.'

'Incorrect. I feel like I've spent my entire life not knowing where I stand with you. You were either super loving and in my face, making up for all the times you were shit, or you were just shit. I feel my entire childhood was waiting for you to come back to me, staring at you when you were either zonked out, or staring out the window, or locked in the bathroom crying, or shut behind your bedroom door. Then after, you'd be cloying, guilty, telling me you love me, love me. But you are not like that with Jack. You'd risk taking him from under my nose, just to do right by him. How do you think that makes me feel?

'I never felt safe with you. You'll keep my son safe, but never me. You know why I kicked off when you took me into the prison? Why you had to start giving me Sleepy? Because I thought you were just going to forget about me and leave me there. Just like you did to Ted. Do you remember Ted, Lisa?'

Ice. In. My. Veins.

'You do, don't you? Oh, yes, Lisa, my teddy who I just loved so much. Like Jack loves Bunny now. Except he's eight and *he* still has his. You've managed not to fuck him up and lose his precious toy, I notice. Go on, let's test your legendary memory. What age was I when you left *my* Ted behind, in prison?'

Two. Jack was just two.

'I bet you never had to give me Sleepy before then, did you?'

I'm so cold. He's right, I know it. Giving him Sleepy started after then. I don't know why I didn't see it. Yes I do. It's because I didn't want to.

It was my last visit to my mum at Holloway prison, before she was moved. It was the only time I'd walked out on my mum during a visit, crossing the visiting hall before the bell, shaming her that I was leaving before our time was up. We'd had a row about something, I can't even remember what, and I was so furious with her, I ignored the crying Jack, thrusting him along in his buggy – *You were so angry, Lisa* – all the way to the tube station. We had boarded our train at Kings Cross before I lost my temper with his crying and moaning and finally noticed him. And I heard him, properly and realised what he'd known all the time: that his precious, most loved, Ted, was left behind in the prison.

I'd try to reassure him. I hadn't yet got a mobile phone but I told him I'd ring as soon as we got home, that the prison officers would send it on, that we couldn't go back – and we couldn't, I couldn't – but he wouldn't be calmed.

Ted did come in the post within a week, sent on by the prison to our home. But Jack never wanted it again. Wouldn't have it on his bed; insisted it stay in his wardrobe. He said Ted had been changed and said Ted wanted to take him back to prison in revenge for leaving him there. It took Nadia's trick of antihistamine to get him to step back inside a prison again.

Jack's speaking now, his voice emotionless. 'Dad tried to persuade me to hold Ted again: but I thought you were just ganging up on me to get rid of me. When I saw Dad in his police uniform, I thought he was going to arrest me and take me to prison. But don't worry, Lisa dear, I don't view Dad as any better than you. He was more interested in his dog than me. And then he was more interested in criminals. And then he was more interested in Anne-Marie, Amelia and Sophie. Did you know this interesting fact? I have never met Sophie. She is nine years' old, was born on the 12th June, but I have never been invited to her birthday, ever. Not once. My sister.'

He draws heavily on his cigarette and regards broken me with amused eyes. 'You *want* me to have feelings. You're disappointed in me because I don't care about stuff. But tell me this, why would I *want* to have feelings with you two for parents? Neither of you even noticed it was my birthday last week. The truth is, Lisa, there's loads of ways like that you've both wronged me. I can't be bothered to explain even one more to you. To explain would be to care. But I will say this: I've never been able to reach you, Lisa. You've never listened to me.'

He smokes, watching my devastation. I can't see him because my eyes are now closed, but I can feel his on me, just as I feel and smell the smoke blown at me.

'Trust me on this, Lisa, it's been a pleasure every single time I've wound you up. It's been worth it to me because it makes me feel alive to punish you. I hated it that you were all perfect and mushy with Jack but not with me. It's an insult. I always had to work so hard to get your attention.

'So, all the effort of the flat, looking after Jack at the weekends, it's been worth every bit of effort, ten-fold. And you can trust me on *that*.'

'You're a psychopath,' I say it aloud, not meaning to. But his reaction surprises me.

He sips his drink. 'Don't let it bother you – it doesn't bother me.'

'It should. The things you've done – it should bother you a lot.'

He shrugs. 'Why would it? It makes my life easier. I don't have to care what other people think. It makes it easier at work; makes it easier with girls. I like being an island.'

I almost gasp aloud at the expression – it's like he's taken my own thoughts.

– I'm an island –

and bent them into a different shape. I made him. He's broken, dangerous, and he doesn't even care. But I care, very much.

It feels vital to me that if I neglected him, then I'm sorry. I want him to know that he can reach me – he always did. I didn't show it enough, I believe him, but I've never not loved him.

With shaking fingers I reach out and do something I haven't done in so, so long, and touch him kindly. He's still my child, no matter what he's done, what've I've done. There's nothing he could do that would make me feel any different. Motherhood has always been both my love affair and my greatest challenge. My fingers brush his jaw but he starts like a bull stung by a wasp.

Irritation burns in his eyes. 'I am who I am.'

'But—'

'No. Don't pity me because I don't need it.'

'I'm sorry for what I did – and didn't do . . .' I touch him again, so lightly.

His irritation brews in his face and I know he's not pretending. He was such an angry baby, such an angry child. He let me take care of him, dress him, feed him, but I could never reach him. I don't think I ever stopped trying, but I certainly stopped believing. Maybe that amounts to the same thing in the end. He certainly felt the gap. We both did.

But I can't stop trying, even now: I take his hand in both of my own. For a moment it rests there, for a moment I think he's going to allow it. With one swift moment he whips it free and, still seated, he must have pushed the kitchen table hard, because it's suddenly slamming into me.

The force of it takes me by surprise and it catches me in the stomach, hard. It pushes me back and I fall back from my chair. As I'm falling I hear another noise:

Bang!

I hear this over the sound of me falling to the floor, over the sound of my *oomph!* as the air is knocked out of me, over the sound of my chair clattering against the tiles. The bang, I realise, is from the back door being slammed open. From the angle of looking up from the floor, the face of the figure at the door is obscured by the table. But I still know who it is, I recognise those legs. My son, I note, doesn't even turn round to see who has arrived.

I think he already knows.

seventy-six:

– now –

'What have you done to her?' Nick bellows, advancing on us. He's above me, reaching down. He takes my hand in his and pulls me up. He checks I'm all right before turning on our son. 'I know what you did!'

At first, I think he's talking about me. All my physical hurts start singing a cacophony of pain, as if trying to be heard over this new, savage stomach pain. I think a lower rib might've been cracked, but Nick is so angry, I can't help but play it down. 'It's not too bad –'

But Nick has left me and has crossed the floor and our son is rising out of his chair to meet the fury of his dad.

'Please, Nick, don't worry about it, it's fine! I just want you to keep your voice down – please don't wake Jack.' And suddenly, I'm back twenty years, reliving our lives all over again. And just like before, no one pays attention to me.

'What's your problem?' sneers our son, now several inches taller than his father.

Nick stands there, just looking at him. He's red in the face and I remember Nick's temper: slow to rouse but then slow to dissipate again. What's happened? I must have asked this question because Nick turns to me. 'You tried to tell me he was the same. I didn't want to believe you, Lisa. I wanted to think it was you,' he says, his voice filled with his fire. 'But it wasn't, was it, because you were right all along. It was because of him. Him!'

Now he turns to our son.

'You tricked me. You attacked your mother as soon as you could; I thought you'd grown out of that crap, but shame on you, you're a grown man and you're still not grown up. You stole police property out of my car boot. You've shredded all four of my car tires and you set me up, you little fucker!' His finger is in his son's face. 'That's police property. That's a massive show of disrespect, my friend. Massive error – *massive*. You've not changed at all. You're just the same, I can see that now. Nicking my car keys, to steal my stuff. You're a thief. I could have you cuffed. In fact, I should. That would change your plans, wouldn't it?'

Very slowly, very deliberately, Jack blows his cigarette smoke into Nick's face before saying: 'Just you try.'

Nick flushes a deeper red like a warning light – since he gave up, he's always hated smoking – and then his face drops to white: the true sign of danger.

'Please, please!' I flap, jumping between them. I'm not sure what's happened, but I don't want them to wake Jack. Being frightened, listening to adults argue, was the childhood I had.

'Why've you got a stinger anyway?' he sneers at his father. The butt of his cigarette glows fire and I'm worried he'll stub it out on Nick's face. 'You're not a traffic cop.'

'None of your business, you little shit. I'm just sorry I didn't listen to your mother.' He turns back to me. 'Are you sure you're all right? And why were you on the floor anyway?'

I don't answer this question because it would do nothing to improve the tension in this kitchen, which is suddenly red hot. 'What's a stinger?'

'A metal contraption deployed by *trained* police officers after drivers fail to stop. They're only supposed to used after *authorisation* and following *thorough* risk assessment. They're used to span a road, so a car who's failed to stop, drives over a series of spikes. But they're dangerous and our son has failed to consider the potential *risk* to road users. He has failed on all sorts of levels. Including keeping his nose out of my stuff!'

He turns back to our son. 'Why was she on the floor anyway? What were you about to do to her?'

'Nothing.'

'You're a liar. And a thief. I had to pack away that stinger and then I had to walk back here, in the dark, for two miles. You know what I was thinking as I did? That I'd be mad to let you take that child. I did always have a sense of unease, but now I've got something on you – theft; assault; criminal damage; intent to cause a traffic accident – I'll throw the book to stop you from having sole custody. Assaulting your own mother – you're an arsehole.'

I'm the shortest and, standing between them, they bookend me. 'Nick! Don't call him that!'

'Why not?' Nick looks at me, daggers in his eyes. 'He tricked me. Jack called me, saying he needed help. I thought he was upstairs, not in Cleasong. But he asked me to get him from the village, said he'd explain. I actually blamed you, Lisa! I was cursing you on the drive out! But about two miles from here I drove over a stinger – out there in the dark. I get out, check all my tyres – shredded by the way, thank you very much – walk back, see the fucking thing, and I'm like, what idiot has left that out here? I'm about to call it in and . . . *bam*! I suddenly get it: I had one in my car . . . and yes, when I look in my car, sure enough, it's missing from my boot!' He jabs a finger over my shoulder into our son's chest: 'He took it. And he doesn't have the decency to even admit why.'

Jack leans forward, his eyes narrowing, and there's a darkness in his voice that I don't like: 'I just wanted a chat with Lisa on her own, if that's all right with you? I needed you gone for a bit.'

'If you wanted your mother to yourself, you only had to say. Instead, you set me a trap and wrecked my car, which by the way, is now stuck on the side of the road. I didn't even have time to call the AA because I thought you were up to something. Which clearly you were – because that's not what grown adults call talking, if you don't know. How am I supposed to get back to my family tomorrow now?'

I knew, as soon as he'd said it, it was wrong. And I saw his face freeze with the understanding that he knew it was wrong, too. Slowly, I turned to see Jack's face.

His face seemed to tighten, but when he spoke, it was light, almost conversational. '*We* are your family.'

It's funny how you can recall your life. Standing there, between husband and son, I remembered our family life in a series of vignettes: eating around the kitchen table; trips out in the car; watching films while eating popcorn. We were, for those first five years, a real family. The good bits glued us, for a while, at least.

'I never said you weren't,' Nick says, now edgy, his gaze flicking towards the door.

'I think you just did.'

There's a single moment when there's nothing. I like to think that Nick didn't move first, but I don't know, I don't know. But there's no space between them really, only me and the frailties of decency, a construct of how family should be.

Then it's gone.

Nick's fist is raised. But his son is quicker and knocks Nick over with an easy move. As Nick goes to right himself, Jack grabs him by the throat and powers him back up against the wall.

It's only at the last minute that I see he has a knife in his hand – the missing knife from the block. I recall the single-handedness of his shaking a cigarette out and then lighting it with his left hand, then lighting one from the other, letting me pour the drinks, and I realise I never once saw his right hand. I realise he must've been holding the knife under the table the whole time. I choose not to think why.

I choose not to think if Nick hadn't arrived back, what might've happened.

I choose not to consider his lies that he was going to leave Jack with me when clearly he had other plans.

But I do remember the yawning missing tooth in the knife block and I do see the missing knife now clutched in his white-knuckled fist, and his arm is now drawn back and I realise—

seventy-seven:

– now –

– I realise that Jack's about to kill his father. 'Don't!' I scream. I jump up onto his broad back. From over his shoulder, I can see Nick's widened eyes, transfixed on the knife in our son's right hand.

Then I hear a *bang*.

His arm draws back, brushing my waist, and I think: *He's going to stab him! Jack's about to kill his father!* But then there's a shout and there's someone standing in the open back doorway. I can't see who it is, because my face is in Jack's neck. I realise the noise has come from the kitchen door being slammed back on itself, again, but this time it's not Nick.

I hear a woman shout: 'Drop the knife!'

As my son turns his body towards the intruder, I'm still hanging on to his back so I turn, too. With one movement, Jack only pauses to fling me aside, before he smoothly steps torwards the trespasser.

It's Erica. She's standing there, eyes narrowed, holding the discarded shotgun better than I ever could. It's so secure in her arms, it looks like she's held it all her life. She shifts her posture a little and speaks again, her voice low and even. 'Drop the knife, you fucker. Don't think I won't shoot you.'

His knife is still raised.

'Dickhead, this is your final warning. I consider you a threat. Drop your weapon or I shoot you.'

He steps forward.

'Step back! Step back!' shouts Erica. There's a stiffening in her posture – she's about to shoot. 'Step back and drop the knife.'

But my son will not do as he's told. Not ever. He picks up a chair and hurls it at Erica. She steps neatly to one side and it hits the ground just outside the back door.

He takes another step towards her. We are all shouting for him to stop. Nick tries to grab him, but he's kicked away. I try the same and am punched to the floor.

He glances over his shoulder at me and then abruptly rushes towards her, knife high in the air.

seventy-eight:

– before –

– *Jack's about to kill his father!* With this realisation, I ran across my bedroom and grabbed the knife from Jack's small five-year-old hands. My son is surprised to see me and lets go of it easily. Shaking, I stared at my bed: Nick lay sleeping. He snorted and turned over, still in his dreams. The light leaked through the gaps in the bedroom curtains, throwing a bar across the bed, but it doesn't disturb him. Nick had long ago got used to sleeping in the daytime, after working night shifts on the beat.

My child looked anywhere but at me and the knife in my hand. It was heavy, one of Nick's fishing knives. I nearly asked him: *why were you standing over Daddy with a knife?* But I didn't want to hear the answer.

Jack was fishing mad and wanted to go fishing early this morning, but Nick refused to take him. It was the first time he'd refused to take Jack on a trip and we all knew it was because Jack had killed Winston yesterday. The usual fishing party of three, would've been, without Winston, the two of them for the first time, and I didn't blame Nick for not wanting to take his son and pretend everything was all right.

Now the dog was dead, it was far, far from all right.

Nick still felt terrible about hitting Jack, had apologised, and as much as he wanted to make good, he couldn't face just him and Jack and no Winston just yet. I totally understood and had supported Nick making a stand despite Jack's tantrums. The words 'social services' hadn't been mentioned again since Irene's bitten cheek, but I thought we were both thinking the words anyway.

I stared at Nick's fishing knife. It was a present from me. He kept it in his tackle box which meant that Jack had purposefully gone looking for it. Its blade was dark and dangerous and I thought of my own childhood. I finally considered Jack, who'd edged away from me and was now standing on the far side of the bed. He just looked back at me, waiting for me to say something. But what could I say when we both appeared to be the same?

No.

I fought back against my shame: it wasn't the same, not the same. I had been frightened; was trying to save my mum. His violence was all I'd ever known and it was getting worse. I used to hide under the covers, listening to her trying and failing not to scream. I could hear what he called her – bad words, so bad. I saw him play with the knife against her: I loved her and I wanted to save her.

Nick was a great dad. Winston a great dog. No, this was not the same. I gripped the knife and marched round the bed. Taking Jack's hand, I led him out of the darkened bedroom.

I settled Jack on the sofa and turned on the TV. I was plaster of Paris: fragile, delicate – even the lightest of brushes could break me.

Before I'd even reached the kitchen, I realised my life was over. I knew then that I would have to lead him much further from this flat. With Winston dead and now this, there could be no remaining here – Nick just wouldn't ever be safe. And if he felt that – knew that – he would call Social Services and Jack would be taken away. Perhaps that wasn't true, perhaps it didn't work like that, but I wasn't prepared to wait and find out.

If I had to choose between losing Jack or losing Nick, then I made my choice right then. I decided we would go away; somewhere on our own. Somewhere where no one could get hurt. I was prepared to risk myself for my son. I also understood there was no one else who could do this for him – there was only me.

I didn't want him to do what I did: hurt someone and then spend the rest of his life secretly suffering.

I stayed in the kitchen. I knew I should speak to Jack, but I couldn't. I had no words. Our life as a family was over now; how could I sleep knowing what Jack could do in the night? Some people would say that it's love that underpins family life, but it isn't.

It's trust.

Wordlessly, I took him a Jaffa Cake and a Ribena. I didn't want to treat him, I just wanted to keep him quiet. I needed time to think. I hid back in the kitchen, found Nick's whisky and poured myself an inch. I downed it and then poured another.

But I didn't drink it. The brute burn of alcohol reminded me I needed to go somewhere, anywhere. I knew I needed to pick somewhere to run to so I could leave Nick safely behind. I gripped the glass; I loved Nick, that'd never been in question. He had his faults, but I still remembered the man before we had our son. It was our love that meant I had to leave. I had to protect him from both his son and from difficult, hideous choices, because, in the end, it's protecting people that's true love. My mother taught me that.

Just as she stepped up, so I decided I must.

I thought of my dad then; so abruptly did he come to me that I put down my glass before I dropped it. He was funny, so funny – just the best sense of humour. Like Jack, he was incredibly talented with art too – drew me a cartoon of anything I asked for. I remember his smell: cigarettes, aftershave and whisky. Jack looks like him, I thought.

I poured away my drink and pulled out the Yellow Pages and let it flop open on the kitchen countertop. I found the map and then located my mother's prison in Send, near Woking. Then looked at large towns within travelling distance. Bracknell caught my eye. Perhaps it could be as meaningful to me as Brighton was. The fact that it begins with B was as good a reason as any.

From the wall-mounted phone, I picked up the receiver and dialled for an estate agent I'd found. 'I wonder if you can help me. I'm looking for a furnished flat – two bedrooms – around the Bracknell area, please.' I realised the car was Nick's, bought by Irene as a present. 'And it's vital the flat is near the train station,' I added, marvelling at how pleasant I sounded – one wouldn't be able to tell that my heart was breaking.

All the time I arranged our new flat, I checked on our son without actually looking at him properly: not even once.

Then I packed our bags, took Jack and left.

I nearly left a note, but I didn't. Mostly because I didn't know what to say.

And Nick peacefully, unknowingly, slept on and on and on.

seventy-nine:

– now –

The noise is sudden and loud. The sound of gunshot. Then there's a metallic sound as a knife – my kitchen knife, I know it is – drops to the slate tiles. He collapses to his knees. I reach for my son and embrace him again, just like I have always done. Before I was holding on to him: now I am holding him up.

Trying and failing.

I can't look at Nick or the intruder; instead I hold on, so tight, eyes squeezed shut, gripping against his back, inhaling his scent of cigarettes, whisky and deodorant; he smells like my father. I'm trying, still trying to save him. But I collapse with him; together we fall.

Really, we were never apart.

Sorry, Daddy.

I love you, Jack.

eighty:

– now –

I climb away from my son – I don't want to crush his breathing – but, even as I clamber off, I know from the blood spreading that it's too late. Close-up shotgun wounds don't leave any room for hope – his chest is meaty and messy.

I look up at Erica in the doorway. She stares right back at me. 'I'm going to call the police,' she says, and she breaks the shotgun and reaches for her phone. 'Dickheads, all of you,' she mutters just before she requests: 'Police and an ambulance.' She's cool as she starts to explain the situation and Nick then takes the phone from her and I think he's doing his police thing. I know that if Erica hadn't shot Jack, he would've killed her.

I think she saved all of our lives. I hear enough from Nick to know that he thinks the same and is telling them so.

He commands Erica to leave the gun outside, clearly broken open. He watches whilst she does it and then informs the operator that it has been done. Then he tells her to sit at the table, with her hands where he can see them. He is communicating with the police the whole time. She is lucky he is a senior police officer. But I'm not going to worry about Erica's future. She did the right thing. The truth will out. I stop listening.

My life is over.

I kneel back down, as close to him as I can.

'Jack?'

His eyes flicker open. 'Lisa?' he says, then, focusing on me, he says the sweetest thing: '*Mum.*' That word he hasn't said in so long. There's so much I want to say. Instead, he's dying. His mouth works, but no sound is made.

I lay a light hand on his shoulder and get even closer. Now it's just the two of us. I ignore the stink of blood. 'Jack,' I falter and try again. So little time. 'Jack. I love you. I'm sorry for what I got wrong.'

He smiles a little but his gaze is vague – it's on me, then not, then back again. 'When I was a little kid . . . I found a newspaper article.'

I shake my head a little. At first I don't know what he means, and then my blood runs cold because I do know.

'I thought . . .' He's struggling to breathe. The blood is spreading from him fast, covering the world, smothering it, ending it. 'I thought . . .' He looks at me with searching eyes. 'Is it true? Did I guess right?'

My hand props me against the floor, now surrounded with blood. It's warm with life. I lean closer to my son. His breath is on my skin and mine is on his. Our eyes are finally together. 'Jack . . .' I don't think I can find the words that convey my depth of feeling. 'Jack, you were always – and will always be – my boy. There's nothing you could do –' I think of losing Nick, my Sunningdale residents and my mother, and know it's disappointingly and painfully true – 'there's *nothing* that could ever make me not love you.' I smooth his hair away from his sweating forehead and even manage a smile. 'You've been the hardest thing I ever had to deal with, but darling, you've always been the best, *best* thing I ever had in my life. I love you, baby.'

'You killed your dad.'

I want to know how he knows, but in the soup of him reading the article, visiting prison all those years with my mum, that last day with my mother when she died and him being as smart and nosy as a jackdaw, I know it's too thick for me to sieve now: there's no time.

'I'm sorry, baby,' is all I say. I don't know how long he has known. I don't know how much it has shaped him or his actions, but I do know it's too late for us. I can stop neither the bleeding nor the reality.

Instead I lift his head; its heavy in my arms, but I rest him on my forearm. He's breathing slowly and I recognise it from the dying. I am at once both professional nurse and loving mother. I kiss his perspiration-slicked cheek and tell him the truth: 'Sweetheart, I have always loved you the most.'

He is still, amazingly, looking at me and I feel like we truly see each other.

His mouth works again: he is trying to say something. I lean lower, my face next to his mouth to try to hear what he is saying. His hand suddenly, with a strength that is shocking, reaches for me and grabs my head and pulls me closer. But then: I feel his lips against my cheek, soft. It is a kiss. We stay like that for perhaps only seconds but the memory of it, I know, will sustain me forever.

Then at once it's over. His grip drops to nothing and his hand and lips fall away and when I can finally bear to look, his head has dropped back to the floor.

His gaze is both fixed and distant.

I ignore it. I ignore that his wound-pocked chest is not rising or falling. Instead I press my lips against his forehead and kiss him back, and just breathe him in deeper. For a moment I can pretend.

But after a while I know.

I know I will feel this loss later, but for now, the fact that my son did love me, means the joy tempers the grief. Love is enough.

Love is enough.

epilogue:

– eighteen months later –

Jack runs across Hove Lawns on to the beach, the pebbles spilling under his feet as he chases our dog; Lennie is yapping around his feet, already hoping for a swim in the sea. Jack is laughing and throws the ball and our dog tears off ahead, with Jack pistoning behind.

I shout good-natured, redundant words into the wind: 'Jack! Don't go far!'

I stop at my usual coffee stand. It is parked up on the wide pavement that delineates Hove Lawns and the busy Brighton seafront road; in another hour the traffic will be heavily crawling as the crowds arrive. I order a hot chocolate and a flat white for breakfast, extra hot with oat milk and, to celebrate, I buy two almond croissants. 'For me and my grandson,' I smile as I pay. Jack is always my grandson now; I can find the answers if people bring the questions.

The barista gets to work and I turn my back on him briefly to check first on Jack and then look out across the crashing waves. It feels so good to be back in what feels my spiritual home.

I accept the croissants in a paper bag. Although Jack doesn't know it, I deserve a treat today: today marks one year of sobriety for me. Coffee is all I allow myself now. I've never had a problem with alcohol, but treatment has helped me understand that I don't want to swap one problem for another.

Treatment has helped me understand a lot, not least that I don't need to be afraid of anything anymore. All my life I've been afraid of something. But not now. All the monsters are gone.

My new therapist, Anya, is such a toughie. She questions my version of events all the time, making me reflect differently on it all. I blurred over the edges of my substance misuse, but she's encouraged me to recognise what I already knew – that I only started taking codeine as a way of coping with my son. When my mother died, it was a major setback, and, whilst I can't rule out another catastrophe in my life yet to come, we do agree that being prepared is part of the battle. I wasn't prepared for what happened to my mum, but that's not an excuse though – many in my situation wouldn't have made my mistakes.

My mistakes are my mine only and I own them.

Many would've coped better with Jack than I did. I say his name all the time now. Many, many people deal with challenging children, and many do better than me. They are my heroes. I think, if he'd been born now, I would've done better. I think there would be a support group for parents like me; I think I could've learnt new coping strategies – even if I couldn't have changed Jack's behaviour, I think I could have possibly found a better way to deal with it than simply to retreat from it.

Anya suggests that people cope with domestic violence in different ways. For a long time I struggled to use that term, but in the end, she made me read the definition off my phone and then challenged me to say why it was different to what I had experienced.

I could not.

We talk about how I grew up with it and then how I suffered it as an adult. It feels like the two things are related. Anya doesn't make suggestions; she just listens to me as I make my own. I know that I took painkillers as a way of escaping my mental suffering. It's hard doing the thinking now, it's hard to think about how my father's violence shaped me and how, in turn, I shaped my son. Somewhere, an ancestor of mine threw a stone into a puddle and the ripples kept going, hitting into another until the ripples hit my father and then hit me and then my Jack.

I know it's still not over: I know that little Jack suffers the considerable loss of his parents, but I'm doing well with him and he's in counselling too and seems to be happy and thriving. When I get down about it, Anya reminds me that I'm doing the best I can for Jack's future. It's not what I'd choose for him, but I also know that lots of people compromise all the time, and I also know that kids thrive every day in the space between perfect and necessity.

I shut my eyes and turn my face towards the salty wind that blows off the sea. I think I've forgiven my father for his behaviour. It's too new an emotion to know for sure, but I feel this forgiveness now, weigh it carefully, and it feels right. Forgiveness always is, I think.

Even better, if I forgive him, then I have to forgive myself because his behaviour and mine are bound so closely and inextricably, together. Besides, I have to have some peace, not just to minimise the ripples hitting Jack, but because I need to feel better about me. Is that selfish? Anya champions the idea that it's not. She says living is more than just survival.

Grateful, I sip my coffee: I don't think I ever got over missing having a decent coffee when living at our little cottage on the hill. Then again, so much of living in isolation wasn't for me. But it served a purpose, I think, as I glance at the marks on my wrists.

The burns were never as bad as I perceived they were at the time; I think that would be a good metaphor for how I've looked at some things over my adult life. My most recent therapy breakthrough was recognising how weak I've always been, how passive. To some people, they might want to shake me, and tell me to stop sleepwalking through things – perhaps that's what Issy wanted to do, all those years ago. She got the perp wrong, but her ideas were right. I have been weak; I can accept that. But I can also accept why that is: when you've committed a terrible thing in childhood it's easy to become scared by the power of oneself. To see one's muscle flexed at its most strong, is overwhelming. I'm not surprised I took a step back and instead stayed timid and safe.

And that timidity – at least in part – might've driven Jack's behaviour. Every time he pushed up against me, I always took a step back. And then another step. And another.

That might be a factor. Possibly.

I accept that my reluctance to challenge bad behaviour might not be Jack's full story. I still don't know why my son was the way he was. Together, Anya and I agreed that it's not appropriate – or within our gift – to diagnose him; instead she suggests it's better to stay with his behaviours. She says it's easier to stick to my truth that way. Nick has his truth and Jack had his – therapy has taken me a long way. With it, I accept that I'm allowed mine.

But I haven't forgiven myself. I never will. Just because I can't understand where I went wrong, doesn't mean that I didn't. All the dead at Sunningdale are testament to that.

Anya says only my behaviour can be a testament to me. Whether or not that's true, it's helping me to look forward.

The sun, released from a cloud, shines brighter and my face greedily absorbs the heat. I'm blessed to have much to look forward to. Jack's stammer is so much better too – not completely gone, but some days I forget he even has one. It means that he's liberated from his self-imposed silence and instead – amazement layered on amazement – it turns out he's chatty. I don't think I will ever tire of him talking. He talks on the phone too, to Nick and Anne-Marie and their children. It makes me feel good that he's got another set of grandparents out there and two young aunties who just adore him. It was even my idea that he stays with them for the last few days over the Christmas holidays.

We are both so settled in our lovely terraced house in Brighton, it feels possible that he could leave me and be fine. I trust Nick better now and he trusts me.

A few months ago Anya asked me why I never told Nick the real reason I left him. She wondered if it caused resentment to sacrifice my adult relationship with my husband in order to protect him from our son. She's asked if it's possible that any bitterness was passed on to Jack. I argued *no* to start with. But of course, *yes*. As a parent to a young child, who wants to give up the family unit? Who wants to shut their eyes at night, never feeling safe even in their own bed, knowing there's no one looking out for them? The end of our marriage was because I was watching out for him, but that meant that no one was watching out for me. A bit of me can understand why I had to knock myself out at night, just to sleep.

But I didn't want to tell Nick because it felt like a betrayal of our son, almost as if – for want of a better word – I was grassing him up. My mum had stayed silent for me and I wanted to do that for Jack, but Anya helped me interrogate the power of how conspiracies trap people: I didn't choose to be complicit in our son's conspiracy and yet I have been all these years. So, I decided that since Nick is alive and Jack is not, I should trust him with my truth. I've always understood that it must've been terribly hard on Nick when we left suddenly. I never lost sight of how it must've felt when we abruptly went and then cut off most of our contact with him. So in the end, three months ago, I decided to tell him.

Nick and his family then came down at my request, and credit to Anne-Marie (who is actually a very nice person) she and the girls took Jack to the pier for the afternoon, without even knowing what I wanted to see Nick about, and I told him about Jack nearly killing him in his sleep and about how I didn't know what else to do but take Jack away from him. I told him that since Jack was prepared to look me in the eye and lie about Winston – and believe it – if he was going to pick up a knife too, then I didn't feel anyone was safe.

I told him it was the only reason I left him. Not because I wanted to, but because I felt I had no choice. I told him it was the biggest single sacrifice I've ever had to make in my life and I still encounter its scar tissue every day.

We both cried and now it is done.

I watch Jack lob the ball across the beach to Lennie. It feels good not to have any secrets.

The sea breeze smarts my eyes as I decide that cleaning up your past is like cleaning out your wardrobe: it becomes compulsive and impossible to stop. Once I started ridding myself of the burden of my secrets, I decided to get rid of all of them, so I told Anya what Jack's dying words were to me: *You killed your dad.* It took many sessions to be able to rephrase it to: *I saved my mum.* Although she went to prison for a very long time, there's enough memories in me to accept that I probably did save her life. Probably, maybe, hopefully.

I guess I was dizzy with relief because I then went even further. I saw a solicitor and together we wrote a letter to the police explaining that I believe it was me who killed my father, when defending my mother. I've been interviewed and I'm not sure it's in 'the public interest' for the CPS to take it further, and of course, at eight years old, I was way below the age of criminal liability. Social services have been notified because of my caring for Jack, but Nick has gone on record for me that I'm a good parent, and that seems to have settled it a little. They keep a distant check on Jack, but Nick, sticking up for me, told them that Jack is with me or Jack goes into care. Nick would do the right thing, I know, but thankfully, it seems that's not needed. The fact I'm solvent, sober, and supported goes far. The fact Jack is happy and thriving goes even further.

Nick also went on record too, for Erica, as did I. Of course, there was a thorough investigation and then a trial. Ballistics and other scene of crime forensics backed up our testimony. She won't be allowed another shotgun license, but she didn't have to serve any time. I think Nick's vehement testimony was a real game-changer for Erica. My mother said she was sorry I married 'a flatfoot'. I'd love to tell her that it has its benefits.

I smile to think of her saying that. My solicitors are hoping that my statement might lead to my mother's name being formally exonerated. Although it feels risky, I can't be sober without cleaning out my most dusty and overfilled top shelves.

I feel like I've done that now. I feel brave and new.

I watch Jack and Lennie playing on the beach and think of what my mother would say about me trying to clear her name. She'd be a little cross, I expect, but I like to think she's looking down at me from heaven and is maybe a little pleased, too.

I watch the fast sprint of Lennie going for the ball and it feels amazing to be back in Brighton. It's been sixteen months since I bought my house. Jack's settled so well into school and has made some lovely friends – we have both made lovely friends. I've made new ones, not looked up any from the past. I don't want to be back there – instead here, in the present, is a wonderful thing for us, and it's just where we need to stay.

But I do often look back to remember my mum – her things are all over our house: the sofa throws, some of the nicer knick-knacks, her photos everywhere; everything boxed up and saved by Nick and mum's neighbour and friend, April Dawes, I have since found out. I think mum was everywhere that awful night too – I think it was her presence I felt in the field, that sense of someone there, pushing me on when I needed to go on and couldn't. I just know it. She never let me give up on anything, and she didn't then either. If she hadn't been there, goading me on, perhaps I wouldn't have made it – perhaps Jack wouldn't either. But she was, and we did. I haven't felt her since, but then I haven't needed her. But it gives me a sense of comfort to know that she hasn't left me; that she is all right and is still looking out for me. Really, that's all she's ever done. She remains my hero.

It's not just my mum who has a presence in our house, but my son, too. We have Jack's photo on the wall above our fireplace. We've brought him in and although he's gone, he's a real part of our family. We both love him.

We always will.

I breathe in the sea-salt smell and drink my coffee and contentment wraps my shoulders.

Seeing my paper bag, Jack runs towards me: 'Croissants!' Lennie runs barking at his feet. Nick tracked the puppy down – Jack had given it to his neighbour, but when Nick explained about little Jack losing his dad, they let us have him again. He's our dog now.

We find somewhere to sit on the beach. Jack hugs me. He's so generous with his love and affection. I kiss him back – I never kiss him just for him, but also for his dad. I hope that somehow the kisses get through to Jack wherever he is. I want him to feel my love, still.

I think also of Selena – I often do. I hope she's pleased with the job I'm doing – in many ways, I'm also doing my best for her as well. We have her photo up too – and Jack has met his maternal grandma. We are making progress in all sorts of ways.

Jack eats his croissant and feeds some to Lennie. He tells me about the different things they found on the beach and shows me the crab claw in his pocket.

When I've finished eating, I hold the claw and open and close it. It's an exciting find, I agree. I think about the hard shell on the outside and the soft inside, hidden from sight. Such a different creature from us – well, from *some* of us, perhaps.

'Can we go exploring again, Granny? You'll come with us this time?'

I take his outstretched hand and stand tall. I remember then, what I thought when my son died, as I feel my grandson's hand in my own and I feel it again. But now it's less of a question or a hope – now it's a certainty.

Love *is* enough.

Acknowledgements

Firstly, dear reader, thank you for the read; I hope you enjoyed it, not least because I loved writing it. I intended to express something around ideas of love and forgiveness; not an original message, but I think, the best one.

The creation of this book – obviously – isn't just me tap-tapping away, but the product of many people. The first who deserves a particular ra-rah! is my editor, Katherine Armstrong. I am in a long queue of people who recognise her considerable talents and I'm not surprised by her continued success. Thank you, Katherine, for not being put off by a ragged dishcloth of a first draft and making it into something so much better. Along with Katherine, my thanks goes to Stephanie Glencross, who has shaped many books that perhaps, dear reader, line your bookshelves. Writing is a mostly solitary (tea, back against the Aga, mind elsewhere) task, but it was fun and fruitful to work with Stephanie and Katherine as a three, solving the tangles together. Stephanie works with the fabulous Jane Gregory, who, as an agent, I trust implicitly. Thank you, Jane, for your support and my thanks is extended to Camille and Mary.

Special thanks to the wonderful people at Bonnier Zaffre for publishing this novel; you are a brilliant team and always so helpful and creative. A particular toast to Ciara Corrigan for her patience.

The world of writing is a very friendly and supportive place – happily and surprisingly so. I'd like to thank those writers and reviewers I've encountered, for their warm welcome and the reads and reviews.

Cara Henwood, thank you for your midwifery knowledge – at short notice. Any mistakes are mine.

Thanks to my parents, John and Jenny, who are unfailingly optimistic and enthusiastic about my writing and always give their love heaped high and unqualified. My sister, Juliet Hunter, is always my first reader and her influence on this book is palpable: thanks for the walks and the talks. My other walking buddy is Dorrie Dowling; an anchor, always. Finally, Cooper and Casper, I dedicated this book to you because you keep me going when the incline gets a little steep. But know this: I'd climb Everest for you both – in my socks. If I have to do that, then I hope you, Brad, are still trudging with me. There's no one I'd rather walk with. And – as always – you're definitely in charge of the compass and map.

Keep reading for an exclusive extract from Kate Bradley's debut suspense thriller that asks: How far would you go to save a child that isn't yours?

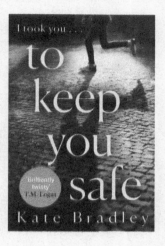

You don't know who they are. You don't know why they're hunting her. But you know she's in danger.

What do you do?

When teacher Jenni Wales sees 15-year-old Destiny's black eye, she's immediately worried. Destiny isn't your average student: she's smart, genius IQ smart, and she's in care. But concern turns to fear when Jenni witnesses an attempt to abduct Destiny from school.

Who are these men and what can Destiny know to make them hunt her?

With those around her not taking the threat seriously, Jenni does the only thing she can think of to keep Destiny safe: she takes her.

Prologue

I hang my legs over the cliff edge and look over so I can imagine your broken body lying on the beach below. I never tire of sitting here. I come even in winter, when the storms seethe, forcing me to grip the scant grass, because I feel that I could die here too. I like that. I watch the crashing waves below, beating against the bluff, pushing and pulling the flotsam and jetsam, relentless, relentless, relentless.

Then I do my own falling. I uncork a bottle and for a while feel the raw pain of my loss.

Walkers have approached me in the past; they see my solo picnic of wine and the inches between me and certain death, and they think I'm going to jump. The police have been here too. Twice they've arrested me under section 136 of the Mental Health Act, determined to get me assessed, but my last psychiatrist intervened. He said that I push all of my grief and guilt onto the clifftop, as a coping mechanism. He's wrong.

As I sober up at home, I spend the night staring at my bedroom ceiling while the world sleeps. I think about my choices, questions writhing like worms in my mind. I replay everything: everything I did and didn't do. What it caused; about the people who got hurt. Who died. I remember blue eyes locked on mine, eyes filled with the pain and the nearness of death. Then the peace, after.

I know I am guilty.

And then when I tire of my self-hatred, I wonder what would've happened if we hadn't come together like a planet spun from its orbit into the path of the other. How different my life would've been. And that's what I can't get over – that's why I cannot know peace.

I turn over what happened to us in my mind, the memories getting no less worn through the constant re-examination. Relentless, relentless, relentless.

I don't need this clifftop to remember you or what happened that Friday afternoon in May, three years ago, when everything that I'd ever loved, would be gone before the sun rose on Saturday.

I think and I think and I think; thoughts of what I'm going to do next beating relentlessly into the shallows of my mind.